JUL. 6 1

MEN IN ARMS

ALSO BY JOHN CROSBY

An Affair of Strangers
Nightfall
The Company of Friends
Dear Judgment
Party of the Year
Penelope Now

John Crosby

STEIN AND DAY/Publishers/New York

First published in 1983
Copyright © 1983 by John Crosby
All rights reserved, Stein and Day, Incorporated
Designed by Judith E. Dalzell
Printed in the United States of America
STEIN AND DAY/ *Publishers*
Scarborough House
Briarcliff Manor, N.Y. 10510

Library of Congress Cataloging in Publication Data

Crosby, John, 1912-
  Men in arms.
  I. Title.
PS3553.R55M4   1983   813'.54   82-40168
ISBN 0-8128-2885-2

-1-

— Cassidy slunk down Demarest Street, his coat collar turned up like Humphrey Bogart's, thinking surveillance is a mug's game.

The man he was following was very big, very sure of himself, and he carried a black suitcase. Demarest Street was full of the usual dreamers, and the big man breasted them like waves, moving briskly with high purpose, something not seen much in this part of Greenwich Village.

The man had turned off Demarest into Market under the viaduct at the edge of North Village where the dreamers mingle with the truly poor, enriching neither. The vegetable carts were cheek by jowl under the viaduct, piled high with potatoes, leeks, spinach, tomatoes, the air heavy with the smells, the big man pushing through the shoppers, unseeing.

Not once had this purposeful man looked around to see who was following—or if anyone was. He didn't seem to give a damn.

He crossed Market and plunged down Forensic whose high loft buildings had once been warehouses and were now full of writers and other riffraff. Cassidy followed after, his hands deep into the pockets of his threadbare black coat. *If I had a decent coat I wouldn't be doing this.*

Cassidy caught a glimpse of himself in a shop window: skinny as a hawk, nose like a beak, shoulders bent, head sunken like a turtle. *I'm about as inconspicuous as Groucho Marx, last person in the world I'd pick for surveillance. Why on earth did Alison pick me? Why didn't the CIA do its own dirty work? Because they weren't supposed to operate in Manhattan. Or anywhere else in the U.S. My ass! There were deeper, darker reasons . . .*

The big man was only forty feet ahead now, and Cassidy felt naked. Nobody else on Forensic at all.

The big man bounded up brownstone steps and disappeared into the building. One minute he was there, the next not. Cassidy picked up the pace. At the foot of the brownstone, Cassidy stopped and looked around, giving the big fellow a chance to get out of the vestibule. He could see him through the plate glass, pushing a button, waiting, vanishing through the vestibule door into the front hall.

Cassidy gave him a moment and then followed, not liking what he was thinking. *Why had the big man walked twenty-five blocks carrying a suitcase that looked heavy? If he was going to a clear address, why not take a cab? Cassidy had expected a street assignation. The man brushing against someone. Money changing hands. Or drugs. Or information. Or something. But to come to a house!*

Inside the vestibule were the usual row of buttons and names. J. D. Smythe 1B, R. D. Robbins 1C (What happened to 1A?) H. C. Rollins 2A. R. Bartholomew 2B. *All good WASP names. Too WASPish actually. Why no Morenos or Baptistas or Fung Chus?*

He pulled out a key ring. The door opened with the second key. *Too easy. Not much concern with security—and that lets out the CIA, the*

KGB, Mossad, most of my best friends. . . . Cassidy was now in the front hall. On his left was 1B, the home of J. D. Smythe, on the right 1C, R. D. Robbins. Where was 1A? Around the corner under the stairs, and Cassidy guessed it led to another stairway leading to the basement.

An Old Law Tenement, obviously fixed up to conform to the minimum of the law. Not many of those around anymore. The others had long since been pulled down and replaced with more profitable buildings. If tenements survived, it was for a good—or more probably bad—reason. Somebody wanted cover. Or it was owned by some rich creep who'd just forgotten it. Something like that. No smells. That was important. Where were the smells?

Cassidy tried the brontoscope on 1B, then on 1C. No sound. He laid the instrument on the 1A door, not expecting much, the plug in his ear.

"No, I won't . . ." Woman's voice. Very faint.

". . . purple . . ." Or people. Or bottle? Or something. Man's voice. The big fellow? Cassidy didn't know. He'd picked the guy up on Alison's order. Never heard him utter . . .

Scrabbling sounds from below.

Now what was *that*?

Panic sounds. Panic had its own noises, its clicks and glitches, and above all, its own rhythms.

Somebody was coming up the cellar steps fast. Cassidy fled down the corridor and up the staircase. On the second floor he shrank back against the wall.

A woman appeared at the foot of the stairs, slender, olive-skinned, eyes wide with horror, held motionless for a moment by the terror of the moment before, reliving it so palpably that it shrieked to the heavens—whatever it was that had happened down there. Twenty-five or so years old, Cassidy guessed. Even with the horror on her, quite beautiful . . .

She was gone. Down the brownstone steps and north on Forensic.

She wasn't the object of the exercise; the big man was. Still, Cassidy didn't hesitate. He skipped down the stairs, two at a time, ran out the door and up Forensic after her.

The chase was over before it fairly got started. By the time he got to Rivington, on a dead run, the woman had already hailed a cab. He just got a glimpse of her long legs as they vanished into it. Cassidy looked around for another cab but, as always, there wasn't one. He jotted down the license number—TN-68-25—and even as he did so he was assaulted by premonition.

Cassidy shook his head ruefully and walked back Forensic to the Old Law Tenement. He stood across the street from it, shielded by the row of cars, and jotted down the street number, 127. He looked at his watch. 4:24 in the afternoon. He'd been gone maybe three minutes.

The big man came out of 127 Forensic, moving fast now, much faster than he had previously. He came down the brownstone steps, still carrying the suitcase (it seemed much lighter), and headed north to Rivington.

Again Cassidy said the hell with the orders. His orders were to follow the big man. Stick with him, said Alison.

Cassidy didn't. He watched the big man walk rapidly—very rapidly—up to Rivington, hail a cab (*Now* he takes a cab!) and disappear into it.

Cassidy tore up the steps and let himself into the building. Time was of the essence. The big man's haste suggested it, and Cassidy's intuition screamed it.

The door to the basement apartment 1A was not a pushover like the front door. Cassidy tried all the keys in his collection as fast as he knew how before pulling out the Wedemeyer, which would open most anything, but with its electronic digitals and dials was a damned nuisance. It was minutes before he got the door open, and he was sweating. Pure terror, and he didn't know what he was terrified of.

The staircase behind the door was straight and steep and dark. Cassidy lit himself down it with his pencil flash. Stay away from switches! clamoring in his skull.

Steam pipes at the foot of the stairs led off to the right. Straight ahead was an open door, and through that the pencil light showed a very large, very bare room in the center of which lay the body.

Cassidy wasted no time on the body. Switches would be where it would be. Flashing the torch around the white walls, looking for switches . . .

The beam passing a table on which a telephone . . .

Telephone!

Cassidy reached for it convulsively and took the instrument off its cradle. The wire was very short, leading directly to the black suitcase the big man had carried twenty-five blocks, now lying open on the table two feet away. (But he still had a suitcase when he left? Different suitcase?)

Cassidy took out his Swiss Army knife and unscrewed the connection, removing the wire from the telephone. Only then did he begin breathing easily again.

Cassidy put the telephone back on its cradle. Let it ring. It could do no harm now. Now that he didn't have to worry about switches, he turned on the lights. The big bare room was full of packing cases, so full there was barely room for the corpse to stretch out in.

The suitcase was loaded with square flat packages wrapped in unlabelled brown paper. Cassidy picked up one of them and sniffed, wincing. The odor was sharp, almost painful. Lucinite probably. Ten times more explosive than G 4, which was very explosive indeed. Carefully he picked up the suitcase. Fifty pounds at least. (The big man had carried it as if it were full of shirts and ties.)

Enough to bring down the building.

The telephone began to ring and ring. Cassidy grinned at it, showing his yellow teeth, and turned to the nearest packing case. Big packing cases, roughly seven feet long and three feet across, very well built of one-inch oak, held together by screws, not nails. Clearly a class act. Cassidy went to work with his Swiss Army knife, taking his time. The big man would not come back to check if the building had blown up. He was completely confident. A grave flaw in the big man's character—overconfidence and it told a lot about him. Now a fellow like me, thought Cassidy, who thinks nothing is ever going to come out right . . .

He unscrewed the plank carefully and lifted it off. Foam rubber was just inside, a lot of foam rubber. He lifted it off. Inside, packed row on row in slotted oak rests, were what looked like artillery shells. Very peculiar shells—155 mm's—needle nosed and three feet long, much longer than any 155 mm shell he'd ever seen before.

A second packing case contained more of the same. Cassidy counted the cases—twenty-six of them. It looked as if the shells were packed twenty-four to a case. And twenty-six cases full of them . . .

If the Lucinite had gone off, so would the cases full of artillery shells . . .

Cassidy sat heavily on one of the packing cases. He drew in a huge gulp of air, recharging himself. I'm too old for this. Ten years ago I was too old. What am I doing here? I need the money . . .

He sighed and looked at his watch. 4:30. He'd been in here five minutes. Get on with it.

He'd been avoiding the corpse. He didn't like corpses.

Another gulp of air. Whiskey was better, but if air was all that was available, you took the air. Reluctantly, he turned his eyes on the body, thinking: *One more.* Cassidy had a superstition (which he had never told anyone about) that a man was allowed the look of only so many bodies in his life and then, presto, he became one himself so that every new corpse diminished his score and brought that much closer the final body, which would be his own.

As bodies went this was one of the more civilized. Face calm. No torment there at all. Death had taken him too swiftly for surprise. One arm was outflung, the fingers of the hand still closed tightly around the glass. Cassidy sniffed the glass but didn't touch, then sniffed the lips. No odor at all. These modern poisons left nothing—odor, trace, or tension. Better dying through chemistry, to rephrase the Du Pont people . . .

On his knees Cassidy stared hard at the impassive dead face. Long jaw, dark complected. The sadness of twelve generations lay on the features, which meant it wasn't American. American sadness had no such ancestry. This man was . . . Levantine? Greek, maybe, mixed with a little Arab? To produce that shade of melancholy . . . centuries.

He puffed out his cheeks and searched the man's pockets, not expecting to find anything and not finding anything. The big man had been very thorough.

Still he had had very little time and maybe. . . . Cassidy ran his fingers over the body, feeling carefully along the seams where they usually carried it. Nothing. He was about to give up when he thought of the most obvious place. With the Swiss Army knife he pried off the heels of the shoes. Two tightly rolled scrolls of paper fell out, one from each. Cassidy stuffed them in his pockets without looking at them, and left the heels on the floor.

He got off his knees painfully, put his hands in the small of his back, and stretched himself straight again. Too old for these games. On the top of the packing case, he saw a second glass, full of colorless liquid. He bent over and sniffed without touching.

The sharp bite of alcohol and caraway seeds. Aquavit. Well, well. The dead man had no aquavit on his breath (or where his breath had been) or in his glass. Pure poison in his glass unleavened by liquor. How very unkind! Where was the bottle? And the third glass? Hadn't they offered the girl a drink?

"No, I won't . . ."

Turned it down. Smart girl.

Cassidy grimaced. It was giving him a headache, all the possibilities.

With his handkerchief Cassidy turned out the lights, wiping off his prints at the same time. He made his way back up the stairs in the dark.

The corridor on the first floor was empty and silent. The whole building much too silent. It was getting on toward five. There should be women preparing supper, children coming home from school, bustle. Cassidy stared out the plate glass window of the vestibule door at the empty street where it was starting to snow.

Carefully, he wiped the prints off the doorknobs of the doors leading to the cellar and the two leading to the street. He let himself out into swirling snowflakes and slogged, head down, northward on Forensic to the pay phone where he called the police.

- 2 -

— Alison was aghast. "The *police*!" he bleated—not very loud. They were in the back room at Spumi's, and there wasn't a soul around, not even a waiter. Still, Alison, the fourth man in the CIA, kept his voice down, professionally conspiratorial at all times. "*Why?*"

"It's customary," Cassidy said, "when you find bodies." He sipped the Wild Turkey, enjoying the whiskey and Alison's discomfiture. When was the last time he'd been able to afford Wild Turkey?

"You didn't give your own name?" Alison whispered.

"No, I gave yours. I thought you deserved the credit, Hugh. After all, it was you who put me on to this."

Alison's eyes opened wide—just for a moment. He caught on too late as always. "You bastard! Always the needle! And I always fall for it. God damn it Horatio!" He recovered fast because he had to.

"*When*? When did you make that phone call?"

"Ten minutes ago."

"What was that address?"

"127 Forensic," Cassidy said. "You mean you didn't know?"

"Now I know," Alison said. He shot out of his chair in the direction of the phone booth. In a second he was back. "The Fourteenth Street Station?"

"Where else?" Cassidy said.

Alison vanished into the phone booth. Cassidy watched the pink, well-scrubbed, overfed face through the glass, counting the times he dialed. Not a local call. He wouldn't be calling the Fourteenth Street Station, Cassidy thought. Not Alison. He'd be calling Washington—the corridors of power. The corridors would call—not Fourteenth Street—but police headquarters, and headquarters would call Fourteenth Street and issue the orders. Alison's name would not be mentioned anywhere along the line after the first call. Nobody was better at covering his tracks than Alison. Alison left no footprints—at the Bay of Pigs, at the Shah's palace, in Vietnam, Berlin, Jakarta, or any of the other places.

Cassidy puffed out his cheeks and went to the bar to get himself another Wild Turkey. There were no other customers at the bar, and Henry, the bartender, who still spoke with a German accent after twenty-four years in America, poured the Wild Turkey. "You want to pay a little on the bill, professor?" Gently, not pushing it.

"My friend's buying," Cassidy said. "He has a rich wife, Henry. She could buy your whole saloon with the change in the bottom of her purse."

"Send her around. I sell it to her this afternoon." Henry polished glasses morosely. "Business is rotten, professor. You know why? Cocaine and jogging. The people sniff. They run. You are the last serious drinker left, professor. You are out of style. You know that, don't you?"

Cassidy laughed. "I'll pay you a little something very soon."

He took his drink and went back to the table and sat down. Presently Alison returned, his face serene, the eyes veiled. That was Alison at his most dangerous—when he was cool.

"Why the hell don't you follow orders?" he asked without heat.

"That's what got me thrown out of the CIA, not following orders. You know that, Hugh. Why didn't you get one of your own goons to follow the man?"

Alison sipped his Cinzano and soda, not answering. He rarely answered questions.

"When your wife asks you what time it is, do you tell her?" Cassidy asked, baiting him with his sharkish grin. "I bet you give her the wrong time, Hugh."

"My wife knows what time it is, Horatio," Alison said. "Why do you hate me so?"

"Because you're rich and successful, you bastard. And you hate me back because I'm poor and unsuccessful." It was dangerous to laugh at Alison, who didn't like it, and therefore Cassidy made a practice of it. I have the most intricate forms of self-destruction of any man I know.

"Ours is a truly symbiotic relationship," Cassidy said. "We feed off each other. We bring out the worst in each other, and that's a fact, Hugh. You're hiring me to do your dirty work because you don't want anyone else in the Agency to know what devious games you're up to, and I'm doing your dirty work because I need the money."

Alison remained cool, pulling out his wallet and counting out hundred-dollar bills, three of them. "You didn't do my dirty work very well, Horatio. Where did the man go? What was in that suitcase?"

"Lucinite was in the suitcase."

"The second suitcase, the one he took out with him."

"Money," Cassidy said, "lots of money." He hadn't told Alison about the woman. With Alison it was always best to keep out a little information. You never knew when you might need a little extra.

"It would be nice to know how much money and what currency." Alison had rolled the three hundred-dollar bills into a tight cylinder, and now he took Cassidy's hand, opened the fingers, put the tight cylinder into the palm, and closed the fingers around it.

"I'm only a part-time whore, Hugh," Cassidy said harshly. "You must never forget that I'm a medieval scholar *most* of the time."

"We're all part-time whores," Alison said smoothly.

"Not you. You're a full-time whore, Hugh, even when you're asleep."

The insult rolled off Alison's back as if unspoken. "I want you to pick up the big man again, and this time hang on to him till he comes to roost. That's important, Hugh."

Alison had risen and picked up his soft, brown leather attaché case from Hermes, his gloves from Gucci, his black stick from Kismet with its silver top under which roosted a .38 calibre single-shot revolver.

"Pick him up at the same place you picked him up last time—the United Nations. He's in and out all the time."

"What's his name, Hugh? I've seen that face before." The thought had jumped into his mind just then. Why hadn't it occurred earlier? And where had he seen that face?

Alison smiled for the first time at their meeting. "Wenceslas. We call him King Wenceslas, and we rather suspect he calls himself that, too."

"Mother of God!" Cassidy said. "Did he pick that name himself?"

"Tells us something, doesn't it," Alison said. "Megalomania with a touch of whimsy."

"What's his real name?"

"When you find that out, let me know." Alison made his elegant way across the floor in his superbly cut suit, the black stick tap tapping on the floor, as if this were the nineteenth century.

Cassidy called after him: "I told Henry you'd pay, Hugh."

"I already have," Alison said. He paused at the door and looked at Cassidy. "Shall I send Grace your love?"

"Tell her I love her for her body, not her money."

"She'll be overjoyed," Alison said dryly—and left.

Someday I'll go too far, and he'll shoot me with that .38 single-shot revolver under the silver-headed cane, Cassidy thought. He opened his palm and smoothed out the hundred-dollar bills. Two of them he put in his wallet. The third he tossed to Henry as he walked out. "Put it on the bill, Henry."

He went out into the snowstorm, but he didn't have far to go. The Spumi was a basement restaurant in an old brownstone house.

Directly above it, up the brownstone steps, was Cassidy's apartment, which occupied the entire first floor. Cassidy let himself in with his key. It was an enormous room with fourteen-foot ceilings and two fireplaces, one opposite the front door, the other about twelve feet away in what had once been a separate room. The entire room was lined with books from floor to ceiling. Lucia was stretched out on her stomach on the sofa in front of the first fireplace, her nose inches above her Second Year Latin. Lucia was thirteen.

"I hate Latin," she announced without looking up.

Cassidy kissed the girl on the top of her head and took off his coat: "You can't just take subjects you like. Education is not an exercise in self-indulgence. It's supposed to develop your character as well as your mind."

Lucia rolled over on her back, the book still in her hand, the black eyes in the plain face somber. "Julius Caesar has just accepted the Helvetians surrender, cut off their hands . . ."

Cassidy was going through his black book, looking for the telephone number. "Not *all* of their hands. Just a few selected hands."

". . . and sold the women and children into slavery. This is good for my character?"

"It'll toughen it, I hope." He was dialing the number now. "Our dealings with the Third World are much more enlightened now. We don't cut off their hands or sell them into slavery. We sell them arms, corrupt them, bankrupt them, starve them. Much more civilized." Into the phone, now. "Lieutenant Fletcher, please . . . Fletch, Cassidy. There's going to be trouble from Uncle."

"We got it," Lieutenant Fletcher said. "From the mayor's office. Headquarters is on the scene, and we're off it—totally. We were told to clam it to the papers. To everybody."

"Aaah," Cassidy said. "You kept my name out of it, I hope. I'm an unknown informant."

"Don't worry."

"I need a favor."

"If I got time . . ."

Cassidy read him the license number: "A Yellow Cab. Picked up a woman in a black coat—about 25 years old—at Rivington and Forensic. At 4:24 P.M. The driver would just be coming on duty, so he should have a record. Where did he take her?"

The lieutenant was silent for a long time, letting the obligation sink in. "It would help, professor, if you told us which of Uncle's many arms was pulling the mayor's strings. We like to know who's covering up murders in our precinct. We don't care about anyone else's precinct."

"You can always make an educated guess, Lieutenant," Cassidy said softly. "And who said anything about murder? The word I used was body."

"Yeah," the lieutenant said. "I'll get back to you when I can." He hung up.

Lucia was drinking it all in, the black eyes sparkling. "You've been moonlighting again." An accusation.

Cassidy sat next to her on the sofa and ran his finger down her cheek. He could never get over the softness and silkiness of that young cheek. "I'm going to buy you a new warm coat," he said.

"You need a new winter coat much worse than I do," Lucia objected. "That old black thing you wear . . ."

". . . is a mark of my virtue," Cassidy said. "Anyone that shabby must have the highest standards of virtue."

"Nobody uses the word virtue any more, professor. It's a very old-fashioned word."

"Well, I'm an old-fashioned fellow."

Supper was spaghetti, which Lucia made and served at seven o'clock. Cassidy washed the dishes while Lucia finished her homework—two chapters of *Madame Bovary,* which almost put her to sleep. "I don't know why this is considered the greatest French novel," she yawned.

"You will. Some day." Cassidy sat next to her. "It's better in French. Next time read it in French." Cassidy took the book from her. "Bedtime," he said. "You can finish it at breakfast."

Lucia undressed behind the screen that separated her part of the room from Cassidy's. She had her own wash basin back there behind her screen, Cassidy contributing to her education while she brushed her teeth.

"Flaubert," he said, "was once asked what a novelist's greatest quality was. He said: 'Passion.' And he was right. The greatest flaw in your generation is a lack of passion. Everyone wants to be cool, laid back. I devoutly hope that you will not be one cool cat when you grow up. I would like you to be passionate—passionately alive, passionately concerned, because anything else is just living death."

"Thus endeth the lesson?" The young voice from behind the screen was loving and teasing (where it had once been cold and mocking). Cassidy had no idea how seriously Lucia took his sermons, but at least she listened—that was important. He had a responsibility to the unformed character in his charge and had to try. Cassidy thrust himself out of his chair and went behind the screen for the good-night kiss. An important ceremony. He kissed Lucia on her cheek, a light touch of the lips on that softest of flesh, overwhelming him with tenderness and love, a nightly experience that never changed. My reason for existing.

Lucia sound asleep, Cassidy took out the two scrolls he'd taken from the dead man's heels and smoothed them out. One scroll was blank, and Cassidy didn't believe the blankness. A man didn't put blank scrolls in his heels. There were secrets there if he had the right chemistry. He put the blank scroll in his breast pocket. The second scroll was simply a list of ten names with addresses. The first name on the list was Mohammed el Glasha, 23 rue de Serpentine, Paris.

Cassidy pursed his lips, scowled, thought about it. Mohammed el Glasha. Aaah, yes. The man had been gunned down on a Paris street a month, six weeks ago. Something like that. It had attracted attention because people don't get gunned down on Paris streets all that often. There had been hints in *The New York Times* that Mohammed el Glasha was a part of the nether underworld of armaments. A gunrunner. A hijacker. An agent. A buyer. A seller. One of those things.

If Cassidy were still in the Agency, he'd know a lot more about Mohammed el Glasha, but he wasn't and he didn't.

The second name on the list was Gerald Foster, 167 Front Street,

London. Recognition was swifter here because Gerald Foster was an American. He had been shot at his London home; he'd gone to open the front door and been shot dead on his doorstep, very professionally—about three weeks earlier. Again there was the gossip about the arms underworld—but no hard facts.

The next six names meant nothing to Cassidy though he scowled over each one, searching his memory. The addresses were a Cook's tour—Madrid, Cairo, Rome, Singapore, Tokyo, Capetown. All big cities this side of the Iron Curtain.

The next name on the list made him blink. Jeremiah Wenceslas, 359 Rarity Street, Brooklyn. Well. Well. Well. So the man had a first name, Jeremiah. Why wasn't I told?

The last name on the list was the biggest shock of all.

Hugh Alison, 1678 K Street, Washington, D.C.

It was a very elegant Georgian house in the Georgetown district. Cassidy had seen it only from the outside with its mellow red brick, its perfect proportions and well-painted black shutters; he'd never been invited inside. Alison's very own house. He'd bought it with his own money, not his rich wife's, for some ridiculous sum like twelve thousand dollars back when Georgetown houses were going for those sums and it was now worth—Alison liked to tell people—about half a million. Alison's own, not his wife's (though it was her money that had remodelled it from top to bottom).

Cassidy's lips drew back in a ferocity of a grin. I hate the bastard. I envy him. I disapprove of him. If he's on the list, he probably richly deserves to be. Cassidy looked at his watch. Ten o'clock. Too early for Alison to get home. Cassidy killed a half hour reading from Lucia's copy of *Madame Bovary,* opening the book at random to the wedding. "The procession, at first united like one long colored scarf that undulated across the fields, along the narrow path winding amid the green wheat, soon lengthened out and broke up into different groups that loitered to talk." How the French loved processions! There was the other procession, the funeral procession with dead Emma winding through different fields at the end of *Madame Bovary,* and in *Claudine à l'ecole,* Colette dwelt lovingly on the procession at the end of her school year, pages and pages of it, the French *Tom Sawyer.*

10:30. Alison ought to be home. Cassidy picked up the phone and dialed Alison's private—*very* private—number which, unlike Alison's other two telephone numbers (which were also private but not *that* private) rang only in his study. The telephone was picked up immediately. "Yes," Alison said. (The other two phones he answered by saying "Hello" but on the *very* private phone, the one that received those mysterious late night calls from Berlin, Budapest, Brussels, he always answered with a stiff, thrusting, questioning: "Yes?")

Cassidy spoke without preamble or introduction: "You're on a hit list, Hugh." He let it sink in and then, because he couldn't resist, he added, "If it's any comfort, you're the last name on the list. If they're killing them in order, you're way down the line."

A long silence on the other end.

"Would you like to hear the other names?" Cassidy asked. Alison said nothing. Cassidy read the list anyway with addresses, spelling out the tough ones, because Alison would be taping.

Another silence. Finally Alison said, "Where did you get the list, Horatio?"

Cassidy told him.

"You're holding back on me, Horatio. That's not very nice."

Cassidy sighed. He was holding back a few things—the woman, for instance—but not this: "You shot out of the Spumi before I had time even to unfold the papers, Hugh. I called you the minute I read them." And that was the truth—although why I'm loyal to the son of a bitch, I couldn't say. Yes, I could but it would take all night.

"Would you send me the list, Horatio. There might be something you've missed . . ." The Agency would examine it for everything—paper, ink, microdots, secret writing, fingerprints, radiation, exhalations, emanations . . .

"Your wish is my command," Cassidy said.

"That'll be the day," Alison said and hung up.

Why was Alison on the hit list? He was on a lot of shit lists. He was widely, with good reason, disliked. But a hit list? A gunrunners' hit list?

The phone rang, and Cassidy grabbed it on the first ring to keep it from waking Lucia. "Got a pencil, Cassidy?" Lieutenant Fletcher said. "The cabbie's name is Gariglia, owns his own cab. He took the lady all the way to Brooklyn—very nice neighborhood overlooking the Narrows—and got a ten-dollar tip."

"Address?"

"Rarity Street, No. 359. One of them big nice houses that look out over the bay."

"I'll do something for you sometime," Cassidy said.

"How about right now?" Fletcher said. "Is the lady the one who did the dastardly deed?"

"What dastardly deed is that, Lieutenant?"

"Good night, professor—and sweet dreams." The lieutenant hung up.

Cassidy's eyes were on the slip of paper. Jeremiah Wenceslas, 359 Rarity Street, Brooklyn.

Cassidy looked at his watch and grimaced. 10:45 P.M. The bed looked warm and inviting; outside was snow and cold and . . . Oh, hell. He put on his shoes and his worn black coat. From the drawer underneath the bed, from his pile of shirts, he drew out the Moon-watcher, still on the secret list. Alison wouldn't let him use any of the gadgets any more now that he'd left the Agency, but this had been in his possession when he departed and no one had asked for it back.

Underneath the Moonwatcher were the wallets with his other identities, three of them, one Swedish. He picked out an American one, which had the driver's license for Bradford O'Malley, address 869 Biscayne Boulevard, Queens. He put one of the $100 bills in the wallet and put it in his rear pants pocket.

A ladder mounted on wheels leading to the books on the upper shelves was connected to a rail ten feet off the floor. Cassidy pushed the ladder to a point near the rear fireplace, climbed the ladder, and took out two books on French medieval songs. He reached into the space behind the books and pulled out the .357 magnum. Unaccountably, just then he changed his mind. He put the gun back behind the books. No more of that, he said.

Cassidy came down from the ladder and walked around the screen. The sleeping child lay curved in the bed, the face on the pillow facing downward, washed in innocence, looking much younger than her thirteen years. Cassidy kissed the smooth young cheek, charging himself with fresh energy.

He let himself out the door, triple locking it behind him. Lucia had her orders. Never, never unlock the door for anyone when he was away, not even for the President of the United States.

The snowstorm had got much worse.

- 3 -

— Cassidy drove the rented car as slowly as he dared down Rarity, the park on his right side, the line of houses on the other, the snow coming straight off the Narrows in parallel lines, making the viewing more difficult. Ahead—way ahead—the lights on the Verrazano-Narrows Bridge blinked and winked through the snowfall. The houses were well kept, imposing brownstones with brass knockers on the doors and wrought iron railings on the brownstone steps leading up from the street.

Most of them were dark now. It was getting on toward eleven o'clock, and the Brooklyn burghers were in bed. Cassidy saw the number 359 on the wrought iron fence and cruised past slowly, sizing the place up. It wasn't a brownstone like the rest but a gray stone house, later Victorian with great turrets like a fortress, a round tower in the right forefront with a conical roof, a big front porch, and quite a bit of yard in the front and at the side.

Cassidy drove the rented car around the first corner and looked for a parking place. Cars were parked solid for blocks, and eventually he parked across the crosswalk, an offense if a cop happened by, but he doubted that one would. He turned up the collar on his old black coat and trudged through the snow.

There was no one on Rarity. No cars, no pedestrians. He crossed the street and walked toward the big Victorian house on the opposite side, the snow getting down his back, into his mouth, his eyes. If the lights are out in the house, I'll have to make the play. Two black-bag jobs in a single day . . .

He was now three houses away, on the opposite side of the street. No light at all showed on the gray stone house.

A car cruised down Rarity, its headlights glimmering through the falling snow, the only moving car in the area, as Cassidy was the only pedestrian.

A low brick wall separated the sidewalk from the small strip of greenery called Rarity Park, bordering the bay. Cassidy vaulted the wall and was instantly enveloped in shrubbery and darkness, his low shoes deep in the snow, well out of the streetlights and away from the headlight beam.

The car stopped in front of 359 Rarity. A four-door, light blue, middle-class car, blatantly inconspicuous. If a man was looking to find a car that would attract no attention whatsoever, that is the kind of car he would choose.

The rear door, the one at the curb, opened and a man stepped out. Even at a distance of forty feet, there was no mistaking those broad shoulders, that imposing air of authority. The big man known as Wenceslas turned to say something to whoever was driving the car. Directly under the streetlight, Wenceslas exuded geniality of such warmth Cassidy could almost feel it. A few moments later the big man turned, opened the wrought iron gate, climbed the stone steps, and went into the house. He was carrying a suitcase. As always.

The car stayed where it was, and this was interesting because it was against the law. Rarity was a thoroughfare. No parking. No stopping at any time. Clearly the big man didn't intend to leave the car there all night. He'd get a ticket. Anyway there was a driver in it. Waiting. Waiting for what?

As long as the driver stays there, I don't have to go breaking and entering again. That man has postponed the unpleasant duty because I can't cross the street without being seen by him. But that doesn't mean I can avoid it. It just means I get to bed even later, and I have a class tomorrow. Cassidy passed the time running over his talk to his students at the New School for Social Research. Sorcery and its place in medieval superstition. Among other superstitions Cassidy planned to list Christianity—a categorization that had got him into lots of trouble in the past and would get him into even more trouble in this era of dense religious fanaticism. The President of the United States, Cassidy was thinking, had said that he considered every word of the Bible divinely inspired. I shall remind my little monsters that the Bible is a translation of a translation of a translation and that much of it was divinely inspired by pagan religions from which the Christians pinched any little morsel that suited their fancy.

The snow filtering down his coat collar into his shirt, his shoes now soaked through, the cold smiting his knees, reaching for his chest. I shall tell my little monsters (some of whom I'm very fond of and the rest of whom are brain damaged beyond help) that the Virgin Mary was not a Virgin until she was dead two hundred years. The Christians stole that myth from Athena who had been a virgin for three thousand years before Christ was born and five thousand years before Doris Day was a virgin. I hope that damned driver is as cold as I am. He must be getting very cold indeed because the engine isn't running and there he sits . . .

After the first hour, Cassidy found it hard to keep his humor intact. His eyes were blurred with weariness, and his concentration was going. No light showed in the big house. For the third time, he brought out the Moonwatcher and inspected the gray stone edifice, starting at the third floor, going from window to window, the marvelous gadget dissolving the darkness into red light, bringing out each Victorian gewgaw with stunning clarity, each of the windows dark and empty.

No. Not that one. Cassidy stopped the scope at a first floor window at the extreme left of his vision. The two faces came in bright and clear. Wenceslas was talking and pointing with his superb self-confidence at something out the window. Pointing at . . . what? The house had a nice view of the bay. Is that why it had been selected? To give it a view of the big ships as they came in? Except not many big ships passed that way any more . . .

Cassidy concentrated on the woman, bringing her in to a sharp close-up, her face filling the scope altogether. No longer terrified but clearly unhappy. Beautiful girl, dark eyed, almost olive complexion, with a stillness about her that seemed deep as the ocean. Saying nothing, as the big man next to her chattered away. Disagreeing, though. So thought Cassidy. Whatever he's saying she doesn't like and doesn't approve of. There's moral as well as intellectual disagreement in that face. I'm getting lightheaded in this icy landscape, reaching conclusions that would get me laughed out of the Agency if I were not already out of the Agency . . .

He tore the scope away from the girl's lovely unhappy face and turned the instrument a little to the left of her to see what the background had to say. Books. Floor to ceiling. Just like my place. Cassidy fine tuned the scope until he could read the titles. Some were not books but manuscripts and documents. He looked at the titles: *Arms for the Third World* by James D. Atkinson; *The Soviet Military Aid Program as a Reflection of Soviet Objectives* Atlantic Research Project; *Moscaus Militarhilfe an Die Dritte Welt* Eberhardt Einbeck . . .

That was as far as his reading went. The blow came from behind, sending an explosion of white light through his brain, immediately followed by the most velvety blackness.

His head roared like a typhoon. Deep inside him a bellows expanded and contracted with great solemnity and agonizing strength. Whistling a ragtime tune. Cassidy Cassidy Cassidy in ragtime. Consciousness sent out a small experimental shoot. Warmth. I'm warm, and I was cold. Aah, the splendor of warmth. The bellows expanding and contracting and whistling a ragtime. My lungs, that's what's making those rhythmic whifflings. Breathing is what I'm doing. How very nice. When you stop breathing. . . . That throbbing is my heart. When that stops throbbing you're in big trouble.

Keeping his eyes closed, trying to piece it together. Somebody belted me from behind. And how did they get behind me? Because I wasn't paying attention, that's why. And why was I standing there waiting to be taken from behind? Because that bastard was sitting there in that car, holding me there, immobilizing me until they could get a goon behind me to take me out, that's why, you big dumb lug. They were setting you up with that car parked there. And keep your eyes closed and your breathing regular so they think you're still out.

Warmth. That meant he was inside and from the feel of things lying on something not quite soft enough to be a bed but too soft to be the floor. A sofa probably.

The voices were above him. One voice very close. The other a few feet away.

"Try the shoes." The close voice. Very middle America. Nebraska or somewhere like that.

Cassidy felt his wet shoes removed from him one by one. Why? Searching him, of course. What have I got on me? False identity papers . . .

"Try the heels. That's where they put it usually."

They're going to tear apart my shoes, and I can't afford another pair . . .

"Iss nothink." Now where is that accent from? Germany? Or deeper in the eastern zone, and in the lower class. And not all that bright. Pretty good education from three syllables with your eyes closed.

Now what were they doing?

Cassidy felt the touch, light as the breath of spring, across the base of his nostrils, the most vulnerable spot of all, unbearable. He tried with all his might to resist but . . .

"At-CHOO!"

His eyes flew open in spite of all his resolve and he found himself staring straight into the amused eyes of Wenceslas who sat next to him, feather in hand.

"I rather thought you were awake," the big man said pleasantly. "If you watch a sleeping man carefully, Mr. O'Malley, you can—with a little practice—*read* him. The kind of thoughts he's thinking." All this in a conversational tone as if they were old friends. "You were asking yourself questions. What are they doing? Why are they taking my shoes off? You could almost read it off your eyeballs. Awake questions. Not sleeping questions. Sleeping questions are quite quite different—deeper, more . . . what shall I say . . . dreamlike, more abstract, more intense, more soul searching. I've done quite a bit of research on sleeping."

Cassidy's gaze slithering about during this, taking in the scenery. The man with that Balkan lower-class accent stood a few feet away. Bony fellow, thin as a blade, who looked as if he hadn't smiled in thirty years.

"How do you feel?" Wenceslas asked.

"Terrible," Cassidy said. He didn't feel all that bad, but it was best to exaggerate your infirmity, to get the other side to let down its guard . . .

"You could feel much worse. Mr. Slovik is an expert at the business, applying just enough pressure to put you away and not so much as to do damage. It's a very great gift."

Cassidy tried to sit up. "I'll be running along now. I've got an early class tomorrow . . ."

The big man put his hand on Cassidy's chest and pushed him prone, which wasn't hard. Cassidy's muscles were like water.

"A few questions first, Mr. O'Malley. If you don't mind . . ."

Cassidy tried to match the geniality because he had no choice. "Always glad to be helpful to any man who coshes me in a snowstorm. After all, you got me out of that snowbank into this nice warm room. Very kind of you."

He could see his wallet now, on the table beside the sofa, his fake driver's license lying next to it with his name and picture in it, and next to that the Moonwatcher.

Wenceslas picked up the Moonwatcher. "Where did you get this delightful toy, Mr. O'Malley. I've always wanted one."

"Try Macy's," Cassidy said. "They have everything at Macy's, and they won't be undersold."

Mr. Wenceslas' geniality dimmed just the tiniest bit. "I'll tell Colonel Khaddafi," Wenceslas said. "He's been trying to buy some of your night-seeing devices for years, but your arms control people are very narrow-minded about Colonel Khaddafi."

"Oh, you know Colonel Khaddafi, do you?"

"I know everyone, Mr. O'Malley. I know far too many people in all walks of life all over the world. It's a very great burden."

"I'll get out of your life, Mr. Wenceslas, if you'll just let me up."

Wenceslas pushed Cassidy back down absently, as if he were a child. "Don't rush off. We have much to talk about."

He'd picked up another object from the table. Oh, Jesus! thought Cassidy. Why did I bring *that* along? I should be shot at sunrise and probably will be.

It was the little scroll of paper he'd taken from the dead man's heel.

"You can't get this at Macy's, Mr. O'Malley. Very special paper indeed. Fortunately I've encountered it before, and I know just how to deal with it."

The girl came in then, bringing along her miasma of unhappiness so piercing Cassidy could smell it. She carried a small brown bottle she handed the big man without a word. Wenceslas pulled out the cork, which had a wire with a soft felt brush on the end. He brushed the felt against the piece of paper and instantly brown lines appeared on it. Cassidy could see the writing from the underside. Mirror writing, it looked like.

The girl with the olive complexion and the miasma of unhappiness had walked out of the room, stiff with what Cassidy devoutly hoped was disapproval.

"Where did you get this, Mr. O'Malley?"

The easygoing charm had vanished. Wenceslas was very much more interested in the piece of paper than in the Moonwatcher, Cassidy was thinking. That gives me a little edge. Wenceslas is not going to knock me on the head and drop the body in the bay until he finds out where that piece of paper comes from.

"My mother," Cassidy said, "writes me these little notes to remind me I'm to bring home some knockwurst."

The big man rose from the sofa, looking eight feet tall. "Mr. Slovik," he said, "the pentothal."

"Kapitsch," the Balkan said, and left the room.

"It won't work," Cassidy said. "I'll talk your arm off under sodium

-33-

pentothal but you won't hear anything you want to hear because I don't know anything. You'll probably have to listen to all ten of my lectures and unless you're very interested in medieval literature, this can get very boring."

The big man rocked on his heels, his eyes on the little piece of paper Cassidy had taken from the heel of the dead man on Forensic Street. Two minutes later, the needle entered Cassidy's arm, and he drifted into Never Never Land in a state of exhilaration beyond the reach of coherence.

He began talking immediately, his CIA resistance training still firm and vigorous. The trick was to talk and talk and talk and never listen, Ulysses and the Sirens in modern dress. Where Ulysses plugged up his ears to keep the Siren call from him, Cassidy plugged up his brain with the hypnotic sound of his own voice, prattling on and on, the urge to talk irresistible under pentothal, not listening to the questions, not hearing them even, blanking them out with his own superior wisdom, which, under the drug, seemed to be the voice of God, immensely wise, omniscient, encompassing the universe, and all the other universes, babble babble babble . . .

Eventually silence and slumber.

He awoke slowly, his brain still buzzing, his nerves blissful with the pentothal. Later would come the reckoning; now was the bliss. Total darkness. He sat up, swung his legs around to the floor. A bed. A cot of some sort. His hands probed the blackness for what they could find. On his left a wall, on his right another. Behind him, still another. Very small room. His right hand encountered a bit of cord hanging above him. He pulled it gently, and a light came on overhead.

He was in a closet. No windows. No anything except the bed. He was in shirt and trousers. No jacket. No shoes.

Exhilaration ebbed. What did I tell them? What *could* I tell them? Plenty. Did I tell them about Alison? The body on Forensic Street? The artillery shells? He couldn't be sure. The resistance method worked well up to a point, but between babble and blackout there was an interval when the man under drugs felt such bonhomie for his interrogators that he would tell them anything they wanted to know, give them the shirt off his back, his money, his wife . . .

Cassidy tried the door. Locked.

His watch was missing. What time was it? Late. Very late. Cassidy had an interior watch in his skull. He could wake up in the middle of the night and, with intense concentration, guess the time within a minute or so. Five A.M. He could be wrong because the drug might throw his interior clock awry. The sound of the silence was that of 5 A.M.

In another couple of hours, Lucia would awake, find him gone . . .

Into the sound of the silence came the breathing.

Just outside the door. Very light breathing but so still was the house that the faint sound carried through the wood. Breathing. Inhale. Exhale. Cassidy stood up weakly, hand on the wall. No condition to fight. The big man could take him with two fingers.

The sound persisting, just the other side of that door. Inhale. Exhale. And with it something else—indecision. I can smell indecision. The person on the other side of that door is torn by indecision. Now isn't that interesting?

A faint scrabbling noise like mice in the pantry. The key in the lock. Cassidy flattened himself behind the door.

The door opened, and Cassidy sprang his hammerlock.

"Don't!" the woman said softly, sharply.

Her perfume in his nostrils. Violets.

Cassidy removed his arm from her neck. "Sorry," he said.

She stood before him, reproachful, his shoes in her hand, his jacket and worn black coat over her arm. The complexion olive, faintly so, a brush of olive. Olive on one side of the family but not on the other. The eyes dark.

She extended the shoes to him. "We must be quiet," she said.

Cassidy sat on the bed and put on his shoes, whose heels had been put back in place. She handed him his jacket, which he slipped on. His tie and his watch were in the side pocket.

His mind clamoring. This is a bit too much of a good thing. Why is she doing this? Look for the con. Aloud he said, "My wallet?" How would she handle that? Anyway he wanted to hear her talk, any- thing . . .

"I don't know what they did with that. I'm sorry." A little trouble with the R's there. Sorr-ee. Unable to let go of the R's. She spoke English with too much precision. Clearly it wasn't her first language. She was dressed in a simple red wool dress with big patch pockets, which meant she'd changed clothes since he'd seen her last, gotten undressed and dressed again, whatever that meant.

She reached into one of the big patch pockets and pulled out a gold money clip. She peeled off four bills and handed them to Cassidy. Brand new bills. Hundreds. Cassidy picked off the top bill and extended the other three in her direction. "I only had a hundred dollars on me."

She shook her head. "Keep it," she said indifferently, "to pay for your wallet, the damage they did to your coat."

Cassidy looked at his coat. It looked all right. What could they do to that threadbare old coat?

"They . . . looked into the . . . seams. Everywhere, I'm sorry." Again that trouble with the R's.

Now that was interesting. They were still looking for—what? His identity? He tried a question, not expecting much, still looking for the con (but even the con told you something). "What did I say under the pentothal? Anything interesting?"

The answer he got was totally unexpected. The dark brooding face broke into a dazzling smile, the first he'd seen on her. It made her look much younger. "You said you were Osiris, King of the Dead, and you threatened dire calamities, maledictions, and perditions. I've never heard anyone use words like that in conversation."

"I'm Irish," Cassidy said. "Words are our undoing. Words and whiskey."

Her face was lit by the memory, joyful. "You went on and on and on about the thirteenth century. The discipline and purity of knighthood, the beauty and *innocence* of chivalry. You're living in the wrong century, Mr. O'Malley . . ."

O'Malley.

They still thought of him as O'Malley. He hadn't let his real name slip.

"You're better when you smile," Cassidy said. "You should do it more often."

That ended it. The veil of unhappiness fell back on her face like a lead curtain. "You must go. They'll be waking up soon."

"Just when we're getting to know one another," Cassidy said, not moving. "What's your name?"

She smiled at that, not the radiant, joyous smile of before, this time a sad smile. "Kore," she said. "I, too, am a god, Osiris."

"Kore?" He'd never heard of a Kore in mythology.

"Later they called me Persephone. The original name was Kore. Come on." She took his hand and led him out of the room, pulling the overhead cord, extinguishing the light. They were in a narrow corridor on badly worn carpets lit by the faint glow from street lamps that came through a round window at the end of the corridor. The servants quarters, guessed Cassidy, back when people had servants. Her hand still clutching his, sending electricity to his very toes. Sex shaking its gory locks at me, when I should be keeping my wits about me . . .

A narrow staircase plunged steeply just under the round window. She led him down it, hand in his. At the foot was a door that led to the second floor landing and here luxury obtruded. The carpet was soft and deep, the hallway was very wide with hunting scenes on the wallpaper, everything freshly painted. They were out of the servants quarters into the comfort and ease of the bourgeoisie. Only for a moment. Kore opened a door that led again to the backstairs—narrow, badly carpeted, steep. They were back with the working classes.

The backstairs led to the kitchen—a big kitchen, lit dimly through windows. At one side Cassidy saw a big butler's pantry, its shelves covered with dishes and silverplate. Next to that was the servants' dining room. The kitchen itself contained a big chopping table, its racks hung with copper pots and shiny pans. The stove had nine burners, big as a hotel stove, as if accustomed to cooking for a score or more.

She led him to the door. "Go round that side," she said, pointing. "You're at the rear of the house."

Letting go his hand.

"When will we two meet again?" Cassidy asked. Looking for the con. There *must* be a con. The thing was unreal.

"Probably never," she said. "You must go now. I have to go back to bed."

He made a last stab. "What's Wenceslas to you or you to Wencelas?"

She showed a spark of outrage at that. He'd trespassed on her privacy. "Indissolubly linked, Mr. O'Malley. Please go."

That left no room for maneuver at all. Without a word, Cassidy turned and let himself out the back door, and down the back steps, leaving a trail of footsteps behind him in the virgin snow. That was her funeral, not his. It didn't seem to bother her, and it bloody well *should* bother her and that bothered him. Wenceslas was not one to brook interference, and his vengeance was drastic. As witness that body on the floor in Forensic Street. Why was she letting him go so light-heartedly?

Something very rotten in Denmark . . .

Cassidy made his way through the snow to the front of the house, and there his footprints joined another set of footprints. Outward bound footprints. Someone had left the house sometime after the snow had stopped falling, which meant after he was slugged and taken into the house.

There was a set of footprints on the sidewalk. Two sets. One led to the right, the other to the left. Or was it the same set? Someone had gone to the right and returned and gone left. The car that had stood at the curb, blocking his way, was gone. Cassidy went back to the rented car—and the trail of footprints went right along, deviating here and there, to wander up side streets, and then wander back—as if searching for something. The footprints marched directly to his rented car. And stopped. Circled.

His car, so badly parked. A dead giveaway.

All Cassidy's senses quivering now. The footprints crossed the street—and headed back to the house. The con was beginning to fall into place.

Cassidy pulled out the car keys, sorted them out, his eyes, under guise of sorting out keys, shooting this way and that, looking for what he could see, which was nothing. He unlocked the rented car, taking his time, giving them time to show themselves. Nothing in the mirrors or anywhere.

Cassidy started the car, backed out of the space, his wheels spinning in the snow, and shot down the side street to Rarity, which had been cleared of snow. On Rarity he opened it up, glancing at his mirrors from time to time. Speed would flush them out.

Far behind, he saw the tail, that blatantly inconspicuous light blue car—conspicuous now because it was the only car.

So that then was the con. They'd looked up that phoney address from his fake driver's license, found it was a phoney, and now they wanted to know his real address—and his real name. Wenceslas was trying to wrest from Cassidy exactly what Cassidy was trying to wrest from Wenceslas—his real name, and his lair.

Kore had let him out of that room, not out of kindness but because Wenceslas had told her to let him out so that he Cassidy would show his hand, his home, his allegiance. He thinks I'm taking orders from whoever wrote that piece of paper. He wants to know who it was—and I don't know who it was—or even what it was, which he apparently does.

Well, that was the way of the world. Nevertheless, and in spite of it all, Cassidy felt a deep and crushing sense of disappointment. I should know better, and I *do* know better, but just the same . . . What are you to Wenceslas and Wenceslas to you? Indissolubly linked, she had said. His girl? His secretary? His assistant? All three? I am an Irish romantic unfit for low purpose. Like espionage.

I'll lead them a chase to cure me of my disappointment and show them a thing or two. He put the accelerator on the floor. The car leaped forward, but so did the light blue car behind. Cassidy blazed off Rarity into the side streets of Bay Ridge, through miles of parked cars, on streets not yet cleared of snow, up Seventy-sixth, doubling back on Seventieth to Fourth Avenue, weaving around the girders under the elevated, a sharp right on Thirty-six for a wild ride around Greenwood Cemetery—the light blue car staying stubbornly in his rear mirror.

The driver of the other car—that Balkan low-class clown?—was very good and refused to be buffaloed by the double Felix or even the triple Roger, so Cassidy ran down Seventh, turned left on Prospect, and skidded to a halt under the el at Fourth. The train was a block away, making its infernal din in the quiet hour.

Cassidy abandoned the rented car next to the closed and deserted newspaper kiosk directly under the elevated, sprinted up the stairs, just as the train pulled in. He dropped a token in the slot and strolled aboard. From the doorway he could see the light blue car belting down Prospect, still half a block away.

At Union Square he got off the train and made a call from the phone booth. While listening to the ring, he pulled his watch out of his pocket and looked at the time. 5:38. The garage answered on the fourth ring. A sleepy voice, both mellifluous and slightly querulous. "Yeah, man."

"Mu Mu," said Cassidy. "I've abandoned the car under the el at Prospect and Fourth in Brooklyn. It's so illegally parked that the police will be on the scene within ten minutes."

Silence. In his mind's eye, Cassidy could see the tall, immensely dignified black man assimilating this in his unhurried way. There was no point ever in trying to hurry Mu Mu Talaki. You had to let him go at his own pace.

"What you do that for, Mr. Cassidy?" Always polite under even the most severe provocation.

"The bad guys were after me, Mu Mu."

Again, the long pause.

"Mr. Cassidy, I thought you give up all that foolishness. I thought you settle down to be a prof and a good daddy to your girl."

"Bad companions, Mu Mu, I fell among rapscallions."

"You want me to go out there to Brooklyn and pick up that car, Mr. Cassidy. I can't leave my garage."

"I don't want you to leave your garage. Let the police pick it up and tow it away, and you claim it again tomorrow. I'll pay the fine and the full rate. Let the cops handle it. I don't want that car tracked back to your garage."

"They got the license number. All they got to do is call the police."

"They won't call the police. Not these people. You just leave the car where it is, and don't pick it up until tomorrow. I'm trying to muddy the waters, Mu Mu."

Another pause. Mu Mu's low reproach: "You git back to that little girl, Mr. Cassidy. Hear now."

Cassidy walked from Union Square to his apartment on Thirteenth Street through the silent snowy streets. He unlocked the three locks carefully and quietly. Lucia was still soundly sleeping. Six o'clock. With any luck he'd get an uninterrupted hour and a half. He took off his shoes and lay down on the bed, eyes open.

I don't want any more of this.

- 4 -

— "Death was always present—both in thought and deed, in the giving and in the receiving—in that most terminal, most intransigent of centuries." Thus Cassidy the teacher, Cassidy the actor. Standing straight as a pole, his palms pressed together, as if in prayer, voice stern, features unforgiving.

Even while delivering these pieties, he was counting the house. Sixteen students. Two less than last week. If these losses continued . . . his tongue yapping away at the familiar words, his mind miles away . . . the school would cancel this class. Then where would he be? Or Lucia?

"Death was not the End; it was the Beginning," Cassidy capitalizing the word, playing with it, laying it at the feet of his students for their contemplation and wonder.

Deborah Lofts's mouth, as usual, was open. That was her way of adoring him, to open her mouth. Deborah with the big breasts and stout legs and adoring open mouth. Not my type. But he drank in the adoration because he needed it. The wine of life. Adoration of a young plastic mind.

"In their brief lives—and life was very brief in the thirteenth century—they courted, they contemplated, they lived with *Eternity* . . ." Giving the word roundness and depth. "Eternity gave their lives a richness, a glory, a *douleur,* almost incomprehensible to modern minds."

Next to Deborah, Joshua G. Fairweather, the fat boy, brightest in the class, lips pursed in silent disagreement. Joshua was Jesuit trained. He'll stay after class to argue every word, the little snipe, and today I don't want to. Cassidy's students were of two sorts—the adorers like Deborah, or the disagreers like Joshua. He left no one indifferent. Some students got so irritated, they wrote the Dean—annoying him because he had to reply to all the complaints.

The class ended, and the students filed out. Not Joshua, of course. Joshua approached the desk as Cassidy gathered together his papers, his books. He brought these to class, only as props, something to do with his hands.

The fat boy was bubbling with smiling hostility: "One is tempted to say, professor, that you are almost theological in your contempt for Christianity. A form of religion, wouldn't you agree?"

Cassidy turned his fiercest glare on the Jesuit: "Mr. Fairweather, you'll never make cardinal with such pusillanimity. You must oppose me! Denounce me! Show a little fire! Don't temporize! Bring down thunderbolts!"

That thunderbolt caught the Jesuit amidships and stopped him in his tracks. Cassidy swept out of the room.

Deborah Lofts lay in wait, just outside the classroom door, and fell in step with him. "Professor, you were *marvelous*!"

"Deborah, Deborah, you marvel too easily!" He smiled, taking the sting out. "How are you and Thomas Aquinas coming along?"

"Professor, I'm not *ready* for Thomas Aquinas!"

"Then I have failed you, Deborah."

"Oh, professor, it's not your fault; the fault is in me."

An old argument.

They were out of the school now headed for Fifth Avenue, Cassidy striding through knots of students, Deborah in tow, spreading misunderstanding. They think I'm screwing her, and I'm not. The obloquy is mine without the pleasure; such are the joys of student adoration.

At Fifth Avenue, where he usually lost her, Cassidy turned north. This time she came with him. "You're going the wrong direction," he said.

"I've just moved into a new apartment." Her eyes bright as stars. "You must come see it. It's beautiful. On Twelfth."

Oh, dear God! Twelfth!

"I'll walk you there," said Cassidy firmly. "I won't come up because I'm in a tearing hurry."

He walked her to the brownstone, which was beautiful and, he guessed, expensive. East Twelfth was not cheap. Deborah then must be pretty well off. "I'd love to cook you dinner sometime, professor."

They had been through this before. It was going to be harder to get out of it, now that she had moved into the neighborhood. He used the old stall.

"I've got a thirteen-year-old daughter. I have to help her with her Latin, her math—and then it's bedtime."

"Bring her along."

Cassidy smiled at the plump and passionate adorer. "Someday, Deborah, I will. But only when you're ready for Thomas Aquinas."

He strode off toward his pad on Thirteenth Street, feeling her adoration on his backside like sunshine. I love teaching for all the wrong reasons, but nevertheless my passion is genuine. I would be lost without my teaching, not only financially but emotionally.

At Fourteenth Street, Cassidy bought *The New York Times* and ambled bonelessly back to Thirteenth Street, his eyes running down the news summaries. Nothing about a body found on Forensic Street. Or boxloads of projectiles. On page 16 there was a story that caught him by the throat: "The London *Times* said today that the Israelis were supplying Iran with American-made anti-tank guided missiles, a clear violation of U.S. arms policies and agreements. Both Iran and Israel deny the story."

In his mind's eyes, Cassidy saw again the peaceful poisoned face on the floor of the Forensic basement with its twelve-generational sadness. Iranian? No, the Persians had a hundred generations to be sad about, but he doubted that was an Iranian. At least not a pure Iranian.

At Thirteenth Street again, Cassidy studied his front door carefully. He'd laid four telltales, hairs from his own head, across the crevasses, and they were all still in place. A man might find one or even two and replace them. Not four. Nobody had entered that door since he'd left.

He locked all three locks behind him and called Alison on his top secret private number.

"Yeah," Alison said.

Cassidy let him have it without prior ado: "I want out, Hugh. This guy is too dangerous for me. I've got a thirteen-year-old daughter dependent on me, and I don't want to play these games anymore."

"She's not your daughter."

Cassidy's temper flared: "She *is* my daughter, God damn it, Alison. I adopted her."

"Okay. Okay." Alison was instantly placating. "I didn't know that, Horatio. I'm sorry."

Cassidy was not mollified: "You'll have to find someone else to do your dirty work, Alison. I've had enough."

"What happened?"

"I got knocked on the head and pumped full of pentothal."

"Jesus, you didn't . . ."

"I don't think I told them anything, but I don't want anymore of this. Wenceslas wants something out of me that I'm unable to give him. I don't know what he wants me to tell him. But he'll go to any lengths to get what I can't give him."

"I'll be in New York this afternoon. I'll meet you at the Spumi at four o'clock."

"No, damn it, Alison. I don't even want to be *seen* with you . . ."

Alison had already rung off.

Cassidy rolled over on the bed, his hands underneath his head, and thought about things. Presently, he got off the bed and pushed his ladder on its wheels to the far end of the room. He climbed the ladder and brought down a book, *Arms Sales as Historical Process*. It was full of turned down pages containing bits he had planned to put into some of his lectures.

In the modern world arms sales increasingly have little to do with attack and defense or even with war. Arms making is as much a matter of public policy as bridge building. The making and selling of arms is diplomacy by other means, fulfilling the function once filled by actual warfare. Arms are part of the process of industrial growth, and woe betide the nation that neglects the technical offshoots of the development and manufacture of modern weapons. In addition, armaments— their manufacture, their possession, their *display*—have functions far removed from national defense. They are part of the nation's psyche, its national pride and prestige, as intrinsic to national dynamics as the building of cathedrals to the Middle Ages.

To Cassidy, the scholar of the Middle Ages, that last sentence was a flash of blinding white light.

"Where does Wenceslas live?" Alison asked.

"First you got to tell me a few things," Cassidy said.

They were in the back room of the Spumi at four o'clock, the quiet hour before the drinkers arrived, Cassidy with his Wild Turkey, Alison with his Perrier and ice. Both playing it tough.

"You're holding out again, Horatio. That's not only unkind. It's unwise." Alison was showing his muscles. Threats, innuendos, bribes. Alison, Cassidy was thinking, was one of the few eighteen-karat sons of bitches he'd ever known. All the other sons of bitches were to some degree diluted with kindness, generosity, decency. Alison was the real article. Pure bastard all the way through and a yard wide.

"I don't enjoy having to resort to patriotism, Horatio," Alison was saying.

"That's supposed to be the last refuge of scoundrels, not the first."

Alison didn't blink. "This whole operation is part of an intricate, ongoing, very delicate bit of our diplomacy . . ."

Diplomacy. The word rang in Cassidy's skull. *Diplomacy by other means . . .*

Alison still talking. "When the diplomats get on the scene, you must realize, Horatio, motivation gets very deep. The American shipment of F 5s to North Yemen to match the Soviet MIGs to South Yemen had nothing to do with defense. The Yemenis couldn't even fly the things. It was done to strengthen the American position in the Salt talks. And to show Congress what a tough bargainer our dear President was."

"Cut out the generalities, Hugh. That son of a bitch Wenceslas was prepared to blow up the building, which probably would have demolished the buildings on either side of him and might have killed a dozen people. Why don't we arrest the guy?"

"For what?"

"Murder for one thing. There was a dead man on the floor."

"Don't be sentimental, Horatio."

"Sentimental! Murder!"

"Keep your voice down."

"Who was that poor sad-faced wog on the floor? What's his nationality, and what did Wenceslas want to kill him for?"

Alison rubbed his nose muttering: "I can't tell you that."

"Then I won't tell you where Wenceslas lives. Loosen up a little, Hugh, if you expect anything out of me."

Alison's mouth, set in that smooth, too well shaven face, was hard as cement. Silence for a very long time, neither man giving much. When Alison gave, the words came out slow, as if they hurt him inside. "It's a question of balance and imbalance in weaponry. If one side has SAMs, the other thinks it needs glide bombs with terminal guidance, and perhaps they can't afford them or just plain can't get them. Therefore they will do what's in their power to stop the first guy from getting the SAMs."

"Those weren't SAMs. What were they?"

Alison shook his head. "I've given you a clue. Now you give me something back, Horatio."

Cassidy thought it over. I shouldn't be negotiating. I should just tell him to fuck off. What the hell am I doing? Nevertheless he took out the four brand-new hundred-dollar bills and counted them out in front of Alison: "Brand new, consecutive serial numbers."

Alison's face lit like a fuse: "From Wenceslas?" He grabbed for the money, but Cassidy held it close to his chest. "Not so fast. He took my wallet with all the money in it. This is . . . repayment for injuries suffered and this and that." He still hadn't mentioned the woman to Alison. He didn't want to share Kore with Alison.

Alison was in high fever. "Is it money you want?" He had out his own gold money clip and was peeling off hundreds (Uncle Sam's? Or his rich wife's? Anyway not Alison's) and put four on the table. Reluctantly Cassidy handed over his four bills. His last tenuous connection with that olive-skinned lady who said she would probably never see him again.

"We'll hand it over to analysis, put it through the machinery. If it's phoney money, that'll tell us a lot. If it's real, it would tell us even more."

"Your turn now, Hugh? What was in those packing cases on Forensic Street?"

Cassidy enjoyed the pain in Alison's face. Alison hated parting with information even more than parting with his own money. Finally Alison spoke in a low whisper: "Rocket assisted laser guided artillery shells." As if he were handing over the crown jewels.

It didn't mean a thing to Cassidy. "Ours?"

"Nobody else has shells like ours that go a hundred miles, and nobody else is supposed to get them. Do you understand, Horatio?"

"No."

Alison shrugged. "It's what you asked for. Now it's your turn to give. What did Wenceslas want that he put you under pentothal to get?"

Cassidy broke into his crooked ferocity of a grin. The shit is really going to hit the fan, he thought. He told Alison about the piece of paper he'd taken from the dead man's heel with its secret writing.

Alison's face was thunderous: "Holding out again, Cassidy. We could have given it to the lab people, and they'd have figured out that chemical in ten minutes. Now it's lost to us forever."

"Oh, no," Cassidy said. "I read it upside down. Mirror writing. One word."

"What word?"

"*Your* turn, Alison." They were on last name basis now, slugging it out, mortal enemies. "You haven't told me about that dead wog yet. What's his nationality?" A quick pitch. Would Alison . . .

Alison's jaw worked. He chewed on his cheek, hunched his shoulders, scowled. He really hated to give up this bit, thought Cassidy, which means it was important.

"A Libyan Jew. A member of one of the ten Lost Tribes, if you can get any significance out of that, and I'm sure that you can."

"What was that word you read upside down and backwards?" Alison asked.

Cassidy was loath to part with it for obscure emotional reasons that he couldn't sort out at the moment. But if he wanted to wrestle some more information out of Alison . . . Cassidy showed the CIA man the piece of paper on which he had traced out the mirror writing: a single backward word.

Alison held it up to the mirror that formed the rear wall of the back room of the Spumi. The word reversed itself into: CORIANDER.

Alison wrote the word down in his expensive leather notebook from Hermès with his gold pencil from Cartier's.

"Your turn, Alison. Who's Wenceslas working for?"

The answer came so easily that Alison must not have minded parting with it very much, Alison's eyes still intent on that word CORIANDER. "Everyone," he said. "Including us. He's an operator. *Big* operator."

"Jesus!"

"That sums it up very well."

"That's why you don't want to toss him to the lawmen. You're *dealing* with him!"

"It's a very big picture, very complicated."

"You're dealing with the son of a bitch, and you don't even know his name?"

"*I'm* not dealing with him. Others are."

That opened up a lot of vistas. Someone in clandestine arranging for the sad wog to be killed in order that rocket assisted laser guided artillery shells that could travel a hundred miles did not land in the hands of . . . who? Libya? Syria? Israel? A Libyan Jew, a member of the Lost Tribes (if Alison hadn't made that up to throw sand in my face) lying dead of poison on the floor?

"Where does he live, Horatio?"

That was the big one. Why this emotional turmoil? I'm tired, that's all. Big night. The strain of the classroom. Financial worry . . .

"Rarity Street. 359. Big house overlooking the Narrows. You can see all the ships come in." Watching Alison's fingers. Alison was a master of keeping it out of his face, but the fingers always gave signals. The fingers on the gold pencil tightened just a fraction as Alison wrote down the address in the expensive leather notebook. That tells him something, that address.

Alison put away the gold pencil, the leather notebook. From his left hand jacket pocket in the beautiful sharkshin suit he brought out a gold money clip—a *different* gold money clip. "The projectiles are still in Forensic Street. Wenceslas doesn't know—or anyway hasn't done anything about the fact that the building didn't blow up, but that situation cannot be expected to continue much longer."

Alison was now counting out *thousand*-dollar bills—one, two, three . . .

"I'm not playing any more, Alison," Cassidy said harshly.

Alison continued without change in his voice. "The projectiles must be removed tonight, the police have been warned off, Rattigan is there watching the house right now . . .

"I'm too old, and Wenceslas is too dangerous an adversary for an aging professor with a thirteen-year-old girl to take care of. I don't want to get killed."

"You *never* get killed, Horatio," Alison counting out six, seven, eight *thousand*-dollar bills, "although you should have been ten times over."

"I'm not going to do it, Hugh. Wenceslas wants to know who sent that message, and I don't know. He struck out with pentothal, and

next time he'll start pulling my fingernails out. It's not a game I enjoy."
Where did Alison get all those thousand-dollar bills? His wife? The
Agency? There were twelve thousand-dollar bills in a heap in front of
him now. "Why me?"

"Because you got more brains than the others. You'll have Rattigan, Pindar, and Keefe to help, but I want you to run it."

Rattigan, Pindar, and Keefe had all been thrown out of the Agency
in the general housekeeping cleanup along with Cassidy. Alison was
recruiting all the Old Boys from outside the Agency. Why?

"There's not enough money in your wife's bank account . . ."

Sticking it right in his face in the hope he'd get mad and walk out
with all those thousand-dollar bills.

Alison said quietly: "Rattigan's already taken care of the body. I
realize you're squeamish about bodies, Horatio."

"The smell of them reaches to heaven, Hugh."

"You don't believe in heaven, Horatio."

In the end it wasn't the money. It was the romantic foolishness that
swayed him. "*When will we two meet again?*" "*Probably never.*" Well,
we shall see about that. There are possibilities that need to be
explored, my lady with the sad face. There are questions that need
answering. Was it rescue or betrayal that was on your mind when you
unlocked the door to my room? And why? Why rescue? Why
betrayal? What's Wenceslas to you or you to Wenceslas? And why the
sadness?

- 5 -

— Keefe drove the big U-Haul moving van, talking a blue streak, the words tumbling out of him with passion and, occasionally, coherence. "You and I, Cassidy, are the assholes of history through which the leaders of Western civilization defecate over the common people."

"Watch your driving, man!" Cassidy ordered.

The big van had rounded Rivington into Forensic, missing a parked car by a millimeter.

"What I say is somebody has to do it, and why not me because the fact is I enjoy it and so do you, you miserable medievalist. You deceive yourself with your high flown resolve, Cassidy, but never old Keefe."

A huge man with shoulders like a wrestler's, Keefe had gone to Trinity in Dublin and had never stopped talking before or after.

"How did you get out of Castro's jail?" Cassidy asked.

"Money," Keefe said with his big grin.

"Alison's?"

"I didn't inquire. The money in armaments, old sport, boggles the mind. Lockheed paid Khashoggi a *hundred* million dollars for services no one, including Khashoggi, has ever been able to explain. Imagine! A hundred million smackers—if you can imagine such a sum."

"I don't want to imagine such a sum. It's corrupting even to think about that kind of money."

"You are troubled by goodness, my boyo. A terrible affliction— goodness. Causes endless harm to the digestion, the bank account, and the peace of mind. Now me, I am not bothered by goodness. When I was in Castro's wretched jail, lying in the slime and the dark, I used to divide myself into a Good Person and a Bad Person and play myself mental chess, and you know something? The Bad Person won every game. You know why?"

"He cheated," Cassidy said.

"Honesty is the worst policy. We all know that."

What am I doing in this enterprise, Cassidy thought. Twelve thousand dollars? Not entirely. Kore? Not entirely that either. I want to know what Alison is up to, and only God knows that and I don't believe in God.

Keefe drew up in front of 127 Forensic and cut the engine. Cassidy lowered his window, letting in the night air, which smelled of coal smoke. The street lights glowed yellow in the mist and the silence. Two A.M. on the button said Cassidy's watch. In spite of all that errant talk, Keefe was punctual as a metronome.

Rattigan materialized at the window of the van, the eyes reproachful behind the gold-rimmed spectacles in the sad clown's face. "Those tires will not take the load," he whispered.

"You might say hello before you launch on your complaining," Keefe whispered indignantly. "You might inquire after my health, which is delicate."

Rattigan grinned his sad clown's grin. The idea of Keefe's health being delicate was a delicious jest.

Cassidy got out of the van and shook hands with Rattigan silently. A gaunt whisper of a man, Cassidy hadn't seen him in twenty years; an idealist in search of an ideal, as they used to say. "Where's Pindar?"

"On the tug. The three of us will have to do the hauling. Twenty-six boxes."

In the basement room nothing had changed except that the wog with the twelve-generational sadness had gone. Cassidy brought out his Swiss Army knife and screwed down the crate he had opened. Not before Keefe had a look at one of the 155 mm's inside. "God preserve us from the likes of those," he said. "I've never seen anything like that. What's the long snout on him?"

"High technology," Cassidy rasped. "And delicate—like your health. Warfare has got too sensitive for the soldier. These shells are very neurotic—so watch it—or we'll blow up the neighborhood."

Getting them out of the basement was the worst part. The crates weighed three hundred pounds apiece. They put the huge Keefe on the back and the two skin-and-bonesmen, Cassidy and Rattigan, in front and wrestled the boxes up the steep stairs with reverent attention to detail.

After they got the first box stowed in the U-Haul, the three men leaned against the side of the van and huffed and puffed. "Very heavy this high technology. Tell me more," Keefe said.

"Laser guided. Rocket assisted. Each shell cost $50,000."

"What's it doing here? All this high technology? On a nice side street like this?"

Cassidy shook his head. "Come on." They went back up the stairs. Twice on the slushy brownstone steps, Cassidy slipped from one step to another and would have dropped his end but for Rattigan's tight grip. "Sorry," he said.

From behind him, the second time, Keefe called, "I'm at peace with my Maker, but you atheists have no place to go, Cassidy, so for God's sake . . ."

On the second-to-last crate, a board had been pried loose. Not by Cassidy. Cassidy had carefully unscrewed the boards. This one had been pried loose—the screws tearing through the wood. One of the 155s was missing.

"Rattigan?" Cassidy queried.

"What would I want with a thing like that?" Rattigan asked. "The only article I removed from this house was one corpse, which I put in the bay with all the other corpses."

A member of the Lost Tribes, Cassidy thought. Now how did Alison know that about that dead man on the floor. He'd thrown Alison a quick pitch, and Alison had swung on it, unthinking. He shouldn't have known anything about the identity of that body on the floor on Forensic Street unless. . . . It was only a ten minute walk from the Spumi to Forensic Street. He could have gone down and taken a look and then caught the shuttle back to Washington. But why would he want to do that?

The cold was creeping through Cassidy's worn black coat into his bones. With twelve thousand dollars I can buy myself a new coat. Except he hadn't got the twelve thousand dollars. Alison had put it all back in those magnificently tailored pockets. Possession hinged on successful completion.

The second-to-last crate now, Cassidy sweating and shivering, the worst of both extremes. I'm a corrupt Irish romantic, and you can hardly stoop lower than that, Cassidy. Even to call this foolishness corruption is high flattery. You're too stupid and stubborn to be decently corrupt. Somebody else will wind up with the twelve thousand, and you'll end impecunious as a clam and maybe dead.

Last crate on his aching back, his raw palms. Cassidy's eyes on the dark windows of the loft building across the street. If I were Wenceslas I'd be across there right now with an M16 fitted with one of those nice explosive bullets that could blow the stillness to the heavens with one shot. Why isn't he looking after his interests? No explosion in the papers. Why didn't he come to see? Maybe he had . . .

The U-Haul was weighted to the axles, its springs straight as pencils. "I'll drive," Cassidy announced.

"Why?" Keefe asked, aggrieved.

"Because I'm in charge, and anyway it's my turn, you over-educated Irish thug," Cassidy said.

"Over-educated he says. And him a medievalist!" The rest of it—the Irishness and the thuggery—Keefe took as a compliment.

Steam rising from the slush into the cold night air. Is that a face in the dark loft window? A face would be plausible. The absence of a face, implausible. Cassidy pulled away from the curb, carefully, and drove down Forensic, doing arithmetic in his head. Laser guided rocket assisted shells. $50,000 each. Twenty-four to a crate and twenty-six crates makes . . . let's see . . . over thirty million dollars worth of high technology that Khaddafi would give his left testicle to own . . .

Cassidy drove the truck slowly down Forsyth to Canal and turned west. Keefe was in high spirits: "Remember the time we stole the machine guns from the cathedral in Bratislava, dressed as Rosicrucians? You an atheist in God's clothing, Cassidy, blessing the multitude . . ."

It was all a long time ago, when the century and ourselves were younger. Why did Alison recruit four old men? Because we're experienced and expendable . . . above all, ex . . . existential . . . exponential . . . all of those lovely out of date ex's . . .

Hubert Street teemed with eighteen wheelers, all pulled up and parked, their drivers asleep in the little sleeping alcoves of their huge cabs, waiting for the Hudson River to open for business.

"You got your piece, Keefe?" Cassidy asked.

It stopped the flow of reminiscence. "Never without it, old buddy."

"Rattigan?"

The little man hadn't uttered since Forensic Street, his sad clown's face boarded up like a church in Russia. "I'm heeled," he said. "Why?"

"You never know," Cassidy said, his own .357 nestling in his armpit. His mind's eye on Lucia, the black hair on the pillow, the black eyelashes resting on the creamy skin, the mouth open as if astonished by sleep, the mental image calming Cassidy's nerves, focusing his mind, lifting his spirits . . .

The van crawled past the sleeping eighteen wheelers and under the expressway to Pier 26, the U.S. Navy Pier, where lights were lit and people moved behind the wooden palings. Pindar was waiting at the big wooden gate, which he opened to let in the U-Haul.

Cassidy drove onto the pier, stopped, and rolled down his window. Pindar was a Greek from Chicago who spoke twenty-six languages. To no avail, he was fond of saying. He was bald as an apple, thick as a tree, and, behind his cherubic smile, both smart and tough. Cassidy read trouble in the eyes immediately.

"I don't like the look of things one damn bit," Pindar said in a low voice.

There was no time for detail. A man with his hands thrust in a pea jacket and a blue soft cap on his head was waving at Cassidy. "Pull up! Pull up!" he bawled. "You're late."

Cassidy stuck his head out the window and contemplated the gesticulating bellower. "Late for what? World War III?"

"Move up! Move up!" Waving his arms. "To the second ramp."

Cassidy took his time. "We've got explosives. We're going to take it slow." To Pindar: "Who is this guy—the Secretary of the Navy?"

"None of them are Navy. It's a Navy tug but not Navy people."

Cassidy drove the van carefully to the unloading ramp. A U.S. Navy tug in royal blue with U.S. Navy in white painted on its bow. Six brown men in combat fatigues over which they wore pea jackets stood motionless as rocks on the loading platform, looking at the van with round brown eyes.

"Malays," Pindar muttered. "Alison muddying the waters with *Malays.*"

The Greek and Cassidy exchanged a look that contained exasperation, humor, and—the essential ingredient of their advancing years— resignation. They'd been on lots of missions together. Resignation was all. Cassidy unlocked the rear door of the van.

The pea jacket was shouting to the Malays to unload the cargo— and to be *careful.* Clearly they didn't understand. They looked at each other and moved a little back and forth.

"Unlimber one of your Eastern languages, Pindar. Do you know how to say 'Be careful' in Malay."

Pindar approached the men, looked into their brown eyes, and spoke softly and earnestly. They broke into smiles and nodded and laughed as if the sun had come out. In a moment they were around the rear of the van. Two stepped inside the van, four stayed on the ramp, handling the crates as carefully as if they were temple bells.

The man in the pea jacket with the hands in his pocket was bawling at Cassidy during this: "The minute that van is cleared move it out."

Cassidy puffed out his cheek. "Noisy, isn't he?"

"His name's Ferrano," Pindar said.

"Is he a harbor pilot?"

"No," Pindar said. "The harbor pilot's up on the bridge, staying out of it, doing what he's told."

The U-Haul was empty now, and the man in the pea jacket approached. "You going to get that van out of here?"

Cassidy gave him his Number 3 look, which, he liked to think, could burn the paint off a building: "All in good time, Admiral. There seems to be some misunderstanding here." Pindar standing next to him and Rattigan and Keefe crowding in for moral support. "Let's see your orders."

Knowing there weren't any. Alison never wrote anything down, which is why he had lasted through so many upheavals at the Agency. You could never pin anything on Alison when the investigations started.

"Let's see *your* orders." Ferrano challenged. A barrel-chested Italian with flint in his eyes.

Cassidy rubbed his nose and took his time. "Mine are top secret. I'd be only too happy to hand them over if you have the clearance to look at 'em."

A ploy he'd used many times. It never failed to stop them dead in the water.

Ferrano scowled and walked aboard the tug, now covered with crates on every inch of deck space.

"He's going to cut out and leave us standing," Pindar warned. "Unless we get aboard."

"Damn," Cassidy snarled. "I don't *want* to get aboard." His task was finished when he delivered the cargo to the Navy pier. But if the cargo blew up on the way, he'd never get the twelve thousand. Knowing Alison.

"Malays," he blazed. "Wouldn't you know Alison would hire Malays who don't understand English so they can't testify against him in case anything goes wrong, as it probably will."

The two engines on the tug were starting now, two of the Malays on the dock handling the lines.

"The wop can't even give orders to the Malays," Pindar said. "If anything goes wrong with the unloading, any little difficulty, how does he handle it?"

Cassidy looked at his watch. 3 A.M. Lucia alone behind the triple-locked doors on Thirteenth Street. . . . Oh, hell!

"Come on," he said. He stepped on one of the crates that was flush with the bulkhead and skipped down to a small sliver of deck not covered by the crates. Pindar leaped after him, then Keefe, who landed on the steel deck with a noise like a thunderclap. Rattigan, the skinniest, was last, and he had to make a running jump for it, landing with his clown's grin, in Keefe's arms. "May I have the next waltz?" said Keefe to the little man.

"Hey," the Italian shouted from the bridge. "What you think you're doing?"

"Shut up," Cassidy growled. What was he doing? Protecting his investment. Twelve thousand. But it was more than that. Not the money. Not even Kore (though she was part of it).

"There's coffee below," Pindar said.

The four men went down the steep steps to the large galley below deck where black, bitter coffee simmered on the gas burner. Keefe poured a slug of Old Grandad into his and offered it around.

"Go easy," Cassidy said. "Trouble's brewing."

Keefe sipped his coffee and bourbon, leaning against the doorway. "I'll be ready for the trouble when it comes, though, if the truth be told, I'm a little rusty."

The tug was quivering and shuddering as she nosed down the Hudson toward the bay. The four ex-CIA men had taken seats on benches in the galley.

"Where are the Malays?" Cassidy asked.

"On deck," Pindar said. "They don't do anything unless someone tells 'em to."

"Get 'em down here and give 'em coffee, Pindar. Out of the cold."

Cassidy settled on a bench, his back resting against the bulkhead, and pulled out his book—*Arms in the Modern World*—and picked up where he had left off:

Since 1945 there have been fifty wars, all between small developing nations, none between major sophisticated European powers or between the two superpowers. In many of these small conflicts, a slight advantage in technology has been decisive. Around the world as this is written, 150 other potential conflicts simmer away, and many of them will explode into actual hostilities within the next fifteen years. Most of these contests will be won by slightly superior technology—a better tank or anti-tank system, longer range artillery—and all of them will be lost by obsolescent weaponry. The balance of power in the regions hinges almost entirely on the technological edge the small power has over his neighbors or his enemies . . .

Pindar came back with the six Malays whom he arranged on the benches and poured out coffee for, as if they were guests, chattering away in their soft language.

Cassidy put away his book. "Pindar, how many crew aboard besides the harbor pilot and Ferrano?"

"The engineer below."

"One engineer? That's all? Where's the regular captain of the tug? He should be aboard."

"He isn't."

"Very peculiar."

Even more peculiar, Cassidy was thinking, we got that wop outnumbered by—what?—four to three if he truly commanded the allegiance of engineer and harbor captain and Cassidy doubted it. He couldn't even communicate with the Malays, so he could hardly command them. The wop was alone, really, and that was odd because he didn't look the type who allowed himself to be outmaneuvered this way. Perhaps . . .

The tug shuddered harder as it gathered speed, which meant it had cleared the Battery and was out in the bay. Cassidy said to Pindar: "I'm going up on the bridge to have a little talk with our friend. I wish you'd come along—but not up on the bridge. Stay on deck and keep me in view at all times, if you know what I mean."

"I know what you mean. I think the others should come too. We'll cover from three sides."

Cassidy nodded and climbed the steep steel steps to the deck.

The tug was pushing along, enclosed in mist like a cocoon. Off the starboard bow, Cassidy could see Bedloe's Island with Liberty's torch a circle of orange light. Off the port bow was Governor's Island with its ribbon of light barely discernible in the encircling mist.

The tug running along fast, too fast for the darkness.

Behind him, Pindar, Keefe, and Rattigan came up the steel steps and took up their positions—Pindar in the bow, leaning against the bulkhead, eyes on the bridge, Keefe and Rattigan on each side of the deck behind the bridge. The big tug was in the Upper Bay now, and the foghorns were beginning their lonely clamor.

Cassidy climbed the steel ladder to the bridge, silent as a wraith. He wanted no trouble before he got his feet firmly on the deck and his hands free. As his head came abreast the bridge deck, he took a quick look. Ferrano was in the wheelhouse, bent over the chart rack. The wheel was in the hands of the harbor pilot, a roseate, white-haired man who looked as if he had salt in his bloodstream.

Cassidy mounted the rest of the ladder quickly and silently. With his left hand he took out his .357 from his armpit and put it in his left overcoat pocket, keeping his hand on it. He took his place shoulder to shoulder with the harbor pilot but slightly behind him, Ferrano to his left, still bent over the charts.

"Steering by the seat of your pants, Admiral?" Cassidy said. "I can't see a thing."

Startled, the harbor pilot's jaw fell open, his gaze still directly on course. "My goodness!" he said.

Ferrano sprang upright and turned his body toward Cassidy.

Cassidy watching Ferrano's hands, which had been gripping the chart rack.

"Get off the bridge!" Ferrano said coldly.

Cassidy ignored him. "Where we going in such a hurry, Captain?"

"I'm just following this gentleman's orders. We're to be over the Devlin Bank at 3:27 A.M. Just six minutes away. We have to hurry."

"The Devlin Bank?" Cassidy asked. "We don't want to run into it at this speed, do we? We've got explosives aboard."

The harbor pilot smiled. "The Devlin Bank, sir, has been under water for about a million years. It's a point on the chart."

"And you can find it in the dark and the fog just like that?"

"Thirty years on this water, sir. I know the bottom of New York harbor like my own living room."

Cassidy's eyes on Ferrano's hands, which were stiff with nervous tension, held low around the thighs. "Just why do we have a rendezvous at Devlin's Bank in six minutes, Ferrano?"

"Four minutes now, sir," the pilot said.

"None of your business, Cassidy. Your authority stopped at that dock. I'm in command here, and I'm ordering you off this bridge. Now."

Each syllable a little hammer blow. Trying to get me to look him in the eye and take my eyes off his hands, Cassidy was thinking. The hands were clawlike with anxiety, the fingers working. "We've got twenty-six crates of high explosive artillery shells aboard, and you're making a rendezvous with another ship in the dead of night in dense fog in the middle of New York harbor. That's not very sensible, Ferrano . . ."

Ferrano's right hand moved very fast toward the right pea jacket pocket. Cassidy pulled the .357 magnum out of his left coat pocket and leveled it at Ferrano. "Cut it out, or I'll kill you, Ferrano."

Ferrano's right hand stopped just short of the pocket.

"Extend the arms. Keep the hands at shoulder level," Cassidy commanded. "Very good. Looks like you've had practice." Cassidy reached over carefully with his left hand and took the gun from the right hand pea jacket pocket.

"What kind of business is this?" the harbor pilot asked in deep distress—his eyes staying on the compass.

"Just steer the boat, Captain," Cassidy said. "Tell me, where is the regular pilot of this tug?"

"He was taken ill, sir."

"Mr. Ferrano tell you that?"

"Yes, sir."

"Who you working for, Ferrano? Wenceslas?"

The Italian's face was granitic, the eyes opaque with a fury of concentration. This is a very tough cookie, much too assured for his predicament. Why?

The smell of seawater sharp in Cassidy's nostrils, the mournful hoot of the foghorns in his ears, the taste of fear in his mouth. It's not like the old days, thought Cassidy, sadly, when you didn't taste the fear until after the event, sometimes years later. Now . . . Ferrano, a younger man, immobile, hands in the air, fearless, and me with a gun in my hand fearful, the victim of years of experience in which everything that can go wrong does . . .

The harbor pilot reached for the engine control lever and moved from Full Speed to Quarter Speed. The companion lever almost immediately went to Quarter Speed, the engineer below acknowledging the instruction. A moment later the tug slowed, the vibration abating noticeably.

"How far to Devlin Bank, Captain?"

"We're almost there, sir." Eyes on his wrist watch. "One two three four five six." The pilot again reached for Engine Control and moved the lever to Reverse Engines. The companion lever acknowledged the order, and the huge propellers reversed, sending a shudder through the big tug. Cassidy rocked on his heels.

The harbor pilot signaled Engine Stop. The tug's engines ceased altogether, and the tug lay dead in the water.

"We're on Devlin Bank, sir," the pilot said, eyes on his watch, "and it's exactly 3:27."

The cords standing out on Ferrano's neck. Mouth pursed. Cocky bastard, thought Cassidy. What's he got to be cocky about?

The beam of yellow fog-piercing light came with shattering unexpectedness directly in their eyes, over the starboard beam. It startled Cassidy so much his eyes instinctively went in the direction of the yellow light and away from Ferrano's confident face.

Only for a moment, but in that moment, Ferrano's left hand snaked toward his left pea jacket pocket and came out with a .38 special. Cassidy caught the movements out of the corner of his eye and dove to the right, which would make it the hardest direction for a lefthander to cover. He couldn't shoot because the harbor captain was in his line of fire.

The .38 exploded twice.

"Oh!" the harbor pilot said. His eyes went up to heaven, and he dropped.

On the floor Cassidy rolled on his back, both hands on his .357 and fired twice, one shot hitting Ferrano in the left eye, the other in the chest, either of them sufficient for the business.

The Italian showed his teeth in a snarl, spun, and fell heavily on the steel deck, his gun slithering out of his hand.

The yellow light was moving back and forth through the fog, monstrous shadows dancing across the wheelhouse.

On all fours Cassidy poked his head out of the wheelhouse and roared, "Shoot out that light, Keefe. We're being hijacked."

Keefe was already taking aim, having figured this out for himself. He shot twice, and the light went out.

Cassidy on his feet now, turning off the lights in the wheelhouse. "Douse the lights down there!" he commanded.

There were only the red and green running lights, and it took a few minutes for Rattigan and Pindar to get to them and turn them out. Then the tug, heaved up and down in the harbor swell, its engines dead, its decks dark.

Through the fog Cassidy heard a jumble of voices, not one word of which he could understand. Close, very close.

He tasted the fear again, felt it in his belly and his sphincter muscles. It wouldn't take much to blow them sky high. A burst of .50 calibre machine gun fire. Or perhaps that missing shell that had been stolen from the opened crate. Almost anything would set off these highly sophisticated artillery shells, too sophisticated for their own good, as was so much modern machinery of war. War had got out of the hands of the soldiers into the hands of the engineers and designers who didn't understand war.

Cassidy was on the catwalk around the wheelhouse, straining eyes and ears, palms wet with fear. This must be what it was like for those poor sailors in World War II aboard the transports, waiting night after night for the torpedoes. No matter how many trips you took, they said you never got over the fear. You just got used to it. So get used to it, said Cassidy to Cassidy.

Keefe materialized out of the fog at Cassidy's elbow. "They're coming closer, Horatio. Listen."

The pulse of an engine across the water, across the starboard bow, with it the surging swirl of water stirred by powerful propellers. Voices too, low and indistinct, like the chattering of baritone birds.

"If they wanted to blow us up, they'd have done it, when they had the light on us. They're looking to board us," Cassidy said, keeping his voice low. "I'm going into the wheelhouse. Stay here, and keep your ears peeled."

Cassidy felt his way back to the wheelhouse. Once there he brought out his pencil flash and stepped over the bodies. He shined the pencil torch on the Engine Control mechanism, grasped the lever, and turned it to Start Engine. From below came acknowledgment and, a moment later, powerful shudders in the tug as the two engines were started.

Dead Slow, Cassidy signaled. He took the wheel in his hand and spun it to the left, turning the tug's bow away from the oncoming craft.

The tug crept ahead, circling. After twenty seconds, Cassidy corrected and, to the best of his ability, straightened course. He snapped on the tiny compass light. The needle hung over NNE—north northeast. Cassidy shone the pencil torch on the chart and searched for Devlin Bank, searching around Governor's Island and Bedloe's Island.

NNE, he decided would run them aground on Brooklyn, not too far from Rarity Street. In the blackness Cassidy grinned savagely. That would be appropriate. We'll blow up together, Wenceslas. Then and there came her image, the olive-skinned (or half olive-skinned) one with the sadness of face who sent electricity to his toes with the very touch of her, and this was no time for *that*. Pay attention, Cassidy. Talking to myself like an old man.

He spun the wheel again, an arching leftward sweep, until the compass course was due south. With any luck we should pass through the Narrows—if we don't hit Staten Island. At that speed, Dead Slow, it would be quite awhile before they hit anything at all, and they wouldn't hit it hard.

Four minutes passed, agonizingly slow, Cassidy tight as a violin string, waiting the crash of ship on ship. He didn't know what *kind* of ship was out there, how big, how manned, how armed, not anything he wanted to know, only that the light had stabbed at them from about the same height as his bridge, whatever that meant.

Keefe had come off the catwalk and stood at his elbow. "I can't hear a thing over the infernal din of that foghorn. What good's a foghorn? It tells me it's foggy. I already know that." He caught sight of the two bodies: "Mother of God! The two of them!"

Cassidy's eye on the compass needle, keeping it due south. "The harbor pilot got the bullets aimed at me, poor fellow. A very great loss to society. He knew the bottom of the harbor like his own backyard."

"And you, Cassidy. How well do you know the bottom of the harbor?"

"I know it's down there. I'd rather not join it."

"How much experience have you had with oceangoing tugs, old friend?"

"I once navigated a rowboat clear across Central Park lake with magnificent insouciance."

Keefe rubbed his hands together, warming them in the bitter cold. "This is not the time for insouciance, old fellow."

"I'm whistling past the graveyard, if you must know," Cassidy said. "We've got a shipload of highly volatile explosives—and no destination. I have no idea who is supposed to take this cargo off our hands. Here, take the wheel."

"Me!" Keefe said, aghast. "You don't know what you're saying!"

"Just keep it straight ahead, due south. Go easy with that wheel. It's very sensitive."

Keefe reverently put his huge reluctant hands on the brass, keening away: "Dear God above, I trust you will note that this wheel is passing from the hands of an atheist into the proper custody of a God-fearing,

God-loving, properly reverent Christian who devoutly hopes your Divine mercy extends to our protection in this most exigent predicament. Amen."

"Wow!" Cassidy said. He was pulling the charts out of their little drawers.

"Why don't we just dump the load into the harbor and be done with it?" Keefe asked.

"We'd never get our money that way."

Cassidy found the chart he was looking for and turned his pencil flash on it, tracing the path through Rockaway Inlet up Broad Channel to Pumpkin Patch Channel and beyond to Marriott's Grave. His boyhood rose in his throat with delicious sweetness.

"You look like you've seen a ghost, Cassidy."

"I used to fish these waters with my Uncle Joshua when I was twelve. We'd catch flounder and cook it right there on Marriott's Grave, this little grassy island here, and I can taste it on my tongue as if it were yesterday, and no fish has tasted that good ever again."

He was down on his knees now, searching Ferrano's body. The wallet was full of hundred-dollar bills and Cassidy stuffed them in his overcoat pocket because you never knew, you never knew. There was nothing in the wallet to give the man away. There wouldn't be. Cassidy got out his Swiss Army knife and went to work on the heels.

"What the devil are you going now?" Keefe asked.

"Keep your eye on the compass, man," Cassidy said. "And your wits about you."

In the left heel was nothing. In the right was the usual scroll of rolled up paper—blank. Cassidy put it in his shirt pocket. "The son of a bitch had *two* guns—one in the right hand pocket and one in the left. The next time you search a Sicilian be sure you hit all the pockets."

"How do you know he's Sicilian?"

"He's a Sicilian. Square cut body, deep set eyes. I can smell 'em. You know, Keefe, they were Northmen, what we call Norsemen now. Like the Danes who conquered England. Same people. Some of them swept south—to Sicily. Wherever they went they caused trouble, and they're still causing it."

He stood up. "I'm going below to have a word with the engineer, who is the only one left who might know something. Keep up due south, Dead Slow."

"Aye aye, your reverence. I'm gaining confidence with every second I stay alive."

"Not too much confidence, for heaven's sake, man. A little humility in the circumstances." Cassidy looked at his watch. 3:49. Twelve minutes since the rendezvous. The other ship out there, lightless, looking for a needle in the haystack of New York's great harbor.

At the foot of the steel ladder, he found Pindar at the rail, staring at the wall of fog fiercely as if he could melt it with the heat of his gaze. "What's it all about, Horatio?" Pindar asked. "Where am I going and why?"

"We've been set up," Cassidy said. "Round up a couple of the Malays and get the two bodies out of the wheelhouse and dump them in the bay. If we run into the harbor police I don't want to have to explain two bodies."

"Two bodies?" Pindar said.

"Put a little weight on them, so they don't go embarrassing us later by floating right alongside. Where's Rattigan?"

"Here," Rattigan said, which was as many words as Rattigan usually used.

"Go up on the catwalk and keep your ears flapping. If you hear anything that might help Keefe steer this baby, go tell him about it. Understand?"

"Yes," Rattigan said. And went.

Cassidy felt his way along the deck, bumping into crates at every step, his hands on the steel of the boat until he came upon the opening. A faint light from below illuminated the ladder, and down he went into the pulsing noisy engine room with its great brass pipes and steel pistons and gleaming dials, hot and airless.

The engineer in his tan shirtsleeves sat in a wicker chair next to the Engine Control signals that came down from the bridge, his head bent over a book, as if he were a passenger on a cruise. The book was *Sackett's Land* by Louis L'Amour. The fellow was out in the western plains in the nineteenth century as if there wasn't adventure enough in the right now of his current situation about which, as Cassidy was to discover, he knew nothing whatsoever.

He tapped the man on the top of his skull, and the engineer's eyes came off the book and into Cassidy's. A gaunt fellow with hollow cheeks and bitter eyes. A loser, this man. Just what I need at this juncture. A loser in the engine room, a man who would concede defeat at the first opportunity.

"Who hired you?" Cassidy had to yell to get over the thrust of the engines.

"I'm on call," said the engineer, whose name was Wallerby, into Cassidy's ear. "The union hiring hall gets the call, and they call us. This call came at midnight."

"Who called? What name?"

"The hiring hall takes care of that. They don't tell us much. Hundred and fifty for four hours work."

You'd never have collected, Cassidy thought. You'd be in the bay with the rest of us if things had gone according to plan. Aloud, very loud, he said, "How fast does this bucket go at Dead Slow like now."

"Depends on the tides. Maybe a mile and a half an hour. Maybe we're even going backward."

"Where do I find out about tides?"

"There's books and charts in the wheelhouse if you know how to read 'em."

"Lovely," Cassidy said. "Don't *you* know how to read 'em?"

"Not me," Wallerby said. "I'm an engineer." Apologetically he added, "I studied to be a pilot once. I gave it up." That was his first defeat. Or maybe his second. There'd been many after that, Cassidy decided. He was a well-defeated man. "Just keep it Dead Slow," Cassidy said and went back up on deck.

4:30 A.M. The smell was saltier now and oilier. And colder.

Pindar was carrying the body of the harbor pilot, one burly arm around the neck, the other hand on the ladder, coming down from the bridge. The corpse of Ferrano lay on the top of the crates. Pindar reached the steel deck with a thump and put the body on top of the crate next to Ferrano.

"I got a better idea," Pindar said. "This craft has a standup refrigerator with whole sides of beef in it. Why don't we just hang these two by the heels in there. Somebody might want these bodies, Cassidy. People get sentimental about bodies. Wives. Brothers. Sisters. There are ceremonies and burials and things like that that are very important to some people."

Cassidy ran his hands over his face, weary to the bone. "Hang them by the heels if you like, Pindar. Put a little salt on their tails if that pleases your mortuary soul. I find all this necrophilia distasteful, if not downright barbaric."

He climbed up to the wheelhouse.

The fog was thinning, and the deep groan of the foghorn was less frequent now. Inside the wheelhouse, Keefe was steering with one hand and pouring a slug of whiskey down his gullet with the other. He handed the bottle to Cassidy who took a drink.

Cassidy pointed to a string of lights that had appeared off the starboard bow. "That's Staten Island." He pointed off the port bow to another string of lights about a mile ahead. "That would be Shore Parkway in Brooklyn. Head over that way. That's where we're going—into Rockaway Inlet."

"Back to your boyhood," Keefe said.

"I've never left it," Cassidy said.

"Nor have I," Keefe said. "That's all our problem, Cassidy. Pindar. Even Rattigan. Or we'd be home with the children, looking at the TV."

Cassidy went out on the catwalk where Rattigan was staring into the thinning fog. "Keep a sharp eye out for that other boat, any other boat. In another hour we're going to be clearly visible—and so are they."

Rattigan nodded, sparing himself even his usual monosyllable.

Back in the wheelhouse, Cassidy went through the bookcase, searching for books on navigation but his attention was caught by a simple black telephone, hanging on the wall. "Well, well," he said. He picked it up and listened. No sound at all. While he waited, he ran his eyes over the books: *Charts and Surveys, New York Harbor 1970-80. Currents and Tides, 1980, Small Ship Navigation Charts.*

A sleepy female came on the telephone, "Operator."

"Is this the New York operator?" he said.

"Yes. Are you calling someone?"

Ship-to-shore telephone. Cassidy looked at his watch. Quarter to five. He gave the operator Alison's very private number that rang in his study and, after he went to bed, at his bedside. 4:45 A.M. What a fine time to be waking up Hugh Alison and his rich wife.

"Yeah," Alison said on the telephone. Very truculent "yeah."

"Is this the Alison residence in beautiful downtown Georgetown overlooking the Averill Harriman residence and just to the east of all those rich Republicans . . ."

"Cassidy, for God's sake, it's quarter to five. What do you want?"

"Anything I can get, Alison. I'm in the middle of New York harbor floating around with a load of unmentionables and no destination."

Alison was fully awake. "What's going on, Horatio? You should have handed the cargo over to the Navy . . ."

"Somebody has pulled a fast shuffle on you, Alison. We're on a Navy tug, but the Navy is nowhere. We avoided a hijack by the skin of our teeth."

"Whereabouts are you?"

"Not over an open phone, Hugh. The hijacker is still prowling around out there looking for us, and he could be listening to this broadcast for all I know. Get in touch with the Navy and ask 'em where their pilot is and their engineer. I'll call you in an hour or so on a phone that has a little more privacy." He hung up.

The fog was lifting fast now, and visibility had increased.

Cassidy signaled Half Speed on the engine control lever, and a moment later the tug leaped forward.

Cassidy settled down on the leather-covered top of the sonar equipment to read about buoys and tides and currents. His mind was only half on the books. Alison. The most secretive man in a secretive organization. A leak of that magnitude . . .

He put the books aside and went out on the catwalk to join Rattigan. The fog had lifted altogether now, but it was still dark. The tug was making good speed, cutting along about half a mile from the Brooklyn shore.

"Any sign of that other boat?"

"No sign of any other boat. We've got the harbor to ourselves." A long speech for Rattigan.

"Keep a lookout to the stern. We'll keep our eyes ahead."

Cassidy went into the wheelhouse and took the wheel from Keefe. "Sit down and rest yourself, old soak. You can look out the window if you're seeking refreshment. That's Coney Island on our left. You could see the boardwalk if we had any light."

"What did Alison have to say? Anything to nourish the spirits?"

"He was greatly surprised—but at what—ah, that is the question. If you were going to hijack thirty million dollars worth of artillery shells, Keefe, don't you think a more sensible place to do it would be the streets of New York at 2 A.M., rather than a fogbound harbor? What does that suggest to your pixilated Irish mind?"

Keefe took another sip of the whiskey and leaned against the side of the wheelhouse, eyes bright with malediction. "Money! Somebody has been waving thousand-dollar bills in the air. The source of all evil."

Money. Alison didn't need money. He had a rich wife.

The tug was well into Rockaway Inlet now, passing Fort Tilden, which rose in black outline on the right hand side. Presently they chugged under the Marine Parkway Bridge, Floyd Bennett Field, empty and silent on their left, white light streaking the sky, entering Jamaica Bay with its grassy islands and long redolent marshes.

Cassidy swung the tug in a wide sweeping turn to the left around Floyd Bennett Field and headed down the shore. The scene in the pale light was one of watery desolation: on one side the bulrush marshes, on the other the Flatlands neighborhood of Brooklyn. Off the port bow Cassidy could see a dragger, as they called the little trawlers of that area, bottom fishing for whiting, butterfish, fluke, and flounder, dragging its nets in a manner not much different from that of the Greeks twenty-five centuries ago.

In the days before high technology made monkeys of us all, Cassidy thought.

The light was stronger now, and he caught sight of Mill Basin at least a mile ahead. A long rickety pier jutted out into Jamaica Bay on which were several ramshackle structures. Some would be bait shops, one with a great Exxon sign on it sold fuel to the fishermen and the pleasure boats; at the end, the biggest building, faced with brown shingles, had great windows looking out on the bay and a sign on its roof SEAFOOD.

"We'll have breakfast," Cassidy proclaimed.

"Six A.M.," Keefe objected.

"The baymen have been out fishing since four, you landlubber," Cassidy said. "Have you ever had oyster stew for breakfast? It illuminates the soul with its radiance."

"EE-yah!" Keefe commented, hunching himself into his great shoulders. "How much experience have you had landing forty-foot oceangoing tugs at a pier?"

"There always has to be a first time."

At a quarter mile away Cassidy signaled Dead Slow and crept on to the pier like a cat on a bird, drifting almost motionless into the pilings, which the tug struck with the smallest of shudders. The Malays swarmed onto the pier with the lines and made fast.

"Beginner's luck," Keefe observed.

Cassidy was on the catwalk searching the horizon, for he knew not what except that he'd recognize it if he saw it. The draggers were out in force, and he knew it wasn't them. Salt water stretched far as the eye could see, streaks of silvery light on the vast flatness, smelling of fish and marsh gas, the early morning air fresh with its own sharp tang.

"I feel reborn, Keefe," Cassidy said. "That is the craze of the moment—being reborn. Born again. The Second Coming of Everyman."

"Let's go have some oyster stew," Keefe said gently, taking Cassidy's elbow as if it were glass. "We'll talk about the death of kings."

It was a big restaurant with long, bare wooden tables, which had been scrubbed down with soap and water so many times the wood gleamed like soft marble. The walls were hung with stuffed sailfish, and the pictures of saints with much blue and gold and silver paint on them hung in ornate plaster and gilt frames. The place was totally empty of people except for the proprietor, a square-cut Italian with a mouth full of gold teeth.

"You're very late or very early," the Italian said, flashing his gold teeth. "The draggers have been out hours ago, and the sports fisher-men won't be in for another four hours. Take that table by the window. It gives the best view."

They were all there except the engineer, who was still in his engine room reading Louis L'Amour. "Somebody go get him," Cassidy said. "Pindar, explain oyster stew to the Malays if you can."

On the Italian Cassidy turned all his charm. What a nice place! Had he been there long? He got the full history. The man had fished out of Sicilian ports, Palermo, Castelammare del Golfo, and then had moved to America forty years ago, and here he was in his seventies enjoying the best of health and twelve grandchildren.

Cassidy was eating his oyster stew and doing a lot of sympathetic listening, smelling out the lay of the land.

He was into his second cup of coffee before he began asking questions. Did he know Marriott's Grave? Of course! Of course! the Italian flashing his gold teeth. He'd fished there many times. Was the big overhanging willow still there? Aah, *beautiful* tree! Of course! Of course! Then the hard one: "Do you know any harbor pilot we might rouse at this hour?"

The Sicilian's flashing gold smile dimmed and went out. A calculat-ing look came into the eye. "Well now. . . . It cost you money for a harbor pilot. You know that? Two hundred dollars a day?"

Cassidy took out the roll of bills he'd taken off Ferrano and counted out two of the hundreds. "I see," the Sicilian said. "When you want him?"

"Now," Cassidy said.

The Italian went to the telephone that hung at the end of the bar, and Cassidy watched him speaking into it. In five minutes the restau-rateur came back. "He'll be here in half an hour. Name of Gitano. Very good man. Knows every shoal like his own backyard and all the places to fish."

"Can I use your phone?" Cassidy asked.

"Be my guest," the Italian said.

6:30 A.M.

Cassidy went to the phone and called his own home number. It rang eight times before Lucia came on sleepily. "Lucia, it's me."

"Daddy," said Lucia, who never called him daddy except when she

-75-

was scared and needed a daddy. Otherwise she called him professor. "Where are you?"

"Never mind. Listen to me closely. Do you remember where I keep the .38 special?"

"Yes," Lucia said.

It was on the topmost bookshelf behind the third volume of *The Decline and Fall of the Roman Empire.*

"Go up and get it and fill it with bullets, which you'll find in the drawer of my bedside table."

"Daddy . . ."

"Just listen, Lucia. I'll be there as soon as I can get there. In the meantime, I don't want you to go to school today. Just make yourself breakfast and read a book with the gun near you. If someone tries to get in, kill him."

"DADDY!"

"I don't expect it to happen, Lucia. I just want you to be ready. Now don't panic. The door is triple-locked. Probably nothing at all will happen. I'm just . . . taking precautions."

"When will you be home, Daddy?"

Cassidy thought about it. "I hope—an hour. Maybe an hour and a half. Chin up."

Cassidy went back to the table and took Keefe aside. "You're in charge. The harbor pilot has got his own boat. Make him tow it behind and leave you at Marriott's Grave under that big tree where you'll be well out of sight of the helicopters . . ."

Keefe didn't take to it lightly. "You're overreacting. Why don't we turn the stuff over to the Navy and be done with it?"

"There's been a massive leak somewhere on a very high level. I don't trust any of them. I want to know what's going on." But of course he had to explain a bit more than that. "It's not like the old days, Keefe. I've got a vulnerability now. I've got a daughter to raise, and if this bastard knows about her, he'll use her for all he's worth. There's a ruthlessness here that is . . . extraordinary."

"Why?"

"Money," Cassidy said.

- 6 -

— Cassidy caught the Woodlawn Express at Flatbush and Nostrand and settled down to read *The New York Times,* all seventy-six pages, himself full of oyster stew and foreboding. Reading the *Times,* he decided, was like picking your way through a crab, 90 percent of it unedible shell and gristle, but the crabmeat was delicious when you could find a bit.

He found a bit of crabmeat on page 26:

Senator Myron Kuhn of the Senate Arms Control Committee charged yesterday that Libya's Colonel Khaddafi is spending millions in this country to buy American weapons, which he gives to the Palestine Liberation Organization, including top secret munitions our own armed forces don't yet have. American businessmen are known to be drawn into this illegal enterprise by the huge sums of oil money Khaddafi is spreading around, the Senator said.

Cassidy tore out the item and put it in his overcoat pocket.

His eyes met those of the only other passenger on the train, a chic black girl in a yellow leather coat and yellow thigh-length boots who stared at him with total contempt, repaying him for the slights her great-great grandmother had suffered at the hands of the honkies in 1882. Very sexy, the hatred in a black girl's eyes.

Cassidy put aside the *Times* and turned to *The Daily News*. A whole new world. From the high crimes of the *Times* to the low lusts of the common man. Rape, mostly. Everyone getting raped in the most interesting ways, and Lucia thinks I'm paranoiac to teach her kung fu and how to handle a gun. We are back in the seventeenth century again. Life is *dangerous* every minute of the day and, if nothing else, interesting.

He was glancing down the gossip column when the item leaped at him, all but biting his eyeballs: "Grace Alison is filing suit any day now. Her husband is such a big CIA secret that you never heard of him, but the Other Side has. She inherited six department stores in Chicago . . ."

Cassidy read it twice and then rolled the *Daily News* into a tight round billyclub and stared across at the black girl in the yellow leather boots without even seeing her, which evened the score.

Alison's rich wife suing for divorce. Taking her leave. And her money. It changed all the equations. The balance. The motivation. The codes. The ciphers. Everything would have to change. It was a whole new ball game.

If true. Gossip is never altogether true or altogether untrue. Who'd said that? Alison himself. Alison had always claimed that the mere *printing* of an item, even if you made it up, made it in some respect true because now it existed as rumor, buzzing about the marketplace, changing the odds . . .

Looking right through the black girl, which is what the blacks always accuse the whites of doing, not realizing the whites did it to themselves, too. We're all alone with our private fears . . .

Cassidy got off the subway at Fourteenth Street and walked back to his apartment on Thirteenth Street, picking up the pace because it was getting on toward seven thirty A.M. and the foreboding was eating away at him.

He took the precaution of knocking: "Lucia, it's me myself in person. Don't shoot!"

Lucia unlocked the three locks herself and engulfed him in her long skinny arms, chattering away bright-eyed. "I was *petrified*! I was quivering!"

"You can't both petrify and quiver. It's a contradiction in terms," Cassidy said, holding his armful of thirteen-year-old just a bit tighter than usual because it had been a long night, and he was entitled to his moment of exquisite sensibility.

Right away she tried to break loose. That's the way it went between them. If he didn't hold her, touch her, she missed it and complained. If he held her too tight, she wriggled loose, accusing him of sentimentality. The ground always shifting under his feet.

He pulled the black suitcase out from under her bed and began filling it with the essentials—her wool skirt, the sweatpants she wore to skateboard in (though she'd be doing no skateboarding), her T-shirt with *Here's Trouble!* on it, the stuffed elephant she slept with, her brush and comb . . .

She saw there were none of his things going in the case, only her things, and she became stiff and silent and grown up and deeply hurt. So he had to explain the inexplicable. "I don't want you to think that anything is going to happen because probably it isn't. I just want you out of sight so that I can concentrate. Otherwise I'll be incessantly worrying . . ."

"Why can't I come with you?"

Himself packing her toothbrush, her Second Year Latin, her *Madame Bovary*. "Someday," he said quietly, "we'll do just that. Not this time."

"Why not this time?" Stiff and defiant. Hating him.

He hadn't time to quarrel. He picked up the telephone and got information to give him the number and called it. "Deborah," he said, turning on all the Irish charm. "I've a great big favor to ask."

Of his plump eager student who had been dying for him to ask anything and everything of her.

He delivered Lucia in person.

"It's just for a few days, and I'm afraid I can't explain, but Lucia must stay off the street and out of sight all that time."

Deborah's apartment was large and empty, the way they liked them these days—no rugs, not much furniture, a great deal of light on the bare floors and white walls, eighteen-inch thick mattresses on the floor, very Japanesy and sterile and austere.

The two girls sized each other up like boxers on opposite sides of the ring. Waiting for the referee to get out of the way so they could spar a few rounds.

"You won't be taking your class then?" Deborah asked. "The students won't like that."

"Some of them will be overjoyed," Cassidy said. He kissed Lucia's stiff unyielding cheek and said: "I'll call you tonight."

To Deborah: "Don't stand for any nonsense, and make her study her absolute ablative, which is very shaky . . ."

Cassidy caught the shuttle to Washington, slept all the way, and an hour and a half later was in the Senate Office Building with an old acquaintance named Harry Dixon, now an investigator for the Senate Arms Control Committee. They shook hands warily, trying to bridge the years. Harry was a survivor. A thin, wry man of bottomless disillusion who had been with OSS, then ISS, and a dozen other international agencies and groupings, mostly government financed, sometimes straying into the private field.

"The last time we laid eyes on one another . . ." Cassidy said, trying to remember.

"A good restaurant on the shore of Lake Geneva," Dixon said. "The Veau d'Or. You had the veal, and we talked about gunrunning in Nigeria. Fifteen years ago. Seems like yesterday. What can I do for you, Horatio?"

Cassidy took out the item he'd clipped from *The New York Times* and showed it to him. Dixon glanced at it and handed it back. "Yeah," he said in the way of government men who have a thousand things on their mind and don't want to be bothered. "What about it?"

Cassidy had his eyes on his own palm, running the index finger of his left hand over his right palm, as if reading his own future. "Why was the senator sounding off at this time, Harry?"

"You know senators, Horatio. They sound off. All the time."

Cassidy avoided looking at him: "May I speculate a little, Harry?"

"Go ahead—we do it all the time around here."

"It sounds to me," Cassidy said, "as if the senator was fishing for information. I just had a hunch the senator might be sending up signals for someone to come off the street and tell him a few things he didn't know."

"Do you know something we'd like to know, Horatio?"

"I might. Tell me this, Harry. What kind of top-secret munitions our own armed forces don't have is Khaddafi looking for?"

"Anything he can get—F 16s, SAMs, ATGMs, artillery shells with terminal guidance and single-shot kill probabilities . . ."

"Hold it," Cassidy said. "Right there."

"Where?"

"Artillery shells with terminal guidance and single-shot kill probabilities."

That set Harry Dixon's antenna to quivering. He'd been leaning back in his chair, eyes on the ceiling, just talking. Now he leaned forward, put his feet on the floor, and focused his eyes. "Just what made you zero in on that particular thing, Horatio? The FBI would be very interested in any character who just happened to drop that particular name at this particular time."

Cassidy scowled and rubbed his hands together: "Let's not have any loose talk about the FBI in here, Harry. It gives me indigestion. May I resume my . . . speculation?"

"Resume."

Cassidy looked around wearily. Big office. The desk itself was tremendous, piled high with papers, documents, letters, all the disorder of government. Thousands upon thousands of these offices all creating work for each other and falling everlastingly behind. "Some of these . . . artillery shells with terminal guidance and single kill probability have disappeared."

Harry Dixon was listening intently now, jaw clenched tight.

Cassidy still talking: "Now it's my *hunch* that someone in our government, with the best of motives—at least in his own eyes—had helped filch these artillery shells to give to some of our friends but that he had to do this secretly because arms control regulations, to say nothing of arms control investigators, and also arms control reporters on the national press might kick up a storm which would kill the deal."

Silence in the big paper-strewn office. Harry Dixon got up from his chair and poured himself a cup of coffee from the coffee maker. He poured out another one for Cassidy, brought the two cups back and handed one to Cassidy.

"If you got the shells, Horatio, give 'em back. We won't ask any questions."

Cassidy sipped his coffee: "Who was *supposed* to get the shells?"

"For God's sake, Horatio, who do you think. It's always the same people, isn't it?"

"Israel," Cassidy guessed. "Are these shells a big technological secret?"

"They're so secret you're not even supposed to know they exist, and how come you do know they exist? I thought you were out of the Agency."

"Nobody ever quite leaves the Agency altogether, Harry. You should know better than that." Cassidy's voice had got dry and nasal. "It's like trying to resign from the human race, getting out of the Agency is. It's in your bloodstream." Until it came out of his mouth, Cassidy hadn't suspected he harbored such terrible thoughts. He ran his fingers over his eyeballs, wishing he hadn't given tongue to them.

"Jesus," Harry Dixon commented. He was looking at his watch. "I haven't got a hell of a lot of time, Horatio, I'm due in the Committee Room in ten minutes." He rose and started stuffing papers in his briefcase.

"Why is arms control in this highly illegal enterprise, Harry?"

Harry Dixon's face darkened. He didn't like that crack, and it opened him up as Cassidy hoped it would: "It's *not* illegal. The Israelis paid for these munitions, and we have the right to grant them. They were intended to give the Israelis a little technological edge over Syria so the Syrians would think twice about rebuilding that nuclear plant because this time it could be taken out by artillery. It's diplomacy by other means, Horatio . . ."

"Yeah," Cassidy said skeptically. "Diplomacy. But you just asked me to give them back to you, which sounds like you don't know where these shells are. What happened, Harry?"

Dixon kept packing his briefcase, turning the thing over in his mind. Finally he said: "Somebody pulled a switch on us. Presented false credentials at the Keswick arsenal in New Jersey." Savagely, he added: "If the God damned thing hadn't been so hush hush, they'd never have got away with it. We were outwitted by our own secrecy. What the hell are you doing, Horatio?"

Cassidy was removing the piles of documents, books, papers, manuscripts from a long, leather-covered sofa in the office and stacking them on the floor. "I'm presuming on our old friendship, Harry. I didn't get to bed last night, and if this office is going to be unoccupied for a couple of hours . . ."

He stretched out on the sofa and turned his most winning smile on Dixon.

"Horatio, there are secrets in this office I'm not willing to share with you . . ."

"Harry, look at this place," Cassidy waved his arm at the pile of paper, documents, dusty piles of paper on desk, filing cabinet, floor. "How could anyone find a secret in here? How do you find your own secrets?"

Dixon shook his head and sighed. "Government," he said, "is a very messy business." He headed out of the office and had his hand on the doorknob when Cassidy asked him, "Do you know a man who calls himself Jeremiah Wenceslas?"

Dixon had the door opened, but he closed it again and walked back to stand beside the sofa. "Horatio, if you're mixed up with that son of a bitch, I'm going to throw you right off that sofa."

Cassidy grinned his ferocity of a grin. "I'm glad we're on the same side, Harry. Wenceslas and I are not friends. You might say we're mortal enemies."

Dixon looked down on Cassidy, thinking the thing through. "We've got to have a long talk, Horatio. I'll be back in a couple of hours."

"I'll be gone. I've got other people to see . . ."

Dixon was rummaging about on the top of the desk, throwing papers about: "What about five, five thirty?" He'd found an engraved card, and he showed it to Cassidy: "I've got to make a ceremonial appearance at this thing. You come too. You'll find it very interesting. Among other guests—your mortal enemy, Jeremiah Wenceslas."

Dixon walked out of the office and closed the door behind him.

Cassidy was left staring at the card. The gold crest of the Illyrian Embassy. Cocktails at five to seven. To meet Hassim el Kariq. Now where had he seen that name? Somewhere.

Cassidy rolled over on his left side, facing the rear, and closed his eyes and was almost asleep when he remembered where he'd seen that name. It was one of the ten names on the hit list he'd found in the dead man's heel. It didn't stop him from falling into deep satisfying sleep . . .

Cassidy walked down K Street in the winter twilight, past the eighteenth-century red brick building that changed hands with every change of administration, the prices mounting to the stars. Not so many decades earlier, it had been an all-black area. Then the white honkies had bought it, driven the blacks out, and ruined the neighborhood with their money.

The big trees were bare of their leaves in the gray winter light.

Not a soul on the street. As always, Cassidy felt the eyes on him from behind all these Venetian blinds. You were always terribly visible when you were on foot in Georgetown.

Alison's house was one of the bigger ones, the red brick glowing softly and expensively in the twilight. Four fifteen. Alison should still be at work. The front door was black and freshly painted, the bell brass freshly polished. Cassidy pressed the button, and Grace answered the door as if she'd seen him coming and had lain in wait.

Regarding him with her venomous look, which was permanent, and, as she liked to tell people, not meant personally.

"One little gossip item brings out all the vultures," she said.

"Only one vulture at the moment, Grace. Might we have a quiet cup of tea together?"

"Oh, come in! Come in," Grace said irritably. "Everyone up and down the street behind those blinds is looking at us and making book—Her lover? Her lawyer? Her blackmailer? That's what they're saying."

Cassidy had never set foot in Alison's house before. The inside was hushed, Persian carpeted, the walls satin covered, the furniture, of which there was much too much, all burnished mahogany, satinwood, rosewood, softly lit like a movie set.

But no soul, thought Cassidy.

"You don't really want *tea*, Horatio?" Grace asked.

"I do! I do! I have promises to keep and many miles before I sleep."

"You forgot the best line. 'The snow lies dark and deep,'" said Grace, her face relaxing a little bit, only a little.

A maid appeared in proper black with a little white crepe apron like someone out of a 1936 movie. Grace Alison ordered tea, and before the maid left the room, launched, without preamble, into a tirade that must have been simmering in her for twenty years.

"We always get taken, Cassidy. Every rich woman I know, and I know 'em all, Cassidy. We pass up the nice mild little fellows who adore us and fall for the con men, the connivers, the self-seekers, the bastards—every last God damned one of us. I could give you a list as long as your arm of rich women who got taken . . ."

Spitting out the bitterness with that beautiful diction learned at her mother's knee, Madeira, Sweetbrier, the Junior League. The beautiful diction made it much worse . . .

Twenty years ago, Cassidy was thinking, Grace had been beautiful, rich, witty, self-confident. God help the girl who is born with everything because she has nowhere to go but down.

"We all knew each other, Cassidy, all the poor little rich girls from New York and St. Louis and Chicago. We all went to school together, and we all went to each other's weddings, and we all had the same idea: 'Why is she marrying *this* bastard?' and I'm sure that's what all my bridesmaids thought at *my* wedding, but of course you don't say those things aloud . . ."

Tea came and was poured by Grace Alison, who kept the diatribe going while pouring very well, as she'd been so well taught. Something was missing here, Cassidy knew, some key element that provoked this outcry, something she wasn't telling . . .

Cassidy drank the tea and waited until Grace ran all the way down.

"It's true then. You're leaving him."

Grace emitted a laugh like a bark. "*Me* leaving. He's left!"

Cassidy was so startled he spilt his tea all over his trousers. "He's gone!"

"Not physically." As if he had a bad smell. "The *body* will be home in an hour if you want to see it. I certainly don't. I'm only here until Thursday. Then I'm off to Honolulu where I have a house. This house is his. You know that."

"Yes, I know that." Everyone in Washington knew that. Alison made sure of that. "What do you mean he *left*, Grace?"

"Spiritually he left. You didn't know I was interested in things of the spirit, did you, Cassidy? Well, I damned well am. I may have lost my looks, but the spirit still vibrates . . ."

"The looks are not bad, Grace, if you'd just calm down." Still a piece missing. The library reeked of the unspoken . . .

The lines on Grace's face—deep, tight, long-standing—loosened a little. Grace sipped her tea, smiling faintly for the first time. A little bit of that Grace he'd known twenty years earlier peeked out of the eyes.

"He was so damn tied up in that Agency and all his power plays. Still, I put up with all that. Spiritually, you can push me around only so far . . ."

Who would have thought the old girl had so much spirituality in her?

"There are things you do and things you just damned well *don't* do, Cassidy. You Agency creeps justify your crimes by all this high-minded patriotism, but I've never bought that crap. He's over the line, Cassidy, way over."

She shut up tight, as if she'd gone too far.

Cassidy took his time. "How many other vultures have appeared on your doorstep today, Grace?"

"Not one. He's got them all in his pocket, Cassidy, except you. He never had you in his pocket. What brought you, you failed Irish romantic? He accused me of lusting after you once."

"And did you?" Cassidy asked.

"Well, only a little!"

"Why?"

"Well, you were attractive in those days. Young and handsome. Not any more, God knows. Look at you. You look like an IRA gunman who has already starved to death, Cassidy."

That hit Cassidy in his funny bone, and he leaned back in the deep, brocaded sofa and bellowed with laughter. After a bit she joined him, both of them laughing away, and that eased the tension. She poured him more tea, which he drank. He asked the big question: "When did you cut him off, Grace?"

"Cut what off—his balls? his legs? his money?"

"Money," Cassidy said.

"Just before Christmas. Six weeks ago. Not another cent, I said."

Cassidy got off the sofa then and walked around the living room looking at all the expensive Chippendale, the paintings, the bric-a-brac. "He can't live without money any more than a fish can live without water, Grace."

That brought forth another torrent: "He's *got* money, the son of a bitch. He's rolling in thousand-dollar bills, the bastard." Here the bitterness took a new turn. These rich women, Cassidy was thinking, hate being loved for their money, but they hate even worse their husbands getting off the hook and finding their own pile, getting off the dependence. It's their weapon, and when they lose it . . .

"He's in over his head this time, Grace . . ."

"*I'm* not going to pull him out. Are *you* going to pull him out? He wouldn't pull you out. You know that, don't you?"

Cassidy wandering about the big furniture-crowded living room, between the highboys and the end tables and the bronzes, all giving off their soft glow, on Persian carpets overlaid on other deep carpets, as if one carpet wasn't enough. One curtain wasn't nearly enough for the windows either. There were thick velour curtains with elaborate large flower patterns, lined with silk, and under them fluffy white glass curtains, and under those Venetian blinds, all keeping the world at bay, the inhabitants cocooned by expensive fabrics.

"Yes, I know that," Cassidy said after awhile.

"Then why . . . ?"

Cassidy shrugged. It was not anything he could explain to this embittered woman and hardly even to himself. He and Alison had been together for a great many years, neither friends nor enemies, but *colleagues,* members of the same club. Cassidy enjoyed the spectacle of Alison floundering out of his depth, but he wouldn't enjoy the spectacle of Alison sinking out of sight—if for no other reason than that it would end the game.

Cassidy said: "What was the final immorality you couldn't stomach, Grace?"

"Do your own dirty work, Cassidy!"

She's close to tears, thought Cassidy, this tough dame, and I'm nowhere. "I'm trying to help, Grace. If you'd give me a clue . . ."

"Killing women and children is what he's doing, and that I won't stand for. Instead of giving me a child, which is what a husband is for, he's off murdering the children of other women . . ."

That last line bubbled dangerously, so full of emotion that the very air trembled; Grace Alison swept out of the room and up the stairs, eyes huge with unshed tears.

Cassidy picked his worn black coat off the richly brocaded sofa and put it on. He let himself out the newly painted black door and walked down K Street in the twilight, the street lights just coming on. She's watching me out the window, thought Cassidy, and shook his head dolefully from side to side to give the woman some interesting reaction to look at.

Killing women and children? *Alison?* It seemed highly unlikely, if only because Alison wouldn't like to get blood all over his Gucci gloves.

- 7 -

— The girl at the table checking the lists looked fresh as a flower—laundered, pressed, coiffed, scented. And smiling. Mostly she was waving the guests in, old familiar faces who showed up at many of the Washington receptions. And me, thought Cassidy, not out of my clothes for days, with the stink of New York harbor still about me. He smiled at the pretty girl and handed her Senator Kuhn's gold-crested invitation.

"Name?" she asked.

"O'Malley," Cassidy said, not wanting his own name bandied around the Illyrian Embassy.

While she looked for O'Malley on the list—and not finding it— Cassidy slipped past her, down the curved marble stairs with its gilded nineteenth-century ironwork balustrade into the great reception room with its crystal chandeliers.

Illyria was a very small, oil-rich, radical, and pugnacious country, and it got a mixed bag of guests. Arabs in their burnouses and Arabs in Bill Blass suits, black people and brown people and white people and yellow people (no red people). Pretty girls from senators' offices and from committees and commissions but not many senators, committee members, or commissioners. The small fry, not the big fry, because Illyria was rich but not that rich.

A white-coated waiter thrust a trayful of champagne at Cassidy. He waved it aside and headed for the two enormous tables at the rear of the room where the food was. When had he last eaten? It seemed like days. To get at the food table, Cassidy had to shoulder his way through clouds of Chinese who always seemed to get to these receptions early and ate like Chinese locusts. Cassidy elbowed a Marxist out of his path, picked up a plate and filled it with roast beef rolled in little cones and tied together with toothpicks, two crabcakes, a lobster tail, six shrimp, and four pieces of buttered rye bread.

He used his elbows again to get free of the table and pushed his way slowly through the crowd, eating, looking, and listening all at once.

"That's the Ambassador's last year's girl friend in last year's dress," a pretty girl said, clinging to a glass of champagne.

"Oil glut," her companion explained. "He'd had to economize."

Little circles of people, all of whom seemed to know each other, chattering away. Cassidy stayed just outside the circles, listening and stuffing food into himself.

"He was once full of ideals," a nice-looking girl with tired eyes said. "He's now full of shit."

"That describes almost everyone in the room," complained her companion, a sharp-eyed man who looked younger than she did.

Another white-coated waiter offered Cassidy a champagne cocktail, and this time he took it, holding it in the same hand that still clutched the plate, a feat of legerdemain that defies the laws of nature, but which any cocktail party habitué has to learn. "Where is the guest of honor? Hassim el Kariq?" he asked the waiter, the safest person in the room to show curiosity to. The waiter pointed to a corner of the room where quite a crowd had collected around a moustached, smiling man, an Arab in a Bill Blass suit, not a burnous. He was holding court. Cassidy pushed his way over and joined the court.

Mr. Kariq was doing all the talking in Oxford English. "The Somalis now have the Russian KTG heat-seeking missiles that they can't afford, don't need, and don't know how to operate, so now it's up to the Americans to sell the Eritreans *their* version of the same weapon that the Eritreans can't afford, don't need, and can't operate. That way we keep everyone equally unhappy—otherwise known as the balance of power."

He got quite a laugh with this jape. He'd got both the accent and the argument at Oxford, thought Cassidy. You had to hand it to these upwardly mobile Arabs. They were going to the best universities, wearing the best clothes, and getting on the best hit lists.

Cassidy was being looked at. He could feel the look as if it were sunshine. He lifted his eyes from his plate, just as he stuffed the last piece of rye bread in his mouth, and looked directly into the looker's eyes . . .

Kore.

She was standing just outside the circle of Mr. Kariq's admirers, holding a glass of champagne in both hands, using the champagne as something to do with her hands rather than a beverage to drink. She was wearing a white dress edged in gold that showed off her olive skin to a sensational degree and diminished not at all the pool of sadness that surrounded and isolated her. She seemed, even in this crowded room, all alone.

Cassidy caught hold of a waiter, put his empty plate and glass on the man's tray, and took a fresh glass of champagne. He moved over to the woman in the white and gold dress, she watching him over the lip of the glass.

"You and I were never going to lay eyes on each other again, and here we are," Cassidy said. Not the opening he'd planned but one that just popped out of him.

She sipped her champagne, a glint of amusement in the brown eyes. "You do get around, Mr. Cassidy." In that too perfect, meticulously controlled English.

Cassidy, thought Cassidy. Not O'Malley. They'd cottoned on to his real name. He wasn't surprised.

"I'm afraid I don't know your last name," Cassidy said.

She looked into her champagne as if seeking her last name there and made him wait a very long time. "Condorcy," she said finally. "Very alliterative. Kore Condorcy."

Condorcy. It could be a lot of things—English, French, even an Anglicization of Arab.

"I was going to look up Kore in my mythology books, but I've been very busy," Cassidy said.

"You're always very busy, Mr. Cassidy," Kore Condorcy said, with a little bit of a smile. "Mr. Wenceslas is very cross with me for letting you out of that room."

"Is he now?" Cassidy said. "I rather suspected he'd told you to let me out."

"You have a suspicious nature, Mr. Cassidy."

"Where is the big man?"

She glanced left, and there he was in his own circle of admirers, the big confident voice booming away, though Cassidy couldn't catch the words.

"Always dominates the group, doesn't he?" Cassidy asked.

"Not you, Mr. Cassidy. But I wouldn't push your luck."

"My fatal weakness," Cassidy said. "Pushing my luck."

He strolled over to the Wenceslas group. Sheer bravado, he was thinking. Showing off in front of the lady. Not very smart.

The big man caught sight of him in midsentence and was discomfited not a single bit. "Mr. Cassidy," he boomed. "What an unexpected pleasure. The last person in the world I expected to see in this motley throng. What are you doing here?"

"Buying," Cassidy said, with a great Irish smile. "And you're selling, of course?"

"Always," the big man said. He'd grasped Cassidy's hand and was pumping it in his self-assertive style, a great smile on his wide face. "Well, we must have a little talk, mustn't we? Some place more private than this." To his circle of admirers: "Will you forgive me?"

Not waiting for forgiveness, grasping Cassidy's right elbow with one hand and his right hand with his other hand, Wenceslas propelled Cassidy in the direction of another of the room's curved staircases, this one a bit smaller than the main staircase.

A bit too much of a bum's rush for Cassidy. At the first landing, Cassidy swung himself loose of those proprietarial hands and turned back to the room to look for Kore Condorcy.

"I thought we might ask Miss Condorcy to join us," Cassidy said. "But I don't see the lady."

Kore had vanished, but Harry Dixon entered Cassidy's field of vision, looking squarely at him. Just at that moment several beautifully dressed women came down the stairs and the big man had to step aside to let the women past, and in doing so his back was turned to Cassidy. Cassidy formed the word "Help!" on his lips, throwing it right at Dixon for several good reasons. For one, Wenceslas was calling the shots a little too tightly. For another, he didn't relish Dixon getting the idea he and Wenceslas were great buddies.

He turned and followed Wenceslas up the stairs.

On the second story landing, Wenceslas again took charge, propelling Cassidy in his jovial style through an oak door into an empty office with a big walnut desk, oak panelled walls, leather sofas, and several paintings by Raoul Dufy.

Cassidy sat on a red leather revolving chair beside the desk and leaned back quizzically. "The Illyrians won't like our taking over the embassy office, Mr. Wenceslas."

Wenceslas was helping himself to a cigar from the humidor. "I assure you, Mr. Cassidy, the Illyrians' hospitality is boundless. The Illyrians and I are *very* old friends."

"I keep forgetting how many old friends you have, don't I?"

"Yes, you do, Mr. Cassidy. You consistently underestimate me and also misunderstand me. At the same time I must confess I both underestimated and misunderstood *you*. The little piece of paper I found on you was very misleading. I had thought that was your—uh—piece of paper. I have since discovered that you had—uh—taken it from someone else. I apologize."

Cassidy tried a shot in the dark. "You're on a hit list, Mr. Wenceslas. You know that, don't you?"

Wenceslas bubbled with exuberance. "I'm on several hit lists, Mr. Cassidy. Charming as many people find me, others do not."

The same shot in the dark. "When you saw that piece of paper you thought I was the hit man."

"A natural mistake, Mr. Cassidy. But if that wasn't your mission at my home—one of my homes, I have many—what was?"

Cassidy stirred in his red leather chair and swung himself back and forth. "I was just taking a walk in the snow when I was slugged outside your house."

"Come *on*, Mr. Cassidy."

"Might I ask a question? Why did you want to blow up thirty million dollars worth of very sophisticated artillery shells."

"O-ho," Wenceslas said. "O-ho." He said O-ho with great authority. Not many men could pull off O-oh with such élan in modern times. He was walking back and forth now, thinking furiously and almost visibly. Clearly he had been caught by surprise.

"Well, well, well, well," he said. "I thought . . . a malfunction in the . . . uh . . ." He fell silent.

"You thought the telephone exploding device somehow didn't work. No, it would have worked. It was disconnected."

"By you?"

Cassidy said, "If that building had gone up, you'd have killed a few people, Mr. Wenceslas."

"Mr. Cassidy those shells were intended to kill women and children by the hundreds in small Syrian villages. Yes! You didn't know that I was on the side of the angels, did you, Mr. Cassidy? Oh, I confess I'm not always on the side of the angels, but in this case I very much am."

Killing women and children is what he's doing and what I won't stand for. Grace Alison shouting.

The big man had picked up a footstool and placed it about four feet away from Cassidy, and now he sat on it with remarkable agility, flourishing his cigar. "So *you* took the artillery shells. You're not buying, Mr. Cassidy. You're selling, and I'm preparing to buy. I will offer you one million dollars paid into your Swiss bank account, and if you don't have a Swiss bank account, I'll open one for you, by tomorrow morning. Now don't shake your head at me, Mr. Cassidy, I am always surprised but nevertheless always prepared for incorruptibility . . ."

Wenceslas had taken out a sawed off .38 from a shoulder holster and leveled it smilingly at Cassidy's face. Without missing a beat in his booming voice, "I have found, Mr. Cassidy, that most people can be bought, but for those few who can't be bought I offer not only the carrot but the stick. If you deny me what I wish I will kill you, Mr. Cassidy, and your body will be deposited in the Potomac and no one will ever even associate your demise with this embassy. As I remarked earlier, the Illyrians and I are very old friends. They owe me many favors, and they have diplomatic immunity and no scruples, and you can't beat that combination . . ."

The oak door swung open, and Harry Dixon walked in. "Horatio, I've been looking all over for you."

The big man leaped to his feet. Cassidy rose from his red leather chair. Wenceslas' gun had vanished.

For a moment no one said anything.

Cassidy uttered a little sigh and performed the introductions. "Do you know Mr. Wenceslas, Harry? Very persuasive fellow. This is Harry Dixon, a member of Senator Kuhn's staff on the Arms Control Committee, Mr. Wenceslas."

Wenceslas pulled on his cigar imperturbably: "I know the senator very well."

"I keep forgetting you know everyone, Mr. Wenceslas. Well, we'll be running along. I'll think over your offer. There are *ethical* considerations that must be kept in mind."

"I assure you, Mr. Cassidy, ethical considerations are always at the forefront of any of my dealings."

Cassidy could think of nothing at all to say to that. He walked out of the office, puffing out his cheeks. Harry Dixon followed him.

The two men walked down the curved staircase. "Thanks, Harry," Cassidy said.

Dixon's thin countenance was wry. "The dialogue was so fascinating I hated to interrupt, but when he threatened to kill you . . ."

"Yeah," Cassidy said, "he's on the side of the angels, and ethical considerations are always at the forefront of any of his dealings. Those are always the most dangerous men in the world."

The two men collected their coats and walked out of the embassy. Harry Dixon's car was parked thirty feet from the embassy's front door. They climbed into the front seat.

"I want to see who he leaves with and where he goes, Harry."

Dixon leaned back in the car seat. "We'll freeze if he stays at that party too long."

"I don't think he will. Meantime, we can have that little talk you said we should have. Tell me about Jeremiah Wenceslas. Why is he so self-confident?"

People were leaving the embassy party, summoning cabs, some of them in their own limousines. None of them Wenceslas.

Dixon was saying, "He's the biggest private arms dealer in the world, Horatio. He sells to both sides like Basil Zaharoff used to do before World War I, but he's much more mysterious than Zaharoff ever was. No one knows his real name."

Cassidy's eyes were glued to the embassy door. "Arms are almost exclusively controlled by governments now, mostly even *made* by governments. How does a private citizen get into the act?"

"Wenceslas buys the stuff when some little war ends or when some country is reaching for a higher technology. For instance he bought all of Lebanon's Russian Kalishnikoff rifles when the Lebanese moved on to K 47s and sold the rifles to *both* sides of the Nigerian war, and when that war ended, he bought them back at bargain rates and sold them to Liberia and then acted as agent to sell them to both sides of the Lebanese war. They're now killing the very people who sold them to Wenceslas in the first place."

"Very ethical," Cassidy said.

"He deals in cash. He thinks nothing of paying off a million in cash out of a suitcase. Or he works out of Swiss banks."

A million in a Swiss bank account. If you don't have a Swiss bank account, I'll open one for you.

"What is he selling the Illyrians that they love him so dearly?" Cassidy asked.

"SAMs. He sold the Iraqis some very nice used Mirages he bought from Israel after the Israelis went to F 16s. Now the Illyrians want Russian SAMs he bought from Nigeria in order to shoot down the Iraqi Mirages if the need arises."

Cassidy said: "There he is."

Wenceslas had come out of the embassy, waving his cigar over his head, a signal for someone to pick him up. He was wearing a black overcoat that went to his heels. It had a huge beaver collar. Kore Condorcy, expressionless, was on the big man's arm.

A long black limousine pulled to the embassy door. Wenceslas helped Kore Condorcy in and followed her. The limousine pulled away.

"Don't follow too close," Cassidy said.

"I've never done this in my life," Dixon said. He started his car and followed the limousine out into Connecticut Avenue.

Another car pulled between the limousine and Harry Dixon's Saab. Dixon cursed.

"Never mind," Cassidy said. "Use the other car as cover. How does Wenceslas operate in this country? I thought everyone needed to go through the Office of Munition Control. There are all kinds of controls."

Harry Dixon's voice turned savage. "Don't you *know*? Come off it, Horatio!"

"No, I don't know. Harry. That's what I came to Washington to find out."

Dixon held his right hand up to Cassidy's nose, forefinger and middle finger tightly together, eyes glinting anger. "He's like *that* with the Agency. Your old Agency. He's pulling the same trick Zaharoff pulled in World War I. Zaharoff worked with British Intelligence. He knew just what arms the Germans had because he'd sold them to them. Same thing with Wenceslas. He's telling the Agency just what the Iraqis or the Eritreans or the Illyrians have because he sold it to them and he knows what condition the stuff is in and the state of training of their armed forces. The CIA won't let us move on Wenceslas because he's *their* pigeon. He's pulling the same trick everywhere else. In France you have to clear arms deals with the DMA—

Delegation Ministerielle pour l'Armament—but Wenceslas is slipping information to French intelligence about what's going on in Chad so that Foreign Office won't let anyone touch him. We don't know how many intelligence agencies he's dealing with. Probably all of them."

The big black limousine was out of Embassy Row now and proceeding down Indian Lane, past stately private homes with big lawns.

Dixon was still talking in tones of bottomless cynicism. "Wenceslas has got his own foreign policy. He'll tell you if you want to listen that arms are good for the little countries to help nudge them into the modern world. And he's got his own intelligence agency, which is himself. He's a one-man operation. Does it all himself and still has time to go to the parties."

The big black limousine pulled up at one of the stately homes and stopped.

"Keep going," Cassidy said. "Drive right on past him."

He slid down in the seat and buried his chin in his overcoat, only his eyes showing. It was an imposing Georgian house of red brick—*One of my homes. I have many*—and on a lighted iron column were the numbers 4678, which Cassidy tucked away in his mind because he had to get back there.

Dixon drove to the end of the block and turned left. "Now where?"

Cassidy looked at his watch. It was only six thirty. "Let's go to your place, Harry. I'll cadge a drink off you and maybe another hour's snooze on your sofa."

"When was the last time you spent the night in an old-fashioned bed, Horatio?"

Cassidy laughed hollowly.

- 8 -

— Jeremiah Wenceslas took off his big black overcoat with the wide beaver collar, transferring the cigar from one hand to another as he slipped his arms out of the sleeve. Behind him, ready to receive the coat, was Zucchi, who was Burmese, half the size of the big man. Zucchi took the coat from his master carefully and draped it over his arm.

"Any calls?" Wenceslas asked.

"Three," Zucchi said in his light voice. "The names are on your pad in the library."

Kore Condorcy was taking off her own coat, a long sealskin with huge sleeves, which she hung up in the hall closet.

"Are you having dinner in, Jeremiah?"

He was already on his way to the library, his hand on the knob of the door. "I won't want dinner, my darling. A cup of coffee in the library right now, if you would be so kind."

She frowned. "A cup of coffee is not nearly enough, love. You didn't eat anything at the party. I watched you."

He laughed and patted his stomach, which was flat and hard. "I am not exactly starving to death, my darling. We all eat too much. If I'm hungry I'll pick up something later. Some place."

"Some place? You're not staying in?"

"It depends on the phone calls." The big man vanished into the library.

She lowered her head submissively and stood for a moment, motionless. After a long ten seconds, she sighed and went into the kitchen. Zucchi was already ahead of her at the coffee maker.

"I'm making the coffee, Missy," he said.

"Make me one, too, Zucchi. I have acquired Jeremiah's bad habits. A cup of coffee when I should have a meal."

"I have some fish, Missy. I could broil you a fish with a boiled potato and some salad."

She sat down at the big kitchen table. "Perhaps later. What were the calls, Zucchi? Trouble?"

"I think plenty trouble, but you know Mr. Wenceslas. He thrive on trouble."

"Yes, but I don't," the sad-faced woman said.

In the library, Wenceslas was making the first of three calls.

"Slovik, where are you?"

"I'm following." Slovik was driving a rental limousine that had a telephone.

"What area?"

"Chevy Chase, heading northeast."

"Try to do better than you did last time, Slovik."

"Yes sir."

During this exchange there was a steel asperity in the tone of voice quite different from Wenceslas's public affability. He hung up and dialed another number. "Will you get Mr. Kariq, please. This is

Wenceslas. You'll find Mr. Kariq in the middle of the party. I just saw him there." Wenceslas hung on, penciling notes on his desk pad. "Ah, Mr. Kariq, I just got your message. Where shall we meet? . . . Yes, that's all right. I'll pick you up there and we'll just drive about in my car and have our little chat. These days I don't trust anyone else's car. Bugs in all of them."

Kariq said, "You're not safe in your own car anymore, Mr. Wenceslas. When the Americans can pick up what Gromyko told Brezhnev in Brezhnev's own limousine, then nothing at all is safe any more."

The big man laughed. "I don't think you and I are quite as visible as Brezhnev and Gromyko. But you're right, Mr. Kariq. Nothing is safe. We are at the end of the age of privacy. Future generations will speak in awe of the days when people actually had secrets. It will be looked on as something impossibly romantic and distant like cowboys riding the range of the Old West." Without a change of inflection. "You'll bring the—uh—imbursement, to invent a word."

"Yes, I'll have that—uh—word. Good word but I've already forgotten it."

"What time?" Wenceslas asked. "Oh, no, I couldn't in an hour. No, let's make it. . . . Is ten all right? Fine." He hung up.

Zucchi came into the library bearing a Georgian silver pot of coffee with sugar and cream in matching silver containers and a cup and saucer of Minton, all on a silver tray. He poured the coffee at the desk. Wenceslas added cream and sugar to the coffee. He pointed to the last name on the pad. Ali Heykal. "When did he call?"

"Half an hour ago, sir. He's coming here. Is that all right?"

"That's all right. When?"

Zucchi looked at his watch. "Well, sir, another twenty minutes unless traffic is too heavy."

Wenceslas sipped his coffee and said, "Bring him in here and give him what he wants. Tea, probably. He's a Moslem. He doesn't drink. I'm going to have a little rest." Looking at his watch. "An hour, Zucchi. I don't want to be disturbed for one hour."

"Yes, sir."

In the big master bedroom on the second floor, Kore Condorcy had taken off her white dress with the gold edges and carefully hung it up in the walk-in closet at the head of the king-sized bed. She slipped out of the only other article of clothing she wore, a pair of panties, and stepped into the shower in the old-fashioned bathroom that adjoined the bedroom.

While she was showering, Wenceslas came into the room, loosening his tie. He undressed beside a chaise lounge at the end of the room, thoughtfully, brow furrowed. At one point he got so involved in his thoughts that the undressing stopped altogether, Wenceslas sitting on the chaise lounge, trouserless, in his underwear and shirt.

Kore Condorcy came in, toweling her slender body. She looked at the big man, sitting motionless. "Darling, you're a million miles away."

He came to abruptly and shook his head. He slipped out of his shorts and shirt and lay down on the bed, which had been turned down on both sides. He slipped his legs under the covers and lay there, naked. She dropped the towel on the floor and climbed into the bed on the opposite side.

"You're having a crisis of conscience," she said flatly.

"I never have crises of conscience, as you call them. Never."

"Yes, you do, Jeremiah."

"No, what you see, my darling, is—uh—a clash of gears, shall we say. The equations have changed. The mathematics of the operation have become more complicated." He rolled across the bed and took the naked woman in his arms, still talking, "Conscience is not the word for it."

He kissed Kore Condorcy absently on the lips.

"It's more conscience than you like to admit, Jeremiah," she said when her lips were free. He was kissing her neck now and moving down toward her breasts. "These things are on my conscience if not on yours."

The big man was kissing her belly button, stroking her slender thighs. "Don't let it," he said. He moved up on her body now, spread her legs, and entered her.

"Are you going to kill Mr. Cassidy?" she asked, arms around his neck, his cheek beside hers.

"Probably," the big man said and kissed her. "He's a stubborn Irish mythomaniac." He kissed her again and after that conversation ceased altogether.

Afterward, they slept, and when she awoke he was gone. The clock at her bedside said eight thirty. She slipped into a white silk dressing gown with a burnous top and picked up the house phone. When Zucchi answered, she said: "I'll have that fish now, Zucchi. Has Mr. Wenceslas gone out?"

"Five minutes ago."

"Bring *The Washington Post* with my dinner, Zucchi."

"Yes, madame."

Cassidy slept heavily for an hour. At Dixon's insistence he had taken off all his clothes, and he slept in Dixon's bed and dreamed that Lucia had called and said she would be at a certain address but he couldn't find the place and he searched and searched through surrealist streets in black and white stretching endlessly to the horizon and horribly empty of life . . .

He woke when Dixon shook him. "Eight thirty," Dixon said. "You look like you could have gone on all night." Dixon had a cup of coffee in his hand, and he put it down next to the bed.

Cassidy yawned and pulled his thoughts together. "That's three sleeps I've had. On the plane, in your office, and here." He sipped the coffee. "That ought to last me a while."

Dixon looked at him skeptically. "Yeah. How long were the sleeps? Forty-five minutes? An hour? You look like you've been disinterred."

Cassidy was already dialing on the bedside phone. "You shouldn't pamper yourself with too much sleep at our age, Harry. Read the obituary page. People our age dying all the time—you know why? Boredom. They've lost their motivation." Into the phone: "Cassidy, Hugh. We got to talk. I'll come to your place." He listened a moment. "I'm in Chevy Chase. How long will that take? Well, I'll be a little longer than that—say an hour and a half." He hung up.

"Lend me your car, Harry, and a map of Washington." He sprang out of bed and started to put on his trousers.

"I'll be back by dawn."

"Jesus Christ!" Dixon said.

"Can I borrow your razor?" Cassidy asked.

Cassidy spotted the limousine on his tail as he was passing the Washington Home for the Incurables on Wisconsin Avenue. Just to test the tail, he swung the Saab off Wisconsin onto Quebec, picking up speed, watching the limousine follow him. He swung right on Thirty-fifth Street, another sharp right on Ordway, and then a tire-screeching left on Thirty-Sixth. He roared around Washington Cathedral and across Wisconsin to Woodley, ran the lights across Massachusetts Avenue to Cathedral Avenue, where he became very decorous and law abiding because the limousine was nowhere in sight.

"Never send a Balkan to catch an Irishman," Cassidy said aloud to no one in particular. "They're too slew-footed." It had wakened him up, made his bloodstream race, sharpened his wits. Nothing like a car race on someone else's tires to focus the mind.

In Georgetown the big problem was finding a place to park. He found a space three blocks from Alison's house. In the unlikely event that Slovik spotted the car, he wanted no connection with Alison, who was in trouble enough. *Are you going to pull him out? He wouldn't pull you out.*

If you turn over every stone in the human heart you will always find some small kernel of self-interest in even the most distinterested act. Thus Cassidy to Cassidy, walking past the Georgian houses, on the empty Georgetown streets. Disinterested is hardly the word. Whatever my feelings for Alison (which fluctuate from loathing to quite unwarranted affection) they are not disinterested.

The streets misty in the lamplight and winter air, the Georgian houses lit and terribly *inhabited.* Cassidy could almost taste their inhabitation, as part of his own uninhabitation. I am an outsider in this most inside of cities. I'm in a maze of conflicting motivations, not the least complicated of which is my own. Who is doing what to whom and why? I'll settle for the what to whom. The whyness can come later or not at all.

Alison answered the doorbell. Cassidy, grim-faced, walked in without waiting for an invitation. Neither man, in fact, said anything.

Alison led the way through the darkened corridors to a landing on a staircase at the rear of the silent house. Here he opened a door faced kitty-corner to the walls that led into his study.

Cassidy walked in, shedding his overcoat onto a brown leather sofa that looked deep and comfortable and terribly expensive. The room was hung with antique weapons—assegais, Australian boomerangs, scimitars, Masai spears, pikes, halberds. All very quaint in the light of modern destruction.

"Coffee?" Alison asked.

"Whiskey," Cassidy said. He threw himself onto the sofa. Alison poured him the whiskey, exuding disapproval. One shouldn't drink whiskey after dinner until eleven thirty at least. That was the Gospel according to the upper classes. One followed the rules or one was a social aborigine.

Alison handed him the whiskey, and Cassidy took a drink.

"I had a talk with Grace earlier," Cassidy said.

Clearly Alison didn't relish the idea of Cassidy having words with his wife, but he ignored it and went right to the heart of the matter. "Where's the stuff, Horatio?"

Cassidy took a deep drink of whiskey and felt a flood of warmth to his belly. "It's safe," he said finally. "What the hell is going on, Alison?"

Alison stood on tiptoe to reach and bring down a short, wide, straight sword. He showed it to Cassidy. "Have you ever seen one of these, Horatio? That is a Roman short sword, one of the most murderous and effective weapons in all history." Alison flourished it in front of him and then made a stabbing motion straight ahead of him, stopping just short of Horatio's chest. "The Romans subdued the known world with this weapon, which was technologically superior to anything else in its day."

Cassidy growled, "I didn't come here for a sermon, Hugh. Especially one as dumb as that. I want to know what's going on."

Alison was looking down the length of the sword, testing the blade. "So do I."

"Let's have a review of the bidding, shall we," Cassidy said. "The munitions were destined for Israel. Someone hijacked them to keep them out of the hands of the Israelis. Wencelas tried to blow them up, presumably also to keep them out of the hands of the Israelis, so I don't see how he could have been the one who hijacked them. We moved the stuff out of Forensic, and someone tries to hijack us in New York harbor. Now it appears to me there are *three* interests here: the Israelis; Wenceslas, who implies he's acting on behalf of the Syrians to keep the stuff out of the hands of the Israelis—if you believe him and I don't; and a third wild card, the ones who tried to hijack the stuff in the middle of the harbor, who *don't* want to blow the stuff up or the Israelis to have it."

Silence. Cassidy sipped his whiskey. Alison examined the Roman short sword. Cassidy prodded him. "I'd like to hear your thinking on the subject, Hugh, just to see how you're going to lie your way out of this one."

Alison sighed. "Let's keep it civil, shall we, Horatio." He looked Cassidy in the eye for the first time. "As you very well know, Cassidy, our public actions don't always square with our private actions. This case is even more complicated because nothing is public. Privately the U.S. government has agreed to slip the rocket assisted laser guided shells to the Israelis, but even more privately we don't *want* them to have them because we don't trust Begin around the corner with anything as hairy as 155 mm shells that fire a hundred miles. Are you following me, Horatio?"

"Very closely."

"So what one very private U.S. *actor*—that is the going word in the arms trade these days—what one private U.S. *actor* is promising the Israelis, another even more private U.S. *actor* is taking away, if you get my meaning, and I think that you do."

He's opening up, Cassidy thought and, when Alison opens up, look out. Aloud he said, "What about the wild card?"

The study door crashed open. Grace stood there, eyes like coals. "*He's* the wild card." Pointing her enameled finger at Alison like a gun. "He's been suborned by the Israelis to kill little children."

Alison closed his eyes as if the sight of his wife was more than he could bear. "Grace, for heaven's sake . . ."

A torrent of words Grace Alison had been holding in for a long time: "He's killing little Syrian children as he has killed little Guatemalan children and little Iranian children and little Cambodian children. A trail of little skulls follows wherever he goes."

All very unlikely. Cassidy said, "Grace, where did you get this wild talk?"

"Anonymous letters," Alison said wearily. "She's paying attention to anonymous letters!"

I know who wrote those letters, Cassidy thought.

"She's full of neurotic guilt about not having children," Alison said, holding the sword in front of his face as if to fend her off, her and her accusations.

"He's been paid off by the Israelis to do their dirty work!"

A white light lit up in Cassidy's skull—but he had no time to think about it. Alison was saying, "I'm living on my own salary for the first time, and she hates it. She has kept me in subjection to her money for years, and now she can't do it any longer and she hates it."

"Calmly, my children," Cassidy said. "Lets have a little calm."

Grace Alison was beyond calm. "You're the only whore in Washington who is his own pimp, Alison. Getting paid off by both sides!"

The Roman sword went high in the air over Alison's head. Cassidy leaped and wrestled Alison in a half circle so that when the blade crashed down it came down on Alison's desk, slicing deep into the polished walnut rather than through Grace Alison's skull.

That sobered everyone up. For a moment there was no sound except that of Grace Alison's heavy breathing, as if she'd run a race.

Alison said quietly, "Thanks, Horatio. She's been trying to provoke me to murder her for a long time, and she almost succeeded."

Grace Alison paid no attention to her husband. She had a strange little smile on her face. She seemed to be listening to something not audible to Cassidy as she tiptoed across the study and flung the door open. A young woman in a red bathrobe stood there, very calm in this maelstrom of emotion. Grace Alison grabbed the woman's arm and pulled her into the room with such ferocity that the young woman hurtled across the study and landed in a leather armchair, an exercise that seemed to amuse her more than anything else.

"There she is," Grace Alison said. Not shrieking anymore. Speaking low and slow. "My husband's guinea strumpet."

Grace Alison walked out of the room, slamming the door after her.

Alison crossed the room swiftly and took the young woman's face in both hands. "Are you all right?"

It was the first time Cassidy had ever seen Hugh Alison show genuine emotion for anyone's welfare but his own. A landmark and not necessarily good news. The woman was young, nineteen or thereabouts, raven-haired, very self-assured. "She gets very angry, that woman," she said with a flashing smile, all teeth and vivacity, like a young Sophia Loren. She rubbed her fingernails against her dress in a gesture that was as old as Italy. "I think she hates me very much." She threw her head back and laughed a full-throated laugh.

Alison was looking at her as if the world had stopped spinning in its orbit and taken a new direction, and that was all that mattered.

"Introduce me," Cassidy said.

Alison was reluctant but he had no choice. "This is Giuletta Gitano," he said.

Gitano!

"Horatio Cassidy."

"I'm an old friend of the family," Cassidy explained. "*Both* sides of the family. Are you living in, Miss Gitano?"

The girl threw her head back and laughed again as if it were the greatest joke in the world.

"It's *my* home," Alison said. His proudest possession—his only possession. Except this girl.

Cassidy sighed and shook his head. "You might have waited, Hugh."

Alison looked around a little wildly as if the answer to all this was somewhere in the room just out his reach. "Tell that to Giuletta," he said. "I tried. She's an impulsive girl." He looked like someone in a trance, trying to find his way out. He was paying no attention to Giuletta now, only to Cassidy. "I didn't want this breakup, Cassidy. Grace might have shown some compassion. This is one of those things that a man gets into at my age and then, with a little bit of understanding, gets out of. But I've had no . . . understanding."

He was ignoring Giuletta's feelings in this declaration but far from resenting it, the girl seemed triumphant in her own sexual mastery.

"Gitano," Cassidy said to the girl. "It's a Sicilian name, isn't it?"

The girl flashed her reckless smile. "What else?"

Possibilities, all of them dreadful, flashed through Cassidy's mind. "Miss Gitano," Cassidy said, giving her the full charm treatment, "I'm going to have to ask you to leave us alone for a little while. Mr. Alison and I have things to discuss."

He bowed her out as if she were the Queen of Sheba, getting a good look as he did so at the breastworks, the frame, the ass, the skin. There was no doubt about it; Giuletta was in the full flower of her sexuality. In another five years—no, two—she'd be over the hill, the body and face fleshing out, the wild wanton subdued. At the moment she was pumping desire into the very air. She had her hands in the pockets of her red bathrobe, a mischievous smile on her face, full of herself.

Alison watched all this, his face wide open. Alison, the most closed-up person Cassidy had ever known! Wide open! Everything fluttering out. Alison, that cold, self-seeking operator in the grip of the grand passion!

Cassidy shook his head in wonderment, "It just goes to show you never know anything about anyone."

Alison's voice was very low. "You never thought I'd get into such a thing, did you?" A note of pride in his voice as if it were reprehensible but nevertheless wonderful.

"I never thought you'd endanger your career, no."

Alison pulled the Roman short sword out of the walnut desk. Cassidy had closed the door to the library, but now he opened it and looked down the corridor to be sure there weren't any more eavesdroppers.

"I need that *matériel,*" Alison said. "I've made promises . . ."

"To the wrong people," Cassidy muttered.

"You don't know who I've made promises to."

"I can make a pretty good guess."

Alison ran his finger the length of the sword blade. "If I don't keep my promises . . ."

"You'll get killed," Cassidy said.

"I didn't say it. You said it."

"You're on a hit list, Hugh." Cassidy was walking around the room looking at the weapons on the wall, the assegai spears, the flintlocks, the daggers, the history of killing writ plain.

"I need to know some things," he said. "Coriander." He opened the library door again just to be sure there was no one listening. "What did you find out about Coriander?"

Alison pursed his lips and scowled and ground his teeth like a miser parting with his gold. "PLO," Alison said finally. "Muslim secret society. They killed Mohammed el Glasha in Paris and Gerald Foster in London."

"And you in Washington when they get around to it," Cassidy growled. "Who controls Coriander—Arafat?"

Alison shook his head. "Control is in Tripoli. Maybe Khaddafi himself. We don't know. We're working on it."

"You got a gun, Hugh?"

"In the safe." Alison pointed to a painting by Seurat hanging over the fireplace. Trust Alison to hide his wall safe behind a priceless painting.

"What the hell good is a gun in a safe? If Muslim terrorists walk in here . . ."

"At the moment I'm much more afraid of Grace than of Coriander. If she had a gun, she'd kill us both."

Both men grinned at that.

"If you're not using the gun, lend it to me. Just for tonight. I couldn't get a gun on the airplane."

"Why do you need a gun?"

"It's going to be a long night."

Alison swung the Seurat to one side on its hinges and worked the combination. He reached in and pulled out a .357 magnum and handed it to Cassidy.

"Where are the artillery shells, Horatio?"

Cassidy dropped the weapon into the side pocket of his black coat. "For your own protection, Hugh, I'm not going to tell you. I will tell you this. This thing smells to high heaven of olive oil if you know what

I mean, and I think that you do. Whatever you do, don't tell that Gitano girl anything at all. Not even what day it is."

Cassidy walked out of the study, down the corridor and out of the house.

- 9 -

— "Professor, where are you?"

Cassidy smiled and felt much better. If she was calling him professor, she was over her fear and anger.

"I'm in a telephone booth in our nation's capital. How are you and Deborah getting on?"

"I think you should marry her, professor. She's a marvelous girl! She taught me the most *super* game! Cribbage. Can you play cribbage, Professor? I'll bet I can beat you. I've beaten her twice."

"She's just letting you win . . ."

"No, she isn't. She's playing as hard as she can. Aren't you, Debbie? She says yes she is. When are you coming home?"

"Presently. Let me talk to Deborah. . . . Deborah, did she study her Latin?"

"Tomorrow, I'll make her study all morning. Today, she was excited and nervous about you. She watched TV."

Cassidy groaned. "I don't even allow it in the house. Tell her to get on with the absolute ablative. Put her on. . . . Lucia, you *must* study your Latin and French because you're missing school."

"I'll work my butt off tomorrow." She sounded happy and full of vitality. "Can I go outside tomorrow? I go crazy here alone! Please, professor!"

Cassidy was torn by the "Please, professor." Lucia said "Please" from the bottom of her soul—not saying it so much as singing it, elongating it into a three syllable word Pul-ee-uz full of longing and passion, irresistible.

"Where would you go outside and what would you do?"

"I'd take my skateboard to Washington Square . . ."

"Not Washington Square. Too public. Take your skateboard down to Twelfth Street and stay on Twelfth. Don't go anywhere near our apartment, and if any strangers try to talk to you . . ."

"Professor, I've had the don't-talk-to-strangers bit dinned into me for *years*."

Cassidy choked it off because he didn't want to alarm the girl and probably he was seeing bears under the bed. "I wish I could kiss you good night."

"You're getting very sentimental in your old age," she said primly.

A woman prowled back and forth outside the phone booth, waiting her turn. Cassidy let her wait. He hung up the phone, and kept his hand on it, not looking at the woman. In a few moments he took the receiver off the hook and dialed operator, looking at his watch. Ten o'clock. When the operator came on, Cassidy gave her the New York marine number of the Navy tug.

"It's ringing," the marine operator said.

Cassidy let it ring twelve times before he gave up. Damn! He should have arranged a time to call with Keefe before he left. Nobody up on the bridge where the phone was ringing. Damn! Damn! He strode out of the telephone booth to the Saab sitting at the curb, under a sign: "No parking at any time."

The three men were playing three-handed gin rummy at one of the long tables in the galley of the Navy tug. At the other long table five of the six Malays were playing a Malaysian game called *teka* on a homemade board with poker chips in place of the ivory counters used in the East.

Keefe was singing "Underneath the Bamboo Tree" in his Irish tenor and shuffling the cards. Pindar was keeping score, scowling because he was losing. "How much do you owe me, you eggbald Spartan?" asked Keefe.

"Sixty-two dollars, and you're not going to get any of it until Alison pays us, if he ever does."

Rattigan was looking at his watch. "Ten ten," he said. "Tapi should have checked in ten minutes ago."

Tapi was the sixth Malay who was on watch, and the ruling was rigorous. The man on watch was to check in every half hour, if only to stick his head in the galley for five seconds.

Keefe stopped the shuffling. Pindar looked up from his scorepad. "Pindar," said Keefe.

"I'm on my way." Pindar swung his legs from under the bench. He was in charge of the watch because he was the only one who could communicate with the Malays.

"Take your gun, but *don't* use it unless you have a clear shot overside."

"Aye, aye, Admiral," Pindar said. He pulled his gun out of his holster and pumped a shell into the chamber.

Keefe had swung his legs over the attached bench on which he sat. He handed Pindar a Navy flashlight. "Don't use it unless you absolutely have to. I'm going to douse the lights before you open that door. Crawl, Pindar."

Pindar made a face and went down on his knees. "You're overreacting," he growled.

"Let's call it an exercise in discretion. Silence, everyone." Keefe switched off the lights. In pitch blackness, Pindar crawled up the galley steps toward the deck. The door to the deck was hinged in the middle and folded back on itself. Pindar opened it, letting in the faint glow from the stars.

In this faint luminescence the silent galley watchers could see Pindar's round creeping bulk pass out of the passageway onto the deck.

Three seconds later came the scream and the shot, the two sounds simultaneous.

Not a wild scream, a controlled scream: "HOO EE! HOO EE!" You could get a lot of distance with HOO EE HOO EE. They had all—Pindar, Keefe, Cassidy, and Rattigan—used it before in moments of emergency. It meant many things. It meant Look Out! It meant I Need Help! It meant Hurry!

"On your knees," Keefe whispered. The two men crawled, gun in hand, up the galley steps. Keefe on the left side, Rattigan on the right. At the deck level, Keefe poked his head very carefully out into the starlight.

Somewhere up forward Pindar's gun roared again. "Easy with that cannon," Keefe shouted and charged the deck, almost immediately tripping and falling over the body of the Malay. Even in the faint light, the upturned face was ghastly—tongue protruding, eyeballs almost out of their sockets. Keefe felt the neck. The piano wire had cut so deep he could barely find it. Rattigan had pulled abreast of him now and was tugging at Keefe's sleeve to show him something.

It was another body, again face up on the deck, Pindar's shot had caught the man in the chest and thrown him over on his back.

"Wop," Keefe breathed into Rattigan's ear. He pointed to the stern of the boat and patted Rattigan on the head. Then he pointed to the bow and tapped himself on the head. Rattigan nodded and crawled toward the stern, as Keefe crawled forward through the pile of crates, keeping his head down.

Where was Pindar?

The air was cold and smelled of salt and oil. The sounds of Manhattan were low and distant. From the harbor no sound at all until . . .

The scrabbling was directly above him. Keefe rolled on his back, gun held in both hands. The shape came off the packing cases, and Keefe fired, straight up, the explosion tearing a hole in the silence big as a train. The man landed squarely on Keefe, matching him feature for feature—the dying skull directly on that of Keefe, the two sets of eyeballs staring into one another, mutually terrified, the mouth of the stranger, opened in an unuttered scream, directly on Keefe's mouth as if attempting resuscitation, the body thrashing in agony on top of Keefe.

For a full ten seconds, the death throes continued—the eyeballs boring into Keefe's accusingly as if saying, "You killed me, you bastard." The dying lips kissing Keefe's, unnerving him altogether. He heaved mightily and the man fell off him and rolled over, facing the stars, Keefe shuddering from head to toe like an earthquake. An omen, he was saying to himself; no good will come of it. He was much given to omens.

He ran his hands over the body. The piano wire was in the right hand. Under his arm Keefe found a holstered gun. Someone had instructed the man to use the wire, not the gun, and this instruction had finished him.

They're coming out of the tree, Keefe thought.

He rolled over on his back and looked up, but in the darkness he could see little. The tree was up there. They'd sheltered under the big willow to be safe from prying eyes, and now the branches were crawling with them. On his back, Keefe wriggled forward, pushing with his legs, eyes straining upward for any more leapers with piano wire, the gun in both hands.

An arduous journey because he kept encountering crates of shells.

He was nearing the bow when a hand grasped his wrists immobilizing the gun.

Into his ear, Pindar whispered, "You'll wear out your ass traveling like that."

"They're coming out of the tree," Keefe whispered. "I want to see 'em coming."

"Where's Rattigan?"

"I sent him to the stern. Where's the bow?"

"You're on it." Pindar held up the flashlight, and pointed upward into the tree. "We'll have a turkey shoot. Ready?" Pindar held the flashlight in his left hand. His gun in his right. Keefe nodded, still flat on his back, his gun pointed upward held in both hands.

The flashlight beam stabbed into the trees, an uproar of light. Six figures, all on different branches. Keefe's gun exploded, and one of the figures went out of the tree and into Big Fishkill Channel. Another explosion almost in Keefe's ear from Pindar's gun, and again there was a splash in Fishkill Channel. The second shots were simultaneous. This time the two bodies fell onto the crates. The last two men leaped from the tree to the deck.

"No guns!" Keefe ordered. "Bare hands."

The flashlight had gone out, and now the two friends prowled the deck in the starlight, searching for the killers with the piano wire, their own clenched fists next to the neck because once the wire got around the neck, the fight was over.

In the blackness Keefe crept forward, feeling his way with his knees. The assault came from behind and Keefe felt the piano wire sharper than a knife cutting the back of his hands. The full force of the man's body threw Keefe forward on his knees, his protecting hands torn away from his throat, around which the wire settled. It was his great bulk that saved him. Keefe threw himself up and backward with all the power of his body. The crack of the man's skull against the crate could be heard the length of the ship.

The piano wire instantly weakened, and Keefe spun his big body around and used his knees on the testicles. The man screamed. Keefe had his hands around the throat, and he applied all of his strength. Dear God, take this poor sinner to your bosom and mend his ways, said Keefe in his mind, laying on the muscle. I am doing unto you as you would have done unto me, this to the contorting figure. Presently the contortions stopped, and Keefe went to help Pindar, who was having a rough time of it ten feet away, the noise of the struggle leading Keefe.

The man was on Pindar's back, pulling tight the wire, which was not around the throat but around Pindar's protecting hands and wrists, and while this had saved his life, it put Pindar's hands out of the action. Keefe took the wire man's head in both of his hands, jerked up and back, and broke the man's neck.

That was the end of it.

The flashlight searched the tree, but there were no more in the branches.

"We're blown," Keefe said. He was sitting in the galley, sipping whiskey. "We've got to get out of here. Those guineas have friends. They'll be back with something stronger than piano wire."

He was talking low to Rattigan.

Pindar was at the other long table, comforting the Malays. The dead Malay lay on the floor where Pindar had brought him. Keefe had placed a napkin over the protruding tongue and eyeballs.

"Where to?" Rattigan asked.

"I don't know. I wish he'd call in."

"Maybe he has. We must set up a watch in the pilot house to listen for the phone."

Pindar came across to them and sat on the bench. "The Malays want out," he said. "They were not hired for this sort of exercise."

Keefe scowled and bit his knuckle. "We can't have them screaming around the docks about this until we deliver the goods."

"To whom and where?" Pindar asked.

Keefe shrugged and ran his fingers through his hair. "Put a Malay on watch."

"They won't do it. They're scared. You can't blame them."

Keefe said, "Mutiny." He reached for the deck of cards, cut himself a card and held it up. King of Spades.

"You bastard," Pindar said. He cut himself a card. Jack of Hearts. Rattigan was last, and he drew the five of clubs.

"Okay, Rattie, you're first watch. Let's see." Looking at his watch. "Ten thirty to twelve thirty. Pindar, you take twelve thirty to two thirty. I'll take the next watch. Two thirty to four thirty—and after that, everyone up and about. We'll move out at five."

"What about the engineer? Why doesn't he stand watch?" Pindar asked.

"I don't like the looks of that fellow. I wouldn't sleep soundly with him on watch." Keefe got off the bench. "I'm going to go sleep in the pilot house just in case there's a call."

"If he calls," Pindar said, "tell him about the piano wire. He'll be very interested in the piano wire."

Indian Lane was in the Spring Valley area of Washington where the streets rambled like country roads, the houses were large, set in big lawns with lots of trees and expensive shrubbery. Cassidy parked the Saab in Glenbrook Road near American University and walked, shivering a little. Madness. The whole thing. I should call the cops and go home. Insanity. If I get killed, who takes care of Lucia? Deborah? Is that why I stuck her on Deborah?

Glenbrook Road was empty of both pedestrians and cars and the houses mostly dark, some of them lit in one room only, the TV shining blue and green and yellow and red through the windows. One thought returning again and again: Alison and his girl friend, endangering his career, wrecking his marriage, maybe his life, all things the profile in his CIA file would have said he would never do.

How about me? Am I not doing the same thing? This nutty enterprise, just to see Kore again.

It stopped him dead, that idea. I'm not doing this to see Kore. I'm doing this as part of a continuing investigation. . . . Bloody hell! Would I be doing it if Kore were not in the house? I've done nuttier things but not recently. Maybe I'm in my second childhood. . . .

At the junction with Indian Lane, Cassidy slipped into the shrubbery. He crossed a lawn and went behind the row of houses, picking his way around the carefully tended lily ponds, flower gardens, and gravel paths, sticking to the silent grass. Wenceslas's house was the third house, and, as he approached, Cassidy slowed way down. For a long period he reconnoitered behind a big elm tree, casing the house and every shadow for guards, for detection devices, dogs. When he came to the house itself he searched it from end to end for signs of burglar alarms.

There were only two lit areas in the big house. On the first floor a light burned in what looked like the front hall. There was a garden door, all of glass, leading directly to the front hall corridor. Like so many American houses, the front door was solid oak, very stout, covered with locks and chains. The back door could be penetrated by a child with a stick.

On the second floor a light shone in one of the rooms, a big room with two windows. From the ground Cassidy could see the outlines of the room and the ceiling. He was at the wrong angle for seeing whether anyone was in it. He looked about. There was a tree not ten feet from the house that looked climbable. Before he did, he took time out for a long searching look in the shadows, for telltale motion, the outline of a person, for gadgets.

He climbed swiftly, swinging himself up into the elm's lower branches with his arms and then going up limb by limb, gasping and sweating with the effort, bits of bark and tree dirt smearing his coat.

He found himself looking into a large second-story bedroom. On the left was a door through which he could see a bathroom. There was a large bed in which reposed one person hidden behind a newspaper. The other side of the bed had been mussed up, the pillows in disarray. Clearly two people had been in that bed.

A white-coated servant came into the room and was saying something to the person in the bed. The newspaper came down.

Kore.

Some sort of dialogue ensued, and the servant straightened the unoccupied part of the bed, patting the pillows into shape, smoothing the blankets. Kore went back to her newspaper. The servant was talking to her, and Cassidy saw her shake her head. The servant went out.

Well, that settled that. Kore and Wenceslas.

He's too old for you, clamored something inside his head. But then so am I. Get to business, Cassidy. He cased the house from end to end. Speculating on how many rooms, trying to work out the layout. Where would he put it? Probably the bedroom. Cassidy smiled wryly. That would be interesting. Looked at his watch. Ten twenty-five. No sign of Wenceslas. The rest of the house dark which meant he wasn't in it—or he'd be in that bed. Wouldn't he?

Cassidy waited until a light came on in a third-floor, gabled room, clearly a servant's room. That would be the white-coated man, going to bed, or anyway getting out of the way. Cassidy clambered down the tree and approached the back door with his set of keys. It was almost too easy, and Cassidy never liked it to be too easy. It meant trouble later. Always. If the beginning was easy, look out later.

Why was it so easy? Wenceslas was on a hit list? Didn't he know? Or suspect? Why didn't he take greater precautions?

Cassidy found himself in the front hall on a black and white tiled floor. On the right was a closed door. He opened it, stepped inside and switched on the light. A study. Big desk without a single thing on it, not even a desk pad. The man works out of his head, thought Cassidy, just like me. Doesn't like little bits of paper. The walls were lined with books and paperbacked manuscripts. Cassidy looked at a few of the manuscripts. *The Political Effects of Military Programs, Some Indications from Latin America,* Rand Corporation, Santa Monica, California; *Wehr und Wirtschaft* 10, *MiG Affaren,* L. Alexandros; *United States Arms Sales to the Persian Gulf,* House Committee on International Relations, U.S. Congress. . . .

Cassidy sat down at the desk and pulled at the center drawer. Locked. He brought out his collection of keys, but there was nothing remotely resembling that kind of lock. From his breast pocket he brought out a slim leather case with tools in it and selected a long sharp implement with a turned down end. He worked this into the lock and felt the edge of the tumbler. He picked out another implement with a longer turn down and that did the trick. He turned it and felt the lock give way. The drawer opened.

"What are you doing, Mr. Cassidy?"

In those too careful tones.

Cassidy sat back in the desk chair and swung around to face the voice. She was in a white silk robe to her heels with a burnous top over her black hair.

"Why do you always wear white?" he asked. "It's very becoming but it's not a color, it's an absence of color, a blankness, an absence of choice."

Only then did he notice the gun. A little .25 handgun, easy to unnotice. Cassidy grinned, baring his yellow teeth. Kore was licking her upper lip, as if tasting him.

She raised the gun from waist level to shoulder level and sighted down it. "I could shoot you down just like that."

"You wouldn't have anyone to talk to," Cassidy said mildly, keeping his eye directly on hers. Very sexy, having Kore look at him down the barrel of a gun. Very perverse, all of it. But then there it was. You never knew about these stirrings until they happened. He felt no fear, only this tumultous sexuality.

"Have you ever shot anyone, Kore?"

"No." Looking down the barrel, the black eyes deep as night.

"You wouldn't like it."

"How do you know? I might love it. I have heard it said killing is the greatest thrill."

"Not you."

"You don't know anything about me."

"Oh, yes I do. You'd spend the rest of your life thinking about it, and it would spoil all the other thoughts. I don't want to cause you that unhappiness, Kore."

Kore laughed at that, and the gun came down from shoulder level and pointed at the floor. "You're thinking about *me* in this situation, Mr. Cassidy?"

"Yes, and you're thinking about me. You're intensely curious about who I am and what makes me operate this way. And I'm intensely curious about you. Very peculiar. Mostly when people meet under conditions of great stress they think only of themselves whereas you and I think only of each other."

Silence in the room.

Kore put the gun in the pocket of the dressing gown. "How many people have you killed?" she asked.

"I lost count."

"Nobody loses count of something like that."

"Perhaps I'd rather not count."

She was looking at him with savage intensity now. "I knew you'd killed. I knew it. It's on you. Like a smell."

Silence in the room. She moved to a cabinet in the wall, opened a door, and brought out a bottle of brandy. She took a glass from a row of them in the cabinet and poured some out. She handed Cassidy the glass without looking at him and poured herself a glassful. She turned and faced him, holding the glass to her eye level. "*Prosit,*" she said and drank. He drank, too. "I know you pretty well, too." She moved her shoulders. "You drink. Drink has always been more important to you than women."

"Oh, I wouldn't say that," Cassidy protested.

"Perhaps I know you better than you know you. But you're quite right about my curiosity. I *am* intensely curious about you. What are you doing here, Mr. Cassidy?"

"I'm looking for a suitcase with a million dollars in it. Or perhaps two million. Have you seen it?"

"I don't know what you're talking about."

"I think that you do. It belonged to a fellow who died unexpectedly in front of your eyes on Forensic Street."

The effect was cataclysmic. She shuddered from head to toe as if the earth had opened up in front of her. Her eyes widened in recollection so painful it shook her to her very roots. She buried her face in her hands, trembling.

"Oh!" she said. Just a single syllable, but it went through Cassidy like a turning knife. He got out of the chair and took her in his arms.

"Easy, girl, easy! *You* didn't do it . . ."

The whisper came from the bottom of her. "I handed him the glass!"

"Oh, that's how it happened! Wenceslas poured it out and handed it to you, and you handed it to him." His arms around the trembling girl, the electricity of her going clear through him to his toes.

She was looking at him now, horror-struck, her eyes inches away from his. "How do you know all this?"

"I was there. I saw you run out. You paused at the foot of the stairs, and I got a very good look at you. And I fell for you. Right then and there."

She looked at him now with those black fathomless eyes. "Oh, you poor soul!" she whispered. "You poor soul!"

Cassidy was holding her like a lover, looking deep into her eyes, where all the secrets were buried, the secrets of herself; the suitcase of money was forgotten altogether. "Poor soul?" he said. "I don't look upon it like that. I consider you a great privilege, Kore Condorcy. I have not felt this way about a woman since . . ." He was not going to tell her that.

Her mouth turned upward in a smile: "Well, you shouldn't feel that way about *me,* Mr. Cassidy. I am a lost lady."

Cassidy smiled and kissed her reverently on the lips. "I have not heard that phrase in twenty years. You're too young for a phrase like that. And you're much too young to be as sad as you are. Why are you so sad, Kore?"

"I'll never tell you that. Not ever." She smiled her sad smile and kissed him as he had kissed her, reverently.

"You'll tell me. Sometime. You said we would never meet again. Remember?"

"I remember very well." Smiling now, as if she were, for the first time in their short acquaintance, happy. "What do you want of me?"

"Everything," Cassidy said. "That's all—just everything."

She took his hand. "All right. Let's have everything. After that, we'll get to the particulars. Because the particulars are important. Don't you agree, Mr. Cassidy?"

"I think under the circumstances, you should call me by my first name."

She led him by the hand out of the study, turning out the light.

"Have you got a first name?"

"Horatio," Cassidy said.

"How very inappropriate."

"What do you think my first name should be?"

"Adam," she said mischievously. "You are the progenitor. The first man." She laughed again. Very peculiar coming from a lost lady.

"Why is that so funny?"

"I'll never tell you!"

"Someday you will."

Afterward, the conversation rambled. She was propped up on one elbow, her body against his. He lay face upward on the pillow, trying to read her face, that infinitely puzzling cuneiform.

"Your color is a contradiction," Cassidy said. "Where did that touch of olive come from?"

"My mother is a Coptic Christian." Her eyes full of colored lights. "We owned Egypt once. The Arabs are very recent—seven hundred years." Shrugging off seven hundred years as if it were yesterday.

"You haven't the Coptic nose," Cassidy said.

"What do you know about the Coptic nose?"

"I'm a historian." Yielding it up reluctantly, both of them clinging to their privacy.

"A historian and a cop."

"I'm not a cop."

"What are you then," kissing his lips, "a thief?"

The conversation ran at cross-purposes with the caresses. On both sides. He was running his hand the length of her naked back. "I'm a searcher after the truth, which should be a profession"—kissing her on the shoulder—"but isn't. If you're thinking of marrying me, I'm penniless."

"I wasn't thinking of marrying you. As I told you, I'm . . . indissolubly linked." Her face fell into the sadness that was its natural bent.

"Where do you get these antique phrases—indissolubly linked? It's something my grandmother might have said."

"Tell me about your grandmother. Was she nice?"

"No. She was stubborn, capricious, self-willed . . ."

"Just like you."

The trouble was that neither of them were especially interested in talking about themselves. Each wanted to talk about the other, which made the conversation leap and stop and leap again. Out of it came fragments of her life, like pieces of colored glass, unrelated to the other bits of colored glass. She was born and brought up in Alexandria and had lived, she said, "in the usual places—London, Paris, Rome, Abu Dhabi . . ."

"Is Abu Dhabi one of the usual places?"

"We go where the money is."

"He's too old for you," Cassidy said bitterly.

That made her laugh. "So are you. I am a woman with a predilection for older men. I am accursed, a lost lady. You have been warned."

She kissed him playfully. He was not deterred.

"How long have you and Wenceslas . . . ?"

She laid her cheek on his chest. "You won't like the answer to that, so would you like to withdraw the question?"

"No."

"Twelve years."

He was shocked to the core. "You're not old enough for it to be twelve years."

"I was thirteen when we started."

"He's a monster."

"Some Egyptian girls start at seven. You Anglo-Saxons are sexually retarded."

"I'm a Celt."

She laughed. "They're worse. Some of *them* don't start until they're fifty. Are you married?"

He didn't want to talk about that and it showed. "She's dead." Clipping it off and ending that subject.

"Children?" she asked.

"I have a daughter, Lucia. She's adopted."

"Aah—a daughter! I somehow knew you had a daughter."

"She's thirteen. She goes to a parochial school in Greenwich Village." But he didn't want to talk about Lucia either. He asked her about Wenceslas, but she would tell him nothing at all. "I will be unfaithful but never disloyal."

A nice distinction.

"How many men have you been unfaithful with?"

"That's none of your business, but I will tell you anyway—you are the first and probably the last." She was kissing him and nibbling at him and laughing at him all at once. "If you believe that, you are the biggest damned fool that ever was—and yet it happens to be the truth—you truth seeker. Truth is a very uncomfortable business. You should get out of it while there is time. It can get to be a very bad habit."

Being Cassidy, he persisted in truth seeking, and when he got too clamorous about it she aroused him skillfully and satisfied him expertly—and that stopped the questions for the time being.

The air was still full of unanswered questions, even unasked questions, when—as had to happen—the woomph of a closing front door put a stop to the questions and answers. Both of them were sophisticated enough to have thought that this would happen and to have thought in advance what to do. There was no word between them. Cassidy leaped out of the bed and, having already selected the window, didn't hesitate because there was no time to hesitate. He threw his clothes, shoes, everything out the window, climbed out on the window ledge, and leaped for the tree. Not even a backward glance. It was not a time for farewells.

She watched all this expertise with sad eyes, not neglecting, in this interval, to slip on her burnouslike white dressing gown. She smoothed the bed and Wenceslas's pillows and climbed back into the bed with her book—John Irving's *The Hotel New Hampshire*—jumping ahead forty pages to indicate it had been a long night's reading.

When Wenceslas entered, she laid down the book and said reproachfully, "Three o'clock, Jeremiah. You have an appointment at seven tomorrow, and you need your sleep." The best defense is a good offense. It was not something she put into words but something that she practiced with infinite guile.

He was full of bonhomie, fuller even than usual, crackling with his special electricity. "I am so very sorry, my darling, to have kept you up to such an hour. I would have thought you were long ago asleep." He was carrying a suitcase (Another suitcase? One she'd never seen.), and this he put into the closet carefully. Only then did he lean over and kiss her on the lips.

"Was it successful—whatever it was?"

"It was successful. It was also exasperating." He was taking off his clothes during this, walking up and down, expostulating. "I found myself embedded in the other man's *patriotism*." Giving the word a special deprecatory inflection as if he were saying *horseshit*. "I have outgrown *patriotism* (again that special inflection) as not only irrelevant but indecent and, in our time, illogical, contradictory—and by that I mean some patriots are tearing *down* their country with their fervor, their idiocy, getting the country into unnecessary wars, that sort of thing."

All this with the immense self-confidence that whatever he thought must be the right thought because *he* thought it. All the time casting off shirt, trousers, socks, shoes, underpants, not missing a word . . .

"Patriotism is not the last refuge of scoundrels; it is the *sole* refuge of idiots . . ."

Outside in the chilly darkness, Cassidy had caught a branch of the tree, only momentarily, breaking his fall, then tumbled on the grass, rolling over twice. He gathered his clothes and put them on behind the tree, out of the light of the window, as fast as possible, shivering in the winter air. The moment he got his clothes on, the sensible thing, of course, would be to get out of the neighborhood before one of Wenceslas's goons hit him on the head again. So, naturally, he didn't do that. He looked up at the window. Wenceslas was barely visible, walking up and down, taking off his jacket, his necktie, disappearing, a moment later reappearing, unbuttoning his shirt.

Cassidy climbed the tree, the most lunatic act in a lunatic evening. Why? he asked himself. Because I must know. You won't like what you find. And *you* ridiculing Alison for being besotted. Look at you! Up a tree! At your age! Thoughts of a middle-aged man climbing a tree to spy upon his beloved and her protector (Ridiculous!) in their intimacy. What an entertainment! What a surpassing divertissement!

He was gazing into the room now from a branch not more than ten feet away. If Wenceslas had looked out the window, he might easily have seen him.

Wenceslas had other things on his mind. Stark naked now, he sat on the edge of the bed and took the woman into his arms with the self-confidence that was his trademark. After the kiss there was a moment of talk between man and woman. She was, Cassidy thought, protesting. But she was also looking at the big man with a tenderness, a complicity, that tore his heart to shreds.

Whatever protest she made was unavailing. The big man crawled into bed on his side, turning himself to her expectantly. Sitting up in the bed against her pillows, she took off the white dressing gown and threw it on the floor. The last sight of her he had was as she turned to her bedside table, naked to the waist, surpassingly lithe and graceful, and switched off the light, plunging the room into darkness and Cassidy into despair.

He climbed down the tree.

Truth seeker, he was saying to himself. If you seek after the truth, you may very well find it, and it serves you bloody well right.

For a long moment he stood stock-still in the darkness, immersed in unpalatable irony. After that he shook himself, like a dog, and got back to the business that he had so shamefully neglected. He had accomplished nothing. (Was Kore an accomplishment? On the matter of information, no.)

He sighed and looked at his watch. 3:05. Cautiously he stepped back on the brick terrace surrounding the garden door, and this time he looked at the glass door with some respect. Kore had appeared on the scene with a gun two and a half minutes after he'd got into the house. Clearly something had tipped her off. Cassidy looked the doorjamb over and found the eye (a minute protuberance at waist level). With his Swiss Army knife he cut the wire underneath the clapboard.

A minute later he was back in the study with the desk opened, inspecting the notebook he'd barely caught a glimpse of when interrupted by Kore.

Telephone numbers. Hastily scribbled, as if done at cocktail parties on the spur of the moment. The names were a potpourri. Turkish, Arab, French, Anglo-Saxon. Cassidy turned the pages, looking for a pattern. Some of the names were crossed out. That one, for instance. Mohammed el Glasha, Balzac 38-67, which meant it was a Paris number. Crossed out. I know that name. Mohammed el Glasha . . . Oh yes. Gunned down on a Paris street. One of the names on that hit list.

Cassidy flipped through the pages looking for other crossed out names, and found Gerald Foster, the American, gunned down at his doorstep in London—and there was his telephone number. 555-2768, a Chelsea number. Now wasn't that interesting? Wenceslas *knew* these victims of a hit list he himself was on well enough to know their phone numbers. But then, of course, Wenceslas boasted of knowing everyone.

Certainly he knew an immense variety of people in the arms trade. Also, he played both sides of the street—*all* the streets. There were names of Israeli arms dealers and intelligence agents (the two were frequently intertwined in all countries) and the names of Arab arms buyers (there were no known Arab arms sellers but plenty of agents for purchase). Mortal enemies were cheek by jowl in Wenceslas's notebook—South Yemenis with North Yemenis, who would have shot each other on sight. Somalis alongside Ethiopians. PLOs next to New York Jews they would love to massacre.

Also, a few assassins. Ali Heykal, for instance. Ali Heykal was a dangerous Arab hitman—sometimes for the PLO, sometimes for Khaddafi. A Washington number. Cassidy took out his own notebook and wrote the number down. While doing it, he noticed the pad with the three numbers on it that Zucchi had written down for Wenceslas.

One of them, the phone number of Ali Heykal. In other words, Heykal had called recently, probably that day. The two other numbers on the call pad were interesting—Hassim el Kariq who had been the guest of honor at that Illyrian cocktail party. Cassidy wrote down that number. Another phone number next to the name Slovik. Dear old Slovik—that slew-footed Balkan. That number was the sort given to radio telephones, most of which were in cars. Cassidy wrote the number down and went back to the notebook.

It was the kind of notebook a person carried in his pocket. Why wasn't it in Wenceslas's pocket? Because wherever he was going that night he didn't intend to do any telephoning. Or to write down any phone numbers.

Cassidy flipped through some more pages, searching for he knew not what except that he'd know it when he found it.

In the middle of the jumble of telephone numbers were occasional quite different jottings. Thoughts. Ideas.

"Arms dependence is the new colonialism . . . 3rd world countries enslaved by one or the other superpowers because need high technology arms supply. . . . Independent arms dealer freeing small countries from enslavement. We are great moral force for good . . ."

Cassidy sighed. Since the beginning of time arms dealers had felt the need for moral justification.

Another sentence caught his eye: "Arms industry is essential ingredient for stability in international relations."

Cassidy shook his head and went back to looking for telephone numbers he knew or wanted to know.

Hugh Alison. There was Alison's *very* private number. Cassidy was not surprised.

Close to the very end of the prescribed phone numbers Cassidy found his own name, his phone number, and his address.

Cassidy wasn't surprised by that either.

He closed the book, put it back in the desk, locked the desk drawer and let himself out the garden door, locking that after him. No sound from upstairs. Whatever erotic exercises had taken place were over and the participants asleep.

- 10 -

— 3:15 A.M. The evening was yet young. Said Cassidy to Cassidy, himself weary to the very soul. He let down the driver's seat of the Saab as far as it would go, lay down on it and closed his eyes, which only opened his mind's eye to the delicious shape of Kore naked to her lithe waist. Cassidy sighed and pulled the curtain down on that image. He set his mental alarm clock for 4:30.

In seconds he was deeply asleep, assaulted by dreams. He was on a train surrounded by Others, and the Others were all prosaic. Shirts and ties and shopping bags. Himself the odd fellow in the group. Everyone staring because he had no jacket, no tie, no shoes, no ticket, and, when questioned by the conductor, no destination. The conductor stood there, hand out for the ticket Cassidy didn't have. Where was he going again? He couldn't remember. No destination?

Cassidy awoke, sodden and guilty, at 4:25. He shook the sleep out of his eyes and drove down University Avenue to the nearest pay phone. That's my destination—a pay phone.

He dialed the Ali Heykal number. Six rings before the sleepy *"'allo."*

"M'sieu 'ey-KAL." Cassidy was suddenly very French.

"Oui. Qui es. . . ?"

"Un ami," Cassidy said and rang off. The assassin was home, which meant . . . any number of things.

Cassidy dialed the number of Hassim el Kariq he'd copied out of Wenceslas's book. No answer. Cassidy dialed the operator. "This is Hugh Alison," Cassidy said briskly. "CIA Code Number 9850921. I'd like to know the street number of the following telephone number. . . . Yeah, thanks." He wrote it down.

A Cleveland Park address. Abu Dhabi could be expected to house their courtiers very well indeed. But no servant to answer the phone? Maybe the phone was turned off after a certain hour. More probably servants' night out.

Cassidy drove to Cleveland Park. Big houses again, set in trees, but neither Federal nor Georgian. These were modern houses as befitted modern Abu Dhabi fortunes. This time he had no trouble parking. He drove right up the driveway and parked behind a Maserati, which looked precisely suited to the personality of that witty, Cambridge-educated Arab, Hassim el Kariq.

Cassidy rang the bell—just in case. If someone came to the door, he had a reasonably glib story. He doubted that anyone would come. No one did. Cassidy pulled out his collection of keys, but none of them fit. In the end he had to use the Wedemeyer. It took a very long time because it was a very modern sophisticated lock.

Once inside, he closed the door and switched on the light. The body lay two feet from the door, face upward, a gush of dark crimson all over the elegant handmade cotton shirt with its monogrammed pocket. Cassidy let out a short sharp exhalation of air. It was not unexpected, but it was always a shock.

He crouched low. Three holes in the elegant white shirt. The assassin was not taking any chances. He'd rung the bell on the servants' night out and, when the victim answered, shot him three times and then pushed the body inward so the door would close. PLO methodology borrowed from the IRA, which used it all the time in Northern Ireland. Cassidy wondered why anyone ever answered the door in Northern Ireland. It was so frequently fatal.

He searched the pockets. A wallet full of an inordinate number of hundreds and a few thousands. A gold American Express card, scores of other credit cards. In the upstairs bedroom Cassidy found the jacket of the Bill Blass suit, inside of which was a little black book full of names—Sarah, Jane, Rebecca, Helen. Busy man.

On a delicate Directoire table underneath an antiqued mirror lay a hand-tooled leather briefcase with gold-washed locks. Cassidy picked the locks and ran through the papers one by one. Much of it was in Arabic. He put these aside. The documents in English he read carefully.

". . . new technologies proliferating widely are inherently defensive —antitank weapons, surface to air missiles, and airborne and over-the-horizon radar early warning systems. These favor human technology where competence is low. Of the new technologies probably the one most adaptable to the Abu Dhabi situation are artillery shells with terminal guidance capabilities and highly accurate single-shot kill probabilities."

A phrase that seemed to recur all over the place.

Cassidy rifled through and found a letter in English to His Excellency Hassim el Kariq from Arkwright Marine Engineering Consultants, Greenwich, London.

"The submarine is thirty-two years old and too antique and slow for modern warfare but for the limited purposes you suggest . . ."

What limited purposes?

". . . in good condition. Its engines have been overhauled and worn parts replaced. Its air-conditioning needs modernization. Torpedo tubes are in fair shape but I gather these will not be needed. The 155 mm rifle on the deck is in tiptop condition, having been rebored recently . . ."

Cassidy sat heavily on the French provincial bed with its hand-painted headboard and footboard in lovely pastel flower designs and wrinkled his brow.

Submarine? Abu Dhabi had barely the technological competence to handle camels. *Submarines*?

Quickly he ran through the rest of the briefcase. A cancelled plane ticket to Zurich, which meant it had been used. A Xerox copy of a receipt for $3,000,000 on the letterhead of Banque de Geneve, Switzerland.

Three million? In the rare upper air of modern arms deals three million was a tip. Not even a very large tip.

Five A.M.

Cassidy backed the Saab out of the driveway and headed for Georgetown.

Ten minutes later, he was seated in Alison's study, the telephone in his hand, listening to Keefe's musical Irish baritone in a highly dramatic recital of derring-do in the hours of darkness in which Keefe's valor shone like a good deed in a world of total evil.

Cassidy said little because Alison sat opposite in his long Sulka dressing gown. He looks drugged, out of his mind, Cassidy thought. That guinea strumpet has been fucking him all night long, ruining his judgment. But then he, Cassidy, was hardly in a position to bring moral judgments, himself having committed a certain amount of concupiscence. . . .

"Cassidy," Keefe bellowed, "you're not paying attention. I'm telling you a story should drive you mad with the excitement and you harrumphing like a disapproving bishop."

"Yeah, man," Cassidy said in tones so neutral that Keefe woke up.

"Ah, you mean you can't talk, is that it?"

"Yeah, man."

"Somebody's sitting there you can't talk in front of? Let me guess. Hugh Alison. I'll be bound."

"Yeah, man."

"Well, what are we going to do? We're on the move, but we don't know where to move. And if you must know we don't know very much about how to navigate in these shoals and sandbars and grassy marshes. We're goin' two miles an hour so if we hit anything we won't hit it very hard, but Mother of God, we have no destination . . ."

Cassidy uttered a yelp of not very amused laughter.

No destination! I'm precognitive, he thought. Aloud he said: "There's books right there on the shelf will tell you about channel buoys and charts to help with the navigating . . ."

"I've dipped into the books and the charts, and I'm telling you, Cassidy, people go to school for *years* to learn these things. Are you expecting me to pick it up in ten minutes?"

"I do indeed, Admiral Hornblower."

"Among other things I have a mutiny on my hands. Five Malays . . ."

". . . and I must remind you of the volatility of that high technology you have aboard. If you blow, there won't be enough of you left to pick up in a teaspoon. I'll be in touch, Admiral, and just take to heart those immortal words—I have not yet begun to fight. Adios." He hung up and faced Alison.

A grand night for Eros, Cassidy was thinking. Eros and betrayal, those disparate elements that so often went together.

Alison had come out of his torpor. "I need that *matériel*," he said, giving it the French inflection, a very Alisonlike bit of snobbism. "And I need it right now, Cassidy."

Last naming him for menace, assertion of authority, change of tone. Alison was being Alison again, one hundred percent shitheel, no longer pitiable. Nevertheless, Cassidy did.

"That girl's poison, Hugh," Cassidy said, sipping his coffee.

"That girl's none of your damned business. She has nothing to do with this . . ."

"Oh, yes, she has!"

Alison's eyes and mouth were thin pencil lines. "I'm prepared to take very strong steps, Cassidy, and you're enormously vulnerable on any number of accounts—your job at the New School, your daughter, your bank account . . ."

Cassidy sighed. And I am just trying to save the son of a bitch from a hitman. His tone remained very mild. "Who you going to sic on me, Hugh—the Abu Dhabi Navy?"

Alison's mouth fell open, which it rarely did even under the most severe provocation. A palpable hit, thought Cassidy. Aloud he said, "Hassim el Kariq was assassinated last night by a very professional gunman. Three bullets in the heart, which is really being a little too emphatic. Kariq won't be bankrolling anybody any more."

Alison's recovery was swift. "I don't know what you're talking about."

"Somebody got there ahead of you, Hugh, and ran off with the money."

Alison's face was a study in control. If I didn't know the son of a bitch as well as I do, I'd say he was untouched. He's seething inside. The hands in the pockets of his dressing gown were clenching and unclenching. Cassidy could see the movement.

"This is very high policy, Horatio," Alison said in one of his swift changes of mood.

"Yeah," Cassidy said. He helped himself to some more coffee. "Whose high policy—yours? Don't give me a lot of crap, Hugh, because I know better. Shall I give you the story thus far—as I see it."

Silence in the room.

Cassidy said, "The State Department told the Israelis they could have some high tech artillery shells even our own forces don't yet have—all very hush hush to keep it out of the papers. The CIA very privately decided those hundred-mile, rocket-assisted shells would just be used to kill little Syrian children."

"Iraqi children," Alison said very low.

"Anyway the Agency spirited the stuff away but you, Hugh, tipped off your pals in the Mossad that this was going to happen, and those Israeli lads hijacked their own shells and put the stuff in that house on Forensic Street that Mossad happens to own. So far so good?"

Alison said nothing.

Cassidy went on with it. "Enter Jeremiah Wenceslas, the biggest private arms dealer in the world. I have no idea how you got wise to Wenceslas, but, after all, you are fourth man in one of the biggest intelligence organizations in the world, so you have access to a lot of information. You put me on Wenceslas's heels to find out what he was up to in relation to those shells. I found out he was trying to blow up the place—and the shells. I don't know why, but I suspect he got a lot of money from Syria or Iraq, both of them well within the hundred-mile range of those artillery shells. Who was that Lebanese Jew waiting for Wenceslas with a suitcase full of money?"

Alison said nothing.

Cassidy went on with it. "And how about Abu Dhabi—a little place with a lot of money. You're not trying to sell 'em an old used CIA submarine, are you, Hugh?"

The air was thick with silence.

Cassidy tossed in the explosive name. "Finally, a word about Giuletta Gitano . . ."

"Cassidy!" Just that and nothing more. Hugh Alison's face was mottled and ugly. The smooth operator who never left traces, this manipulator of truth and people, this passionless Machiavelli held Cassidy by the lapels of his jacket, seething with feeling Cassidy didn't know him capable of. "One more word about Giuletta, and I'll kill you!"

He means it, Cassidy thought. The son of a bitch means it.

The study door flew open. Grace Alison stood there in her bathrobe, stone-faced. "You don't have to worry about that little whore any more, Horatio. She's gone."

Alison's hand dropped from Cassidy, and he turned on his wife. "What did you do to her, you harpie?"

"I just watched. She walked out the front door with her hat and her gloves and her handbag, and she didn't look like a girl who's coming back."

Alison flew out of the room, a man possessed.

"You lovesick baboon!" Grace Alison shouted.

Much good it did. They could hear the rattle of Alison's feet as he tore down the hall and out of the house.

Grace Alison subsided onto the arm of a chair like a punctured balloon, all the life drained out of her.

Cassidy moved about the room, grinding his teeth, rubbing his hands together, scratching his head.

"Coffee?" he asked finally.

She shook her head.

"Drink?"

She shook her head again.

"Has he ever done this before?"

"Once is too often," Grace Alison said.

Cassidy poured himself a glass of Old Turkey and drank it. "They planted her on him, you know. And they pulled her out when they figured he'd about used up his usefulness. A very dangerous time. If you walk out on him now . . ."

"Don't think I won't."

". . . he'll get killed."

"What are you trying to rescue him *for,* Horatio? *Why?*"

Cassidy scowled and walked about the room, touching things here and there, the gold penknife, the Morocco leather pencil holder, the painting that concealed the safe. That reminded him, he had Alison's gun. He took it out and laid it down on the mantelpiece.

"I think they're setting him up for a big scandal, Grace. I think that's why she's been pulled out. I'm just guessing. The scandal is designed to cover up some skullduggery in very high places. The Mob is into this up to its eyeballs."

"Why?"

Cassidy scratched under his arms, ran his fingers over his face and down his neck, working it out. "Money. The world is spending 600 billion a year on armaments. That kind of cash was bound to flush out the Sicilians sooner or later. The arms industry has got all the other elements the Mob loves—it's crooked, it's devious, it's murderous . . ."

He started toward the door. "I got to get that car back."

Grace Alison said, "I told you I lusted after you once, Cassidy. Did you ever lust after me?"

Cassidy picked his coat off the sofa. "Only after your body, Grace. Never your money."

"You say the nicest things, Cassidy. Why do you want me to play nursemaid, for God's sake? What can I do?"

Cassidy slipped on the coat. "Just *be* here. Otherwise he's going to make some bad mistakes. Just calm him down so he reverts to his own snobbish, hypocritical, selfish, lying, lovable self again because otherwise he's going to mess up, and that's going to do great damage to the Agency . . ."

"Why are you trying to protect the fucking Agency, Cassidy? They *fired* you!"

"Well, that's just the way I am. I don't want the Agency hurt, and, if you must know, I don't want the country hurt. I'm a patriot, Grace. At my age, everyone's a patriot. When you're young, you try to tear the country apart and remake it to your own liking, but at my age you just want to hold the damned place together for a few more years. It's the senior citizen's form of selfishness."

"How long do I have to play nursemaid?"

"A couple of days." Cassidy was brushing some of the leaves and bark off his worn black coat. "My problem is just this: I don't trust a single God-damned soul in this enterprise, especially your God-damned husband."

"What enterprise is this, Cassidy?"

Cassidy smiled and shook his head. He couldn't tell her he had thirty million dollars worth of high explosives on his hands he didn't know what to do with. He put on his coat. "All I can tell you is that if the press gets hold of this, God help us all."

Grace Alison showed him to the door. "I still don't understand why you and I—especially *you*—should be rescuing that son of a bitch I'm married to."

Cassidy kissed her on the cheek. "Forgiveness is what the In Crowd is doing this year."

"Fuck forgiveness," Grace Alison said violently.

Half an hour later, Cassidy was in Chevy Chase wolfing down bacon and eggs Harry Dixon had cooked for him along with toast and coffee.

"Submarine in the Persian Gulf?" Harry Dixon was saying, pouring coffee for both of them. "Well, there *are* submarines out there—some of them ours, some of them you-know-who's. But I don't know of any Arab submarines anywhere in the world. Except Khadaffi's. It would upset the balance of power in the straits very badly. If one emirate had one, they'd all want one. They're an offensive weapon, not a defensive weapon—why would they want one?"

Cassidy had an idea, but he wasn't about to share it with Harry Dixon. Instead he asked, "Are there any loose submarines around for sale?"

Harry Dixon sat down in the brightly painted kitchen and tackled his own breakfast. "Hell, yes, there's *every*thing for sale if it's thirty-two years old—airplanes, submarines, destroyers, tanks, artillery. Everyone's constantly updating their stuff. We sell stuff to the Germans—like those awful Starfighters that we wouldn't be caught dead flying ourselves. The Germans unload their old tanks on the dumber South American dictatorships, and they unload 'em on the Africans. Money changes hand at every step."

Cassidy said, "Your committee has got to pass on every sale. Any submarines up for sale?"

"We pass on all the legal sales in this country," Dixon said. "There's lots of other countries where you can buy a submarine, and there's a lot of extra-legal sales. I never heard of any thirty-two year old submarines for sale, but, hell, I don't know everything."

"Yeah, but you got your ear to the ground, Harry. You ever hear of the Mob getting into armaments?"

"The Mob?" he spoke with high distaste as if he didn't like to use such a low word.

"The Mafia, the Syndicate, whatever you want to call it."

Dixon shook his head. "Never. But then it wouldn't surprise me. This is a business where bribery is very important, and the Mob has always been very good at that. You bribe a minister of some little country to buy some weapons his country doesn't need and can't afford. Some of the bribe-takers get money for services so shadowy no one knows *what* they do, if anything. Your friend Wenceslas is both a bribe giver and a bribe taker. He pays out to sell some obsolete equipment to some gimcrack country, and he's been known to take bribes to *not* sell some particularly lethal stuff to some country's enemy. The possibilities for bribery are infinite—and they're all being exploited."

The two men ate in silence for a while.

"Why are we in this murderous business, Harry?" Cassidy asked.

Dixon poured himself more coffee. "Because they're in it, Horatio. You ought to know that. The Russians gave—not sold—but *gave* thirty-eight billion in armaments to thirty-eight countries in twenty years. So we got in the act because the argument went, if we don't sell 'em the stuff, somebody else will."

"They used the same argument in the slave trade. If we don't sell 'em slaves, somebody else will—so why not?"

"There are other arguments that are harder to counter. Arms transfers are reciprocal bargaining instruments on both sides. We want someone else to do the dying—so we arm the Germans so they can die first. The Russians upset our whole African policy by getting the Cubans to do the dying in Angola and Ethiopia—and it didn't cost them a single Soviet soldier.

"Every country has its own axe to grind. We sell Pakistan arms so they can stand up against the Russians, and they buy the stuff to use against India. We need to give the stuff away, but now we sell it because that's the only way we can afford the research to make even more deadly stuff for 1992.

"Nobody fights with spears anymore. Nobody. Sixteen years ago only eight of the wog countries had surface to air missiles. Today forty-two of them have them. In 1965 only fourteen of the wogs had supersonic airplanes. Today sixty-two of them do. Eventually they'll all have viciously expensive nuclear weapons, but by that time the big boys will have figured out a way to explode nuclear weapons in their own silos, and then everyone will want to get rid of the damn things—and then we'll all be broke—and back to the spears, if we can afford the spears."

Cassidy roared with laughter. "You're a cheerful fellow, Harry. How did you get so cheerful?"

"That's what my wife says. She says leave the doom at the office, but it's not easy."

"Where will it all end, Harry?"

"It'll never end. Never. Back in the fifteenth century Charles the Bold of Burgundy ordered Liège to get out of the arms trade, and they wouldn't, so he burned the place to the ground and slaughtered all the inhabitants and you know what? Liège is still in the arms trade to this very day."

- 11 -

— The big man carried the heavy suitcase in one hand, his large
Morocco briefcase with the gold-washed locks in the other, to the
waiting limousine. He was bundled to the ears in his long black coat
with the beaver collar. Slovik held the trunk of the car open and
stowed the master's heavy bag inside alongside Kore Condorcy's bag,
which was already there. Wenceslas kept possession of the briefcase.

It was ten minutes to seven, and the winter air was sharp and
pregnant with incipient snow. Kore Condorcy, wearing her sable coat
with the sable hat rakishly over one ear, was still at the front door
issuing instructions to Zucchi. "The cleaners are coming today, and
they must get the third floor *spotless*. The painters will be coming next

Tuesday, and you must be here to let them in. You know about the sheets and towels?"

"Yes, Missy."

"Stacks of food are arriving the next few days, and you must stay in all day and receive it and put it away, Zucchi."

"Yes, Missy. When you get back?"

Kore shrugged as if he were asking her to name the day the world would end and walked down the concrete path to the waiting limousine where the chauffeur held the door for her. Wenceslas handed her into the limousine and took his place beside her. Slovik climbed into the front seat with the driver, and the limousine moved off.

Kore had settled on the right side of the warm limousine, and she immediately pulled her book out of her bag and started to read, immersed in her solitude like a fish in an aquarium tank.

Wenceslas immediately picked up the car telephone and gave the operator a Washington number, drumming his fingers on the phone. "Ali," he said into the phone, "I'm leaving on the Gulfstream. You're to take the shuttle as soon as possible and report in when you get to New York. Understood? Goodbye." He depressed the receiver, then signaled again for the operator.

While waiting, he glanced at Kore. "Is it good—that book?"

"Very good." Not looking up from the page.

"I must read it."

Absently she said, "Darling, you have not read a novel in twenty years—if ever."

To the operator, Wenceslas was saying, "Two one two seven two seven eight three four six." Then without a break to Kore he said, "I read novels once. You outgrow them when your own adventures exceed those on the printed page. But I read them all long ago— Dickens, Thackeray, the Russians—Tolstoy, Turgenev, Dostoevski. When I was last in Leningrad, I visited Dostoevski's grave to pay my respects to the greatest enchanter of them all. In *The Possessed,* Dostoevski ushered in the modern age in a precognition that surpasseth all understanding."

Kore's eyes came off the printed page during this speech, her solitude pierced. "You never fail to amaze me, Jeremiah."

"When I cease amazing you, I shall be bereft," he said. Then into the phone—with total change of personality, tone, manner, he said briskly, "Monsieur Assad, how are you? Did I wake you? I do apologize for disturbing you so early, but I'm on my way to New York and I thought we might discuss that business. I warn you I'm on an open phone so *prudence s'il vous plait.* If it's agreeable to you, I'll come to you at the United Nations office in—uh—let me see—shall we say two and a half hours. That would make it nine thirty. Would that be all right? Splendid!" He hung up.

Kore's eyes were back on her book. "Don't forget to cancel that appointment."

"My dear, what would I do without you?" He picked up the phone and called another number, pulling it out of his capacious head. "Monsieur Depardieu, I'm desolated but I must cancel our appointment for this morning. The most urgent matter has called me to New York. I do hope you will forgive me for this frightful discourtesy. In mitigation I can only say that one is not always captain of one's soul. . . . Oh, you're very kind, sir. I shall call you the moment I return to Washington, and perhaps we might have dinner. Again my most heartfelt apologies."

"You apologize *beautifully,* Jeremiah," the woman murmured.

Wenceslas put down the telephone and picked up the limousine intercom phone. "One must mend one's fences. Apology is one of the great civilities, and one should do it with grace and passion. It is a fulfillment—a really *superb* apology." Into the intercom, he said, "Slovik, what did you find out about the girl?"

The window between the driver's seat and the passenger's was closed so Slovik's voice boomed back at them through the speaker. "She goes to a parochial school in Greenwich Village, but she's not been to school for several days."

Kore's eyes flew off the printed page.

"We must make further inquiries when we get to New York," Wenceslas said.

"Yes, sir."

Wenceslas hung up the intercom and opened the Morocco briefcase. It was full of money, packed neatly in wrapped packets. On the top of the money was Wenceslas's notebook. He took it out. Kore watched with sad eyes. He was flipping through the notebook looking for a number.

"What girl is this, Jeremiah?" she asked, very low.

"Nothing to worry your little head over, my angel. A little girl of one of my people is ill, and I must show concern."

He found the number he was looking for—Cassidy's. The book held open in front of him, he picked up the telephone again and signaled for the operator. Kore saw the name Cassidy—and the number.

She returned to her book, biting her lower lip, remembering the number. And the address—113 W. 13th Street.

Wenceslas called the number and listened for eight rings before hanging up.

At National Airport the limousine drove to the area where the private jets were serviced and drove right up to the Gulfstream III, which had cost $11,000,000. Slovik transferred the luggage from limousine to plane, while inside the jet the blonde hostess in Alpine green uniform was helping Kore out of her sables. Wenceslas handed the hostess his heavy overcoat, and he and Kore sat side by side at the curved table, their backs to the pilot. Slovik sat forward by himself, facing forward.

The moment the jet was airborne, the blonde hostess brought croissants and coffee. Wenceslas dipped his croissant into the coffee and ate with relish. Kore pulled her croissant apart delicately and ate it, one tiny piece at a time, eyes distant.

"You are a million miles away from me," Wenceslas complained.

"No, Jeremiah," the woman said firmly. "I am never away from you. Not for an instant. Not even for one inch."

The Navy tug was proceeding very slowly up Horse Channel, surrounded on both sides by waving marsh grasses in their winter coat of brownish green. Rattigan was at the wheel, his clown's face dark with concentration. Keefe was on the catwalk outside, binoculars to his eyes, looking for a navigable opening in Stony Creek Marsh. Pindar stood beside him.

A helicopter flew over the tug at five hundred feet, and Keefe swung the binoculars after it, examining it for markings. The helicopter flew straight on toward JFK Airport. Keefe took the binoculars away from his eyes. "Just a helicopter. Helicopters over New York harbor are like birds in the sky. We cannot assume they are ominous."

Pindar, scowling, said, "I assume everything is ominous."

"That's your Greek blood," Keefe growled. "Your lamentable Attic heritage! All those classical heroines shouting 'Ah, woe!' to the unforgiving Furies—it colors your point of view so that every tiny movement is pregnant with significance. You Greeks are out of tune with modern times. The great tragedy of our era is not the significance of things but the insignificance of things."

Pindar took the glasses from him and watched the departing helicopter. "You've been drinking, you Hibernian tosspot. I recognize the orotundities. That helicopter is circling."

Keefe shouted into the wheelhouse, "Signal Stop to that deadhead below, Rattigan. Pindar, go below and ask the engineer how much draft this craft requires."

"Draft?" Pindar asked.

"How much water we need to float, you Greek landlubber."

"Aye aye, skipper," Pindar said. "One night on the bridge and he's talking like Admiral Nimitz himself." He shot down the ladder, Keefe yelling after him. "Get those Malays to help you with the anchor. I want to hold us right here. There's a channel there might hide us if we can get in it."

He went into the wheelhouse and ruffled through the charts.

"What's up?" Rattigan asked.

"I'm looking for depth of water," Keefe said. He bent over the chart. "Eight feet," he said.

"High tide or low tide," Rattigan said.

"Jesus preserve us, must I know things like that?"

"It's in the charts somewhere."

From below came a whistle on the blower. "Engineer says eight foot draft."

"A close fit," Rattigan observed.

"Proceed with reckless caution up that damned channel and devil take the consequences," Keefe said to Rattigan. "What I'm striving for is to be not only valorous but quotable, so that I land in all the history books along with 'Full speed ahead and damn the torpedoes.'"

"Reckless caution," Rattigan said. He signaled Dead Slow on the engineroom. "You expect anybody to quote *that*?"

"Reckless caution is an oxymoron, and all the best writers are flinging oxymorons into their babble to show they know what's what and that they're right in there with the latest thinking. In all the best cocktail parties if you don't drop an oxymoron once in awhile you won't be invited back."

Pindar popped his head in the wheelhouse. "That helicopter is showing uncommon interest."

Keefe went on the catwalk and watched anxiously. The helicopter was miles away and hovering. The Navy tug nosed delicately into the channel, the marsh grasses enfolding it on both sides.

"There's a dock up there looks deserted," Keefe said. He knocked on the curved glass of the window to the wheelhouse calling Rattigan's attention and pointed to the dock. Rattigan nodded and, at the same time, threw up his hands.

"You're the skipper, skipper," Pindar said. "Go land this craft."

"Bejesus!" Keefe muttered. He pulled the bottle from his coat. It was empty. He threw it in the water and looked at the Malays on the foredeck, gathered around the winch.

"Tell those Malays to hold the anchor," Keefe growled, "and get ready with the lines. We're going in, old man—a bit of dialogue I seem to remember from some movie or other."

"From *all* of them!" Pindar said. He shouted to the Malays to desist, and the five little brown faces looked up at him, mouths open like baby robins waiting for mother.

Keefe took the wheel and spun it to the left to correct its drift, but the tug responded not at all. It was slipping sidewise through the waving marsh grasses, propelled more by the rising tide than by its huge propellers which were turning hardly at all. Ahead of them loomed the dock, its wooden beams silvery with age and water and disuse, beautiful in its abandonment.

Keefe signalled Stop Engine and prayed: "Dear God, if you're not doing anything else at the moment . . ." The long tug struck the pier sidewise with a crack that had everyone aboard grabbing something for support. Two of the Malays recovered first and leaped to the dock with the bow line, which they fastened around the stoutest pole. The other three Malays scrambled off the tug and fastened the stern line.

Keefe joined Rattigan on the catwalk. The scene was one of total desolation. A gravel path thick with weeds led from the dock to a rotting shed that had once been a marine repair shop, its windows long gone, its door hanging on one hinge. Two skeletonized gas pumps stood on the pier. A cracked macadam road led from the repair shack off into the waving grass marshes.

"We're here," Keefe proclaimed, "but where is here? The kind of line that made Sam Beckett famous. Also the kind of situation. Where the hell are we and what are we doing here and who are we waiting for and why? The curtain falls with none of them damn questions being answered, don't ya know."

Rattigan said, "When the tide goes out we'll be high and dry in the mud unable to move."

"Anyway we're safe from prying police launches and fisherfolk with wop names."

"Not from helicopters," Pindar said.

"The helicopter seems to have gone."

"It'll be back," Pindar said.

"Lay off, Euripides!" Keefe shouted. "Beware a Greek bearing portents I always say—oh, dear Mother of God what have we now?"

He had noticed the red light attached to the telephone winking away.

He went into the wheelhouse and lifted the phone. "The S.S. *Nautilus,* Captain Nemo speaking."

"Stop showing off your education, Keefe," Cassidy said, the voice crackling thinly over the radio telephone. "How are things?"

"We're tied up I won't tell you where because I don't know. We've been looked over by a nosy helicopter. Wish you were here and even if I knew where here was I wouldn't tell you over an open line. Roger and over."

"Igspray, destray, joddlespray, windlespray," Cassidy said using a childlike code he and Keefe had devised in the Congo.

"You got a map of the harbor?" Keefe asked.

"Hell, no."

"Hellespont, idlepont, iddlespray, edelspray. That should give you a clue."

"You have sown confusion among your enemies. Also your friends," Cassidy murmured.

"Where are you?"

"Never mind. I'll try and join you soonest—jodespray, iffenpont."

"Bring a bottle," Keefe roared. "We're out of the stuff altogether."

Cassidy hung up and walked away from the pay phone into the seething mass at National Airport. The line for the shuttle to New York was very long, and he took his place in it.

Ahead of him, three passengers ahead, stood a tall thin figure who turned momentarily to look at the airport clock. The profile jumped at Cassidy jogging his memory. Hawk-beaked. Sunken eyes. Cassidy turning over the card files of his memory—all those photographs of the really dangerous ones that had been so carefully drilled into him in the Agency. The face should have a beard, Memory said. Cassidy tried to sketch a beard onto the beardless face in the airport line. He couldn't be sure, and he had to be sure. He slipped out of the line and went back to the pay phone, which had a clear view of the shuttle line. Cassidy phoned the airport number. "Operator, would you very kindly page Ali Heykal who, I believe, is still in the airport somewhere and tell him he has a very urgent message and to call his office immediately. That's Ali Heykal."

Cassidy's eyes were on the hawkfaced one whose skinny shape stood out in the shuttle line like a punctuation mark.

The call boomed through the speaker system. "Urgent message for Mr. Ali Heykal. Would Mr. Ali Heykal please call his office. Mr. Ali Heykal please call his office. Urgent message."

It was an old trick, and Ali Heykal, Cassidy knew, was much too wily an operator to fall for it, but what he couldn't manage to do was suppress the initial shock of hearing his name booming forth from the loudspeaker system. The hawkface jerked a half turn in the direction of the voice, the hands went convulsively to the armpit where the gun was. A split second later the man had regained control and was looking straight forward again, resuming anonymity.

That was enough, though.

Cassidy sauntered back to the line.

I've been waiting for the break, he was thinking, and by God, I've got it!

Wenceslas walked under the glittering panoply of flags snapping in the brisk wind off the East River and went through the revolving glass door, carrying the Morocco briefcase with the gold-washed locks. As always, the lobby of the United Nations seethed with functionaries mouthing in many languages the ceaseless talk that brought so little action, the multibabble of a hundred nations, signifying nothing.

The big man shouldered his way to the elevator, nodding and dropping greetings to diplomats of a dozen small countries who basked in the sunshine of his generous smile.

The elevator bore him to the thirty-fourth floor where presently he was ushered into Assad's private office facing over the river, the flag of Illyria with its three white stars on the red and blue bunting hanging from a pole in the corner.

The ambassador was a portly, beautifully tailored Arab with watchful eyes and a commanding manner. He poured a cup of tea and handed it to Wenceslas who said, "You are most kind."

The diplomat picked up his own cup and said, "To get right to the point, we are severely disappointed, Monsieur Wenceslas."

"You have just cause," Wenceslas said urbanely. "A lamentable mechanical failure." He lied—as he apologized—beautifully.

Wenceslas took the Morocco case from his lap, opened it and laid it on the diplomat's desk. "There is your money, sir. Every penny. I do not charge for failure."

Assad barely glanced at it. "Money we have plenty of, Mr. Wenceslas. What we were seeking was . . . something else . . ."

"Yes, headlines," Wenceslas said, "An explosion. The PLO . . ."

The effect of the initials PLO on Assad was galvanic. He put his fingers to his lips and on a notepad he wrote, "The walls have ears."

"How awkward!" Wenceslas murmured. "How does one get any business done?"

"We can talk about most things," Assad said. "Not . . ." He wrote PLO on the notepad.

"Aaah, yes," Wenceslas said. The fiction that Illyria and the PLO were not so allied as to be almost indistinguishable was unmentionable but widely known, even to journalists.

"I have a suggestion that will, I believe, please our friends in . . ." Wenceslas drew a line under the initials PLO on the notepad. "If you'll forgive me." He felt underneath the banknotes of his briefcase and brought out a brochure. It was on heavy cardstock and opened into a single colored photograph of an old U.S. submarine of the Guppy class. At the bottom of the opened brochure were all the statistics— tonnage, length, speed, range, armaments, crew requirements.

"You have the leprosy letter for this?" the diplomat asked in astonishment. The leprosy letter was what they called the export license from the United States Office for Munitions Control.

"It's already had one," Wenceslas said. "That submarine was sold to Brazil ten years ago. I acquired it from Brazil. It's tied up in New Jersey with a skeleton crew. It's seaworthy and ready. On its deck you will notice . . ."

Here Wenceslas reverted to the notepad. He wrote, "155 mm cannon, which will fire those rocket assisted shells."

"Now," he said to the diplomat, "you wanted a headline you shall get one."

On the pad he wrote, "I have one of the rocket assisted shells that will travel 100 miles to a target of the PLO choice. The others are on a Navy tug. I suggest . . ."

He wrote what he suggested in some detail, and it took a long time. Assad studied the memorandum with care, his face revealing nothing.

"How much?" he asked.

Wenceslas wrote it on the pad: "$22,000,000."

He said, "A bargain, my dear Ambassador. You can barely buy a yacht for that."

"Cash?"

"But, of course. We don't want a lot of cancelled checks lying around, do we?"

The diplomat lit a gold-tipped cigarette and blew out a cloud of scented smoke. "Monsieur Wenceslas, your audacity takes my breath away. Now let us understand each other. For this sum . . ." He tapped his finger on the written number . . . "we get not only permanent possession of the submarine but also the action you have suggested."

"Absolutely."

The diplomat handed the briefcase with the money in it back to Wenceslas. "Consider that a down payment. I'll have to consult our friends, of course, before I can give you a final answer. It's their money."

Wenceslas snapped the gold appendages, locking the suitcase, and stood up briskly. "A pleasure to do business with you, Assad. You are a man after my own heart. Decisive, venturesome, and superbly dressed. Not many like that in the United Nations."

The compliments rolled off the Arab's polished exterior like rain. Dryly he said, "Don't you ever feel a little nervous wandering around the streets carrying a million in cash?"

"Exhilarating!" Wenceslas said. "There's nothing more exhilarating than a million in cash except maybe twenty-two million." He bellowed with laughter at his own joke.

He pointed to the brochure of the submarine still lying on Assad's desk. "Put that in the safe away from prying eyes."

Cassidy was now in another long line—the one for cabs at La Guardia Airport, a slow line that made the problem acute. Ali Heykal was in the same line three men in front of him.

Cassidy made a decision. He slipped out of the line, went to a pay station and called Mu Mu Talaki. "Mu Mu, it's me."

"Yeah, man."

"I'm in the cab rank at La Guardia. I need a car and chauffeur urgently and in hell of a hurry. You know anyone in this area can get here in ten minutes, preferably five? Be prepared for a chase."

Silence from the other end. It was always difficult to get a quick answer out of the tall, dignified black man. "I got a friend could do it. He'll need extra bread for that kind of thing you got in mind."

"A hundred."

"Gimme number that phone. I call back."

Cassidy hung up, his eyes never leaving Heykal who was inching forward in the line. In two minutes the pay phone rang. "He on his way. Name's Fodor. He driving a souped up fifty-three Buick that needs a coat of paint. Fodor's bald as the ace of spades, and how many bald niggers you know, Mr. Cassidy?"

"Thanks, Mu Mu. I owe you."

Now the only question was: would the fifty-three Buick get there before Ali Heykal got a cab. He was only third from the head of the line and if he got into a cab before the Buick got there, he would be off and away and that would be that.

Ali Heykal stepped forward another pace. He was now second man. A minute later he stood at the head of the line. A taxicab was already edging down the road to the cab rank.

Cassidy was on the outer roadway, watching. The fifty-three Buick pulled in behind him, and a voice said, "Mistah Cassidy."

Cassidy drew a deep breath. He opened the door and got into the front seat. "Hi, Fodor. Just in time. See that cab. That's it."

"Nothin' I enjoys better, Mistah Cassidy."

The Buick nosed out into traffic.

It was a long chase, across Queens, down through Brooklyn to the Williamsburg Bridge to Delancey, down Bowery to Canal Street and straight down Canal Street to the Holland Tunnel—the black man staying well back. Time and again, they saw Heykal's face peering through the rear window for followers, but the cab had driven on densely traveled roads and there was much traffic to hide in.

Up the Jersey shore the cab weaved past the American-President line, the Delaware and Lackawanna Railroad docks, the Todd Dry Docks, passing railroad sidings, truck depots, the Marra Brothers Line, the Holland-American Line, the Bristol City Line docks, and finally stopped before a rundown building painted Lester Excursion Line. The Arab got out and paid the cabbie.

"Pull right on past," Cassidy directed, "and keep going."

Heykal disappeared into the rundown building.

The Buick stopped at the next line of docks—Pershing Dry Docks. "Wait here," Cassidy said.

A line of ship repair workers was filing into Pershing Dry Docks, and Cassidy joined the queue, picking up a hard hat at a counter of them, walking right past the time clock, through the dark interior of the dry dock shed where the tools were kept, and into the bright sunshine outside where men were all over a large scaffolding, working on the bottom of a docked excursion liner.

A staircase ran up the scaffolding to various levels of the ship. Hard hat on his head Cassidy climbed to the very top, where a wooden walk ran the length of the scaffolding. It gave a clear view of the next dock.

Tied up there was the long black shape of a submarine. A gangplank led to the deck. Ali Heykal was on the deck talking to another man in combat fatigue costume. The two men were standing by the long barrel of a gun. Ali Heykal was spinning a wheel that raised and lowered the tip of the gun, swinging the barrel from side to side to side.

Cassidy descended the staircase, returned the hard hat, and went back to the fifty-three Buick. "Eight East Twelfth Street," Cassidy said. He hadn't held his daughter in his arms for too long a time.

- 12 -

— Cassidy was half reclining in a bean bag of a chair, a kind of huge lump with a hole in it which passed for furniture in the modern age. He couldn't sit up straight in it, especially with Lucia in his lap.

Lucia was complaining: "Boring! *Boring!* BORING!"

Lucia was far from beautiful or even pretty, but she had her own personal electricity, and she was discharging it on him, which he greatly enjoyed. Cassidy basked in her tantrums as if in a summer storm, finding pleasure and stimulation in the heat of them.

"You won't even tell me what it's all *about!*" Lucia whimpered, "as if I'm not old enough to know these things."

"I'm not telling you anything," Cassidy said, "because I'm not telling anyone else anything." He ran his fingers over her thin arms, feeling the satiny smoothness.

"You're in the middle of some marvelous adventure, and you won't *share* it with me."

"I don't want to alarm you." He could have bitten off his tongue for letting *that* bit out.

"*Alarm*! You mean I'm in danger!" Eyes bright. "Well, if I'm in danger, I should be told. It's *my* life!"

"I'm probably seeing bears under the bed. Fathers worrying about their daughters are not always very intelligent." He squeezed her tight to feel the warmth of her and to get her mind off it.

It didn't work. "Why don't you take me along?" She was breathless with excitement.

"Impossible," Cassidy said. He gave a mighty heave and managed to sit up. "Let's get out of this damned contrivance which I refuse to call a chair." He spilled her off his lap onto the polished floor. "Where is Deborah?"

"In class, of course. Where *I* should be," Lucia said. She got off the floor and smoothed her skirt. "What are you going to tell them about my not being in school?"

"I've told them you're ill."

"That's a *lie,* Daddy. I'm not allowed to tell lies. How come you're allowed to tell lies?"

Cassidy had no answer for that so he said, "Have you studied your absolute ablative? Or done any studying at all?"

"Oh, DADDY!"

"I don't want you sitting here just looking at television all the time. Has Deborah got any books for you to read?"

"She's got books but nothing I'd like to read." Lucia pointed to the bookshelf. Cassidy went to it and read the titles. *Zen and the Art of Motorcycle Maintenance, Zoroaster in His Time, The Maharishi Speaks.* Good God! Deborah had gone from one cult to another, from the Seventies to the Eighties, culminating in . . . what? Himself? The Great God Cassidy?

At the bottom of the bookshelf was a book simply titled *Greek Mythology.* Cassidy plucked it out and read what he could find about

Demeter and Kore. They were mother and daughter. Kore, as Kore had told him, was a much older deity than Persephone, and came from an older, more savage, more orgiastic religion than the later, gentler Greek religion, dating clear back to Minoan-Mycenian times, but it was essentially the same story. Kore had been abducted (a nice word for rape) by Ploúton (who later became Pluto) and borne off to the underworld, while her mother Demeter sorrowed and searched for her all over the world. Later mother and daughter were reunited but only for half of each year. Kore had a central role in the Eleusinian mysteries in which she was always referred to as Kore, never as Persephone, and the mysteries were as mysterious today as they were 2,600 years ago. In her day she had been a very great deity indeed, called "The Holy One," associated always with both death and rebirth.

"What are you reading?" Lucia asked, jealous at sharing him even with a book.

"I'm reading about a goddess named Kore." Cassidy put the book back. "Have you ever heard of anyone named Kore?"

"No," Lucia said. "We have some Cora's at school . . ."

"Kore is probably a forerunner of Cora. She's very ancient, probably four thousand years old. Even for deities that's pretty old. Christ is only nineteen hundred years old."

He was looking for his coat.

"What about her," Lucia said sullenly. "Have you met someone named Kore? Is that why you're looking her up?" Lucia could be quick as light about some things and as intuitive as Cassidy.

"Well . . ." Cassidy said, caught off base. He retrieved his coat.

"You're not leaving *already?*" Lucia wailed. "I've been trapped in this hellhole for days on end, and you spend ten minutes here . . ."

Cassidy wrapped his long arms around her, and she stood there stiff as a stick, furious. "Darling, this whole business will be over in a couple of days. In the meantime, you've just got to bear with me . . ."

"I'm *bored,* Daddy. BORED!"

"Yes, and it's going to be even more boring. I want you to stay off the street altogether, even Twelfth Street. I want you to stay in this apartment until I come back."

It produced a storm as he knew it would. Lucia raged. She shouted. She even cried which she rarely did. Cassidy was adamant, probably a little too adamant, but he hadn't time to be diplomatic. He had a dozen things to do and a meeting with Alison in ten minutes, and he hadn't *time*. A mistake, this haste and this adamance, and it was to haunt him later.

Stiff and furious, Lucia refused even to kiss him goodbye.

After Cassidy left, Lucia stood still as a rock for five minutes, scowling her barely teen scowl. She went into the front hall closet, got out her skateboard and, thrilling to the flagrance of her disobedience, went outside and skateboarded up and down Twelfth Street.

It was sunny and warm on Fifth Avenue, but Twelfth Street was in shade. To get into the sun, Lucia rounded the corner and sped down Fifth Avenue, feeling deliciously sinful. Presently, she was at Washington Square where she skateboarded around the great arch and onto the round pond that never had any water in it, the place where the guitar players hung out, where heroin changed hands, where much of the action was, where anyone wanting to learn the score would gravitate . . .

In the big house in Brooklyn, Kore Condorcy dialed the number she had memorized from Wenceslas's book—Cassidy's number. She had been dialing it off and on for two hours, ever since she got into the empty house. As before, it rang and rang. No answer. She hung up and stood at the upstairs window looking out over the Narrows in the sparkling winter sunshine.

No good will come of it, no matter what I do. I am confronted with a choice of evils—to do something or to do nothing, but always the greatest evil is to do nothing.

She got her gray coat, her most inconspicuous one, out of the front hall closet and left the empty house on foot. She took the subway because that was the quickest.

There was a time to push Alison and a time to leave him alone. This was a time to leave him alone. Even in the dim light of the back room at Spumi's, Alison looked terrible—this passionless schemer who had spun so many webs now caught in someone else's, himself engulfed in passion. Alison had no gift for passion, no resources to cope with it, no experience at it.

They were alone in the back room, just Cassidy and Alison.

For an hour they sat there, Cassidy spacing the Wild Turkey carefully because he had work to do, Alison drinking Perrier and ice. The Spumi was a great place for silence. Some of the great silences of Cassidy's life had been experienced there. Once he and Joe Larkin, a newspaperman and philosopher and drinking man, had stood at the bar for four hours, both busy with their own thoughts, each drawing comfort and sustenance from the presence of the other, and left without a word but refreshed and fulfilled by the companionship.

This was not one of those occasions because Alison was not someone he could be comfortably silent with. Still it was for Alison to speak first. If you nudged him he would tell the usual lies. Alison had to nudge himself, and finally, after an hour, he did.

"I told you it was a matter of high policy and it was—the highest," Alison said in a low voice. "The proliferation of advanced weapon technology had upset the ecology of military relationships—if you get my drift."

"I don't."

Alison frowned and explained carefully, as if to a child, the elemental facts of military geometry. "We're getting into third generation ATGMs—that's anti tank guided missiles . . ."

"I know what ATGMs are."

"The introduction of laser guided, cannon launched projectiles requires less and less intelligence of crews. In fact, you can do without the crews altogether. Preplanted weapons, automatically activated, concealed. This is a revolution in battlefield technology and will act as an equalizer between armies. With this kind of weaponry, which is essentially defensive, Ghana couldn't take on the Soviet Union, but the Soviet Union might hesitate to take on Ghana.

"But you must understand we can't do any of this publicly. We are trying to repair the confidence in the U.S.A. shattered by Watergate and by Vietnam and by that damned Jimmy Carter by providing the most sophisticated weapons to Third World countries—but not out loud, for God's sake. For one thing the Soviets would counter it. For another you'd run into a firestorm in Congress. For still another . . ."

He hesitated because this was the deepest secret of all.

Cassidy said it for him, "For another you're dealing out these sophisticated weapons to *both* sides in the Third World to get strategic access and to undermine confidence in the Soviets."

"Where'd you find that out?"

"I have friends," Cassidy said. "Go ahead. I don't want to interrupt."

"We can't do any of this publicly. That's why we dealt through Wenceslas. He can buy the stuff, he can sell it—he can . . ."

Long pause here. Cassidy kept out of it.

". . . steal it if he has to."

"That's how the Mob got into it," Cassidy said.

"I don't know," Alison said violently. "I don't know how he operates. All we know is . . . he did things we couldn't do ourselves, not even under cover."

Cassidy sighed and sipped his whiskey. He told some home truths because they had to be told. "He's a killer, Hugh, a killer with a Messiah complex, the most dangerous kind. He's the one who's the author of that hit list, and he put himself on it simply to confuse the enemy. He's running the whole show, and the hitman is an Arab PLO named Ali Heykal, and you're on that list and you better lay low because Heykal is in town."

Alison's eyes were round balls in the dim light of the back room at Spumi. He said nothing.

"Wenceslas is dealing with both sides and in total secrecy and in cash," Cassidy said speaking very low. "And with the total amorality of a man who thinks he's God himself. He sold those fancy artillery shells to the Mossad for millions in cash, collected the money from that Lebanese Jew in that Forensic Street safe house the Mossad owns, and then killed him."

"Why? For God's sake *why?*"

"Because he'd also contracted with the PLO—again for a lot of money—to cause a very big explosion that would cause some very big headlines. He didn't get the explosion because I disconnected the wires and ran off with his powder."

Alison looked as if he'd been hit on the head with an axe.

"He sold that submarine you so helpfully gave him to Abu Dhabi and collected the millions from that nice Hassim el Kariq and then had *him* blown away by Ali Heykal. I suspect he's now selling that submarine to somebody else—God knows who, but I have my suspicions. He's not a nice man, Mr. Wenceslas. I know he's paid you generously for throwing business his way, Hugh, but I think you should know there's blood all over those thousand-dollar bills."

Alison stood up abruptly and without a word walked into the Men's Room. Well, it had been a long morning, verging on afternoon. The back room at the Spumi was beginning to fill with the luncheon crowd—the well-dressed, well-pressed crowd who ate too well, too often, too much.

Alison returned, white as paper. He'd thrown up, Cassidy guessed. Alison sipped his Perrier and looked hollow as if there was nothing left inside.

Cassidy leaned forward and put a little artificial warmth in his voice because he had to. "I know you'd rather not get into it, but you must. Where did you meet Giuletta?"

Alison looked everywhere but at Cassidy. "Wenceslas. He has a flat in the Seventies. He loaned it to us."

Flat. Alison had lived in England and still used the word flat in place of apartment. The flat and the girl. A sort of girl, a little tip for handing over old submarines.

That left only one thing, and this was dictated by pure curiosity.

"Hugh, you have kept secrets even from yourself. Why, in God's name . . ."

"I suppose I was trying to impress her."

The back room was now full of lunchers, and the two men rose from the table and threaded their way through the tables to the bar where Alison paid the check with his blood-stained money. At the door Cassidy slipped his coat over his shoulders because he was only going to his own apartment directly overhead. Alison put on his beautifully fitted camel's hair.

It was beginning to snow, large white flakes drifting down from the violet sky, blurring Thirteenth Street into a fragile and temporary lyricism.

"Don't answer the doorbell," Cassidy said. "Night or day. Change routes and schedules. Well, you know the drill."

He shook hands with him, an unaccustomed thing, because a handshake was all he had to offer.

"Condorcy," Alison said out of the blue.

"*What!*" It was like being hit in the face.

"That's his real name—Condorcy. The FBI has just passed it along to us. Good King Wenceslas, bearer of gifts."

Alison plunged out into the snowfall and flagged down a taxi.

Cassidy climbed the brownstone steps to the first floor where his apartment was.

Condorcy! he was thinking. Condorcy!

He opened the outer door and stepped into the front hall. Sitting on the staircase, waiting for him, was Kore.

"I thought you'd never come," she said.

- 13 -

— The guitar players and their scrubby girls sat around the round pond that never had any water in it, humming tunes that had no melody. The melody would come later. It was still early in the day. The barely teen girl was doing Immelman's on her skateboard in the winter sunshine, her face full of joy. The round pond was the best audience for Immelman's on a skateboard, the most knowledgeable, the most appreciative.

"Do a wingover!" challenged one of the guitar player's girls, herself now past that sort of thing, regretting her lost youth.

Lucia completed the Immelman and went into the wing-over too fast. She got dumped hard on the cement, and the joy ran out of her.

She looked at her skinned knee, which was beginning to swell with blood.

The girl who had called out to her to do a wingover jumped off the rim of the round pond and came to help her to her feet. "Are you all right," she asked.

Lucia was looking at her skinned knee and her skirt with blood on it. "I'm really going to catch it," she confided. "I'm not supposed to be out. Look at my skirt."

"Wash it out with cold water. You better do it quick, or it won't come out."

Lucia picked up her skateboard. "Thanks." She limped toward the arch, the radiance gone.

Slovik waited until she was almost out of the park before leaping up from the wide steps around the round pond and following her. At the entrance to Washington Park, the limousine was double-parked. Slovik pointed to the girl limping out of the park. The limousine engine started and pulled slowly into Fifth Avenue just behind her.

Cassidy inspected his front door for telltales. Broken, every last one. He grimaced and opened the door, letting Kore in silently ahead of him, avoiding her eyes. Once inside she stood and watched as he went over the place, looking for the signs of which there were almost too many. They'd turned the place over and, of course, they must have found out she went to St. Theresa's parochial school, but that would not help them to trace her to Deborah's. He hadn't told the school where she was.

Kore was offended by the silence. "I tried to call, but there was no answer," she said gravely. "I came because there was no other way."

Cassidy said nothing, still searching.

"You might say hello," Kore said distinctly.

Instead Cassidy said roughly, "Where did you get this address?"

"From his black book. Also the telephone number. I was very worried."

"Why?"

"Because I was worried about your daughter," Kore said angrily. "And I'm sorry I came. You're being very rude."

She walked to the door. Rapidly but not rapidly enough. Cassidy was ahead of her blocking her way. "Why are you worried about my daughter?" Cassidy said harshly. "What right have you to worry about my daughter?"

"I wish I hadn't bothered," Kore said bitterly. She tried to get past him, but he wouldn't let her.

"Did your husband send you here to find out where my daughter is?"

"I have no husband!" Kore cried. "What are you talking about?"

"Condorcy!" Cassidy said, holding her shoulders roughly to keep her from breaking away. "The real name of good King Wenceslas— the man you're indissolubly linked with. The same name as yours— Condorcy. Your *husband*!"

She hit him then, as hard as she could, and burst into tears.

It was not the tears that undid Cassidy but the blow to his face. Always there was that chemistry between them, even when she hit him. He put his arms around her, if only because she was six inches away, and it was not only plausible but almost unavoidable. She laid her head on his chest because that, too, was not only plausible but unavoidable.

He picked her up and put her on the big bed, reverently, as if she were one of those religious talismans he didn't believe in.

"Why are you being so hateful?" she whispered.

Years and years of suspicion, Cassidy thought. A lifetime of suspicion. I've just left a man betrayed by a skirt. A thousand lies, many of them my own. Years and years of training that things are never what they seem. Skepticism deep as the ocean. A mountain of distrust.

What he said aloud was a single word—between his teeth: "Condorcy!"

Her answer to that was totally unexpected. She laughed.

Laughed at him and caressed him with her finger across his cheek. "You're a sexual innocent, Cassidy."

Through the Venetian blinds on the long windows the winter sunlight made parallelograms on the faded carpet and on their faces. Cassidy's blood pounded inside him, warring with his distrust.

The moment was airless.

"I am his daughter," Kore said. "His daughter and his mistress. We are an incestuous union, and there is nothing more indissoluble than that."

The sadness in her spread through the room, rising to the high ceiling like mist.

The Navy tug was high and dry, lying slightly on one side in the mud. In the wheelhouse, Keefe and Pindar had rigged up a table and were playing gin rummy on it, listening to the radio for news.

"New York," Keefe was saying, "is a remarkable city. Where else is a city with Hungarian restaurants and five miles away you can get stuck in the mud in a marsh as empty and deserted as the Congo River?"

Pindar was adding up the score glumly. He was down by hundreds. "In Berlin," Pindar said, "you can have tea by a lake, with cows in hay fields just like in the open country."

Keefe was not to be deterred. "There are only two great cities in the world—New York and London. The others—Paris, Rome, Berlin, Shanghai—are villages next to New York and London. New York finally came of age when it had its heart broken, when it had to go down on its knees and beg for assistance. No city ever quite comes of age until it has had its heart broken. After that it learns humility. New York badly needed a little humility."

"You think Paris has humility? It's been humiliated again and again—by Bismarck, by Hitler—but humility? My God!"

"Down for two!" Keefe said, winning again. "How much do you owe me, you Thracian poltroon!"

"You'll be paid!" Pindar said. "Have I ever not paid?"

"You wait until the money is devalued until it's worth half as much as when I won it. Then you pay."

"That is the Greek way," Pindar said. "Ah, my God, Keefe, how many places have you and I played gin rummy while waiting, waiting, always waiting? What are we waiting for, Keefe?"

"The end of our lives," Keefe said shuffling. "Actually what I'm waiting for right now—specifically—is a bottle. Cassidy is supposed to bring a bottle."

He started to deal. Rattigan climbed the ladder to the bridge and walked into the wheelhouse. He'd been exploring the road that led away from the derelict machine shop.

"It leads nowhere but into the marshes, which get very muddy about half a mile from here. There are some other shanties down there. You can see them, but you can't get to them unless you want to get very muddy feet. Anyway they're not Aztec ruins, hardly worth wet feet."

"Not the place to start the new Monte Carlo?" Keefe said. "I thought maybe we had discovered a bit of priceless real estate everyone else had forgotten and we would all become tycoons rich as Rothschilds."

Rattigan permitted himself one of his little clown smiles. "People like us never get rich as Rothschilds, Keefe."

"I don't know why not. All the other former Agency fellows are becoming millionaires, selling arms to Khaddafi or blowing up diplomats for the Peruvians. Them and their town houses in London, their country houses in Kent. Why are we not millionaires like them?"

"Because of our integrity!" Pindar said and burst out laughing.

"Our stupidity!" Keefe said, laughing.

"Our romanticism," Rattigan said solemnly. "We lead lives of noisy adventure, and we end up—without wives or children—or a future. We live in the present, but when the present is over we have no future whatsoever."

Keefe dealt the cards. "How long have you felt like that, Rattigan?"

The silence had descended again on Rattigan, and he didn't answer that. Instead he said, "There's beans for lunch. Pork and beans and a little water. After that we're going to have to start eating the dead."

He went down the ladder.

Pindar said, "When the speechless ones speak, look out!"

"Waiting for Cassidy," Keefe said, arranging his cards. "Maybe we should just sell the damned shells to the Third World. Buy ourselves a town house in London."

"First we have to get off the mud," Pindar said, "and next we got to get over our romantic foolishness. The second part is much harder than the first." He laid down his hand. "Gin."

"You've caught me with my pants down," Keefe said. He put down his hand, which was full of face cards, each counting ten against him.

The limousine had sped forward and stopped, just the other side of Washington Mews. Wenceslas got out and stood on the sidewalk.

Lucia was walking slowly because her knee hurt her.

"Lucia," Wenceslas said, booming it out to make sure that it was indeed the right girl.

Lucia's head snapped up, out of her torpor, and she saw the massive figure with his great smile.

The consequences of disobedience. She was a very bright child, and the realization struck instantly that this was menace, this was what Cassidy feared for her, this man was the reason she had been stuck in that room for days.

Not a soul in sight. She was alone.

Lucia spun on her heel and ran—straight into Slovik's arms.

"This won't hurt a bit!" Wenceslas said jovially and stuck the needle into her arm.

Blackness descended.

The place was in half twilight, the Venetian blinds drawn tight.

Kore was walking about, quite nude, her slender, lithe form wraith-like in the dim light. She was inspecting his lifestyle as if it were a painting—his books, his bibelots, his ladder, his kitchen.

Talking in fragments—sense and lunacy.

Cassidy lay under the covers, watching the nakedness and the grace of her, listening to the dementia . . .

"You must not think there is anything unnatural about father-daughter incest because there isn't. It's the most natural thing in the world, and there is a very great deal of it and there always has been . . ."

Kore climbed the ladder to the very top and sat on the little ledge up there to read the titles of his books, barely visible in the half light.

Meanwhile talking . . .

"Brother-sister incest was practiced for thousands of years by the Pharoahs and brother-sister marriage was the common situation for the Pharoahs, and after all I am Egyptian. Father-daughter incest is very well documented in our time. They have even had children, not always disastrously. I have read a great deal on the subject."

"I'll bet you have," Cassidy said—his first words. Actually his first feeling had been one of profound relief. He had thought of her as wanton. The seduction by a father at thirteen was somehow more . . . respectable than seduction by anyone else.

A daughter must obey her father, mustn't she? Especially an Egyptian girl.

She had casually destroyed that comfort.

"I hardly knew him. He had abandoned my mother before I was born. He always sent money—we never lacked for that—but he never was around until my mother died. Then he appeared—roaring with good humor as he does. I—uh—succumbed the second night of our . . . acquaintance . . ."

"And the first night?" Cassidy asked.

"The first night he tried and I said no and I cried and he went away. Out of the house. Out of my life. Leaving me alone."

Cassidy scowled and thought about the thirteen-year-old girl, bereft of mother and now deserted by her newly found father.

"He reappeared the second night, and that time I went to bed with him because I didn't know what else to do. He moved permanently into my bed and told me what to do and how often and just what positions to take and how to do everything, and, if you must know, it was a very great relief to have my life so well organized and to have a father so intensely, so passionately involved in my well being."

"Well being," Cassidy said in his dry tone.

She had come down from the ladder and was looking over the screen where Lucia undressed and slept, where *his* daughter lay, inviolate. Nevertheless Cassidy was smitten with guilt. All those caresses he so shamelessly exacted, those kisses, those strokings, appeared now in a new and alarming light.

Kore was examining all of Lucia's treasures—her massive woolly polar bear, her squirrel, her fox, all the animals she took to bed with her every night. (No dolls, Lucia had never shown any interest in dolls, only stuffed animals.)

Kore was looking at the polar bear as if she wished she had one of her own. "If you must know, Cassidy, I would never have gone to bed with you had I not been so thoroughly . . . indoctrinated to father-daughter incest. You are—to me—a father figure and therefore sexually attractive. I am committing incest with you, too. Your role in my life was prepared for by my father. He would not like to think that, but that's the way it is."

"I wouldn't like to think it either," Cassidy said.

Kore lay on her stomach on the bed, looking solemnly into Cassidy's eyes, talking absently as if to herself: "Of course, I soon realized that what I experienced is not what *he* experienced. He has always reveled in our incest *because* it is incest. My father is—in his own eyes and frequently in mine—a god above mundane considerations and mortal laws. That's why he called me Kore. To him I am a goddess not subject to human taboos. My father is his own superstition, and that is why he operates with such disregard of the conventions . . ."

"Up to and including murder," Cassidy said.

Kore lay her cheek down on the bed, facing away from him, her voice muffled.

"I didn't know about the . . . murders until Forensic Street."

Cassidy said gently, "What were you doing at Forensic Street? Why were you there?"

Kore turned her face toward Cassidy, chewing on her underlip gravely. "My father asked me to take that man to Forensic Street to show him the munitions. He didn't want the key to be in anyone's hands but ours. He said he didn't trust the man."

Silence in the room while Kore fought her war of nerves.

"He poured the drink, and I handed it to him. He took one sip and fell like a rock." Kore turned her face away and picked at the sheet with her fingers. "I would have left him forever right then, but I didn't know where to go. He had been my father, my lover, my protector since I was thirteen. Where am I to go, Cassidy?"

Cassidy never had a chance to answer that.

The telephone rang.

The voice boomed forth into Cassidy's ear full of the usual bon-homie. "Cassidy?"

"Yes!" Cassidy said between his teeth because the menace was unmistakable and the dereliction of duty even more so. Lying here naked! He threw off the covers, covering Kore with them, and swung his legs to the ground.

"I have your daughter!" Wenceslas said with that ebullient self-confidence that was his trademark, "right here in my town house in Manhattan. Yes, I have a town house in both Manhattan and Brooklyn, which may seem excessive to you, Cassidy, but the extra one does come in handy, if only because you don't know where it is. Aaah, your daughter is coming around! We had to slip her into the Land of Nod—oh, very carefully, a very small dosage I assure you—and now she's coming round. Would you like to speak to her? Here she is . . ."

"*Daddy . . . Daddy.*"

In the upper registers of terror, faint and drug-filled, but unmistakable.

"Darling, it's all right! It's going to be all right!" Cassidy said.

Kore had thrown off the covers and sat up, round-eyed, round-mouthed.

"I disobeyed you, Daddy! I'm terribly sorry!" Terror running out of the voice like tap water.

"Darling, I don't want you to be frightened," Cassidy said. "Put Mr. Wenceslas back on."

Wenceslas's voice boomed through the earpiece, picking up where he left off as if he were addressing the multitude, "Now here's what you must do, Cassidy, to get your beloved daughter back. I must have those artillery shells you spirited away, and I must have them no later than this evening. We will arrange a little trade, you and I: your daughter for those shells in the middle of New York harbor, this very evening . . ."

Cassidy had opened the drawer of the bedside table and pulled out his .38. He cut into the monologue harshly, sharply, definitively. "Wenceslas!" he said. "Or should I say—Condorcy?"

He had the man's full attention. He could almost smell it.

"I have *your* daughter . . ."

Cassidy dropped the word like a stone. Kore in her nakedness raised her chin from her chest. Right before Cassidy's eyes she became a deity, frozen in marble.

"Would you like a word with her?"

He handed her the phone.

"Jeremiah," Kore said clothed only in her colossal and enduring sadness. "What have you done?"

Cassidy was always to remember that moment. It was awe inspiring, the grandeur of the rebuke, the upside-downness of it. Daughter rebuking father. Not apologizing for her transgression but, goddess-like, asking explanation of his. Daughter inheriting her father's sublime self-confidence and, for the first time, employing it.

Cassidy took the phone from her hand before the moment slipped away. "Condorcy, we shall arrange a trade of daughters, you and I, and I warn you now, if my daughter is harmed, I shall kill your daughter—unhesitatingly. I hold the gun in my hand right now. Understood?"

"Cassidy!" Wenceslas boomed in a voice of thunder that almost shattered his eardrums. "If my daughter is harmed, hell has no fury like that I shall unleash on Lucia."

Cassidy smiled and felt a flood of relief. Until that moment he had not known how much the big man, in his towering ego, cared for Kore or if he cared for her at all. In the anguished roar of that last remark, he knew and was comforted. Two men with a daughter apiece. The price of one was possession of the other, and it was the only price that would do.

Coolly, Cassidy laid out the terms—the where and the when of it.

"*Compris?*" Cassidy said.

"*Compris!*" Wenceslas bellowed.

Cassidy hung up the telephone.

Kore was looking at him with the serenity of her permanent *douleur*. "Would you really shoot me, Cassidy?"

"Yes," Cassidy said.

"You are like my father in more ways than one," she said, "just as ruthless."

"No," Cassidy said. "I'm not."

She kissed him, lingering over it. "You must realize that what you're doing is irrevocable. You're returning me to him for all time. I shall never get another opportunity to get away. You do understand that, do you?"

"Yes," Cassidy said.

"Make love to me one last time," she commanded.

- 14 -

— The Great Lawn of Central Park, the vast greensward, lies just behind the Metropolitan Museum of Art. In winter it is empty except for a few strollers and their dogs; the trees on its edges are leafless, black, and stark, the traffic sounds on its encircling roads are leaden and distant.

Cassidy and Kore walked south to the very edge of the Promenade, where, following the rules Cassidy had layed down, they waited, engulfed in silence. Since lovemaking, they had spoken scarcely a word. Kore had retreated into her perennial sadness. Cassidy was molten with anger—at Wenceslas, at Lucia, at himself, at Kore. He fought down the anger because it interfered with his thinking—and he had to think clearly or he would be undone—and so would Lucia.

How far do I trust the son of a bitch? Not from here to that tree? He'll do anything, anything at all. How far does he trust me? To that blade of grass and not one inch further. Cassidy felt the gun in his overcoat pocket, looking at Kore as he did so.

Two men, two daughters—all else paling into insignificance.

The juncture was to be at the very center of the Great Lawn in an emptiness of grass where a man could see in all directions. It wasn't foolproof because nothing is. Cassidy had put on the vest with the laminated steel strips, bullet resistant rather than bulletproof, another leftover from the Agency. Kore watching quietly. A good shot could hit him in the head, as it had hit President Kennedy, and Ali Heykal would certainly be a good shot . . .

It was one hour since the phone conversation with Wenceslas. Cassidy sniffed the air, his eyebrows beetling, and spoke sharply. "What will you do?"

Kore said softly, "Care for him—as I have for twelve years. You're leaving me no other choice."

"He is outside the law," Cassidy said.

"So are you," Kore said. "When were you ever concerned about law? You are all lawless, secret, and beyond retribution. And you are always forgiven."

"I'm not forgiving anyone, including myself. I should never have got into this."

"Why did you?"

Cassidy snarled the answer. "I wanted a new, warm coat for my daughter." The reason most people got into things; shoes for the children. Ideology notwithstanding.

The black limousine had pulled into the southern perimeter and stopped just the other side of the bare encircling trees.

"There they are," Kore said.

The length of a polo field away.

Wenceslas, vast in his black beaver-collared coat, had emerged from the rear of the limousine and put his arm back inside to assist Lucia, who followed him out of the car. Even at that distance Cassidy could see Lucia's wide, frightened eyes, her round, frightened mouth.

Or was it only Cassidy's imagination based on his total familiarity with Lucia's moods, her wishes, her every facial lineament?

She was afraid, Cassidy knew, not of Wenceslas, not of the dire situation her disobedience had brought about, but of Cassidy and his anger. Hell and damnation . . .

Wenceslas had thrust his right fist into the air, indicating he was ready. Cassidy raised his right arm, acknowledging the gesture. The two couples—the length of a polo field away—started the long march toward each other in the center of the Great Lawn.

Cassidy took short quick steps, his hands in his overcoat pocket, one hand on his revolver. Kore walked abreast of him, face frozen. Cassidy's eyes never left Wenceslas, who was ambling toward him, his two hands clasped behind his back in that very European attitude, looking like Prince Albert on promenade. Lucia was almost running beside him to keep up.

The first fifty yards passed in silence.

From Kore a deathly whisper: "I'm afraid, Cassidy."

"I can smell it," Cassidy said harshly. "Why?"

"He'll not be hoodwinked, Cassidy. He's very clever. If you're up to any trickery . . ."

"If there's any trickery, it's his," Cassidy said angrily. "The son of a bitch kidnapped my daughter . . ."

But Kore had other things on her mind. "What is that sound, Cassidy?"

Cassidy had heard it too and didn't like it. The ratchety, unmistakably nasty sound of a helicopter, flying low, much too low . . .

Cassidy tore his gaze away from Wenceslas and glanced up at the sky, but he could see nothing.

Now the sound pierced Wenceslas's serenity. His hands came from behind his back, his right hand grasping blindly for the little girl at his side.

The helicopter came into view, low over the trees, black and menacing, the sound terrible . . .

"Treachery!" Wenceslas screamed.

"Not my helicopter!" Cassidy yelled in despair, loud as he could, not loud enough. The gun was in his hand, much good it would do him.

Wenceslas had whirled to face the bird, and as he did, with remarkable agility considering his bulk, he snatched up Lucia and held her up in front of himself like a shield.

The two pairs still a hundred fifty yards apart.

A cataract of sound, too much sound, from too many directions. Now there was a second helicopter racheting away, directly over Cassidy's head, roaring into his eardrums, into his brain.

Cassidy reached for Kore to grab her as Wenceslas had grabbed his daughter, but she was too quick for him. She ran directly at her father who was still holding up Lucia, the thirteen-year-old struggling in his grasp like a kitten.

"Drop her," Cassidy screeched, as though any words could be heard in that tumult of noise.

The second helicopter had passed over him headed directly at the black helicopter.

Cassidy leveled his gun in both hands directly at the retreating back of Kore—the slim, concupiscent, warm, living, fragrant curve of it.

It was then that the shot caught him on the chest, right on the laminated strips of bullet-resistant steel and spun him around, the shock of it doubling him over. The second shot caught him in that attitude, right in the ass, which was not covered by laminated steel.

Cassidy fell like a pile of sticks, wailing mortification.

The second helicopter landed right in front of his agonized eyes. Lieutenant Fletcher hurtled out of it, bent over like a question mark and mouthing imprecations.

After that, silence and blackness.

My ass, my ass, my sainted ass.

The words flew around his skull like frightened birds. A wave of nausea came and went, Cassidy's eyes still closed.

Not his ears. He could hear Lieutenant Fletcher's voice.

". . . 155 millimeter shells, laser operated with single-shot kill probabilities," said Lieutenant Fletcher.

Cassidy opened his eyes. Lieutenant Fletcher was standing, bent over a police stenographer who was fiddling with a recording machine.

The pain in his ass was so intense that Cassidy groaned aloud. The two cops turned and faced him.

"Have I been talking in my sleep?"

"Babbling like a brook," Lieutenant Fletcher said.

- 15 -

— In the twilight the Guppy (for Greater Underwater Propulsive Power, with the Y added to make it a fish) Attack Submarine Sailfish slipped its hawser on the Jersey shore and headed down the Hudson. On the bridge stood Wenceslas and the skipper of the sailfish, a small saturnine man with beetling brows, Nicholas Lebouef.

A tug pulled a line of barges slowly upstream. On the far side, in the gloom, Wenceslas saw the dim shape of another craft headed downstream. Otherwise there was nothing. "Is this as fast as this boat goes?" he asked.

"As fast as we can go if we don't want to attract attention. Actually she'll do twenty-two knots on the surface. We can pick up the pace when it gets a little darker."

"How fast under the surface?"

Captain Lebouef pursed his lips and asked, "Are we planning to be under the surface, sir? In New York harbor?"

"How fast?" Wenceslas repeated grimly.

"Five knots."

It had grown steadily darker. The craft on the Manhattan shore had disappeared from view now, and so had the tug and line of barges. The Guppy had the Hudson all to itself.

"I'm going below," Wenceslas said. "Full speed ahead when you think it's wise. We haven't all that much time."

He clambered down the steel ladder inside the bridge to the conning tower and from there to the control room underneath, where the radioman was listening in on the police channel.

"What are they saying?"

"Routine chatter," the radioman said. "They're putting themselves to sleep with procedure."

"You're sure?"

"I used to be a police radioman. I know the drill. It's all in the clear. If they crave secrecy, they go to numbers. Six-o-nine—meaning motor craft acting suspiciously—at A twenty-seven, which would be the location on the chart."

"Have they got any numbers for submarines?"

The radioman hunched his shoulders. "If they do, I don't remember."

Wenceslas walked forward out of the Control Room (which had three men performing the duties normally allotted to twelve) into the Battery Room under whose deck were 120 lead storage batteries, each weighing a ton. Along the sides and underneath the batteries were the ballast tanks used when submerging. Officers' and enlisted men's quarters ranged along the side of the battery room. Wenceslas opened the narrow door leading into the executive officer's quarters, which had upper and lower bunks for the executive officer and a junior officer.

Kore sat at the little table-desk, still reading *The Hotel New Hampshire,* remote as a star. Ali Heykal lounged against the wall. On the upper bunk Lucia, her arms wrapped around her knees, had made a small round ball of herself.

"Ali," Wenceslas said courteously, "would you kindly take Miss Lucia next door into the captain's quarters where I'm sure she'll be more comfortable."

Lucia glowered, tightening her hold on her own knees. "I'm perfectly happy here," she said.

Kore laid down her book on the table-desk. "Jeremiah, the child has been pushed around quite enough."

"I wish to speak to you in private, Kore. Ali . . ."

Ali Heykal lifted Lucia off the upper bunk and put her on her feet. "Come, miss," he said. He led her by the hand out of the little cabin to the one next door.

Wenceslas removed his beaver-collared coat and sat his large bulk on the lower bunk. "You have betrayed me to mine enemies," he said bitterly.

Kore looked him full in the face. "I have been unfaithful but not disloyal, Father," she said.

The word "Father" shook the room like a cannonade. She had not used the word Father to him since she was thirteen.

Lieutenant Fletcher filled the coffee cup with the hot bitter stuff for the third time. "This is the last one for an hour," he said. "Too much and you'll get nerves, and you're going to need your nerves. Why did Wenceslas shoot you?"

"It's his way of showing affection," Cassidy said, his ass still hurting but his brain working again. "You had me tapped, you bastard, and you just damned well better have a court order or I'll get my lawyers after you."

"We had a court order. You want to see it?"

"On what grounds?"

"You're an enemy of the people," Fletcher said, and he grinned malevolently. He was thin and over-educated for a police officer; he loved his work, including every last paper legality. "Let's see, what did I tell that judge? That you were a former CIA covert who had gone into private practice, suspected of being illicit, possibly violent, conceivably subversive."

"Conceivably subversive is good, very good, you bastard."

"Cassidy," Lieutenant Fletcher said, "it doesn't seem to have registered on you yet what I told you before, so I'll repeat myself. We weren't the only ones had you tapped. Somebody else had a line in there ahead of us."

"Jesus," Cassidy said bitterly.

"When you made that date with Wenceslas to meet in Central Park, you were inviting quite a lot of people to the party. Who do you think might they have been?"

"I was going to ask you that," Cassidy said. "After all you have the whole damned police department at your beck and call, and I have only little old me."

"You know your own enemies better than we do, Cassidy. How many enemies have you at the moment?"

"Thousands," Cassidy said. "Why did you let them get away with Lucia? God damn it, you might have realized . . ."

"I was trying to save your life, my friend, and I had only one helicopter. That other helicopter was not friendly, not friendly at all. In fact the first shot that hit you in the chest came from the helicopter. Somebody was trying to kill you. The second shot, which hit you in the ass, came from the trees. Does all this suggest anything?"

"Yeah," Cassidy said. "It all begins to fall into place, Lieutenant."

"Who was trying to kill you, Cassidy, and why?"

"Sicilians," Cassidy said and grinned evilly, "and the reason why is because they're envious of my Irish charm, Lieutenant. They think if they can rub me out they will acquire my legendary *savoir faire,* my *amour propre,* the way African tribesmen eat the balls of their enemies to acquire their potency."

"You're reviving fast," Lieutenant Fletcher said. "Now if you'd just tell us who shot you in the ass."

"Wenceslas," Cassidy said, "because he wants my secrets, just as you do. Everyone's after my secrets." He struggled up on one elbow, which took enormous concentration. "What are we doing chattering away, Fletcher! We got to get on with it! What time is it?"

Lieutenant Fletcher looked at his watch. "Ten past six."

"Jesus," Cassidy said. "Three hours I been lying here. They could be out of the city." He struggled upright and put his feet on the floor experimentally.

"What do you know about submarines, Fletcher?"

Fletcher chuckled. "We got every problem in the world in this precinct except submarines. We don't need submarines."

"Call the harbor patrol," Cassidy said urgently. "We got to get moving."

The word Father hung in the air, making its presence felt against the whiffle of the air-conditioning, the throb of the diesels.

Wenceslas stood up, massively, his eyes blazing. "I would prefer you not to flourish that word even in private."

"It's more than a word, Father," Kore said, repeating the offense deliberately because the thing had to be settled. "It's the truth of the matter."

Looking at him unflinching. If anyone flinched here it was Wenceslas. There was pain in his voice. "Have you told him?"

"No, Father."

A bold-faced lie, which she had never done before. Her loyalty had shifted in that instant from Wenceslas to Cassidy, a terrifying moment, the ground shifting under her feet in the shaky old submarine that whiffled and wheezed and palpitated under her and around her.

The two of them, father and daughter, eyed each other savagely. Same flesh and blood, same genes, facing off like hockey players.

"I am your daughter, Father," Kore said. "No longer your lover. It was something that was bound to happen. You yourself have said it many times."

He had said it to frighten her, and it had frightened the life out of her, the thought of being bereft of father and lover at one stroke. Now it was the other way around. She was threatening; he was threatened.

His eyes were full of fury and pain.

"You are being sentimental," he cried. "We are not ordinary people. We are extraordinary, you and I . . ."

"Speak for yourself, Father. Leave me out of it!" Something she didn't think herself capable of, a declaration of independence, issuing unbidden from the very bottom of her soul.

He knew what the words meant, and he was monstrously angry. He struck her across the face with his open hand, bending her like a stalk of wheat, horrifying them both. Civility had been the essence of their relationship. Even in the transports of lust they had always been deeply polite.

Kore put her hand to her cheek, herself angry now. "You're *jealous,* Father!" Hissing it at him.

He was trying to recover his equilibrium, trying to justify that passionate blow. "Von Clausewitz said the errors from a spirit of benevolence are the worst kind. One must avoid benevolence."

The loudspeaker broke into the confrontation, ringing through the boat: "Captain Lebouef calling Mr. Wenceslas."

The squawkbox hung on the wall, and Wenceslas flipped the switch. "Yeah," he said.

"Police Harbor Patrol boat bearing down with its searchlight directly on us. They're hailing now. What do I do?"

"Dive," Wenceslas said.

Hesitation hung in the air only for a moment. When Lebouef's voice sounded, it was caressingly sexual, the skipper making love to his boat, demanding of it its supreme function.

"Dive! Dive! Dive!"

Even as he was speaking, Lebouef was scuttling down the iron ladder inside the conning tower, spinning the iron rings that sealed the steel bulkhead.

"Rig for silent running!" The command rang through the boat from end to end.

The bow planes slanted hard; air hissed out of the ballast tanks and water gurgled into them; the thump of the diesels was replaced by the quiet hum of the electric engines. The boat tilted sharply, and in the tiny executive officer's quarters Kore was thrown violently into her father's arms. Their quarrel thus culminated in an embrace, Wenceslas's bearlike arms around his daughter, his blazing eyes inches from hers.

"What on earth are you doing, Father?"

"Submerging," Wenceslas said. "It's what a submarine is for. There comes a time when the arms merchant must use the merchandise."

He threw his daughter away from him across the small cabin into the lower bunk and opened the door. Ali Heykal lounged in the narrow corridor. "Bring the little girl in here, Ali," the big man said, "and stand watch over them."

Wenceslas left the cabin without looking at his daughter. Presently Lucia was brought into the cabin by Ali, who then left the two alone.

Lucia was entranced. "We're *diving*! Isn't it marvelous? Listen to the *silence* of it! Like being a fish at the bottom of the sea!"

"Sit here," Kore said. The little girl sat next to her on the lower bunk. "Aren't you frightened?"

"Should I be?"

Kore smiled and put her arms around the girl. "Perhaps just a little bit. It's even more marvelous if you are a little bit frightened. Like the first time on a roller coaster."

"Are you frightened?" Lucia asked. "You don't look frightened."

"Not anymore." Defying Wenceslas. After that there was nothing to be frightened of. Not ever.

The two of them listened to the silent running of the ancient submarine, its whoofing and whiffling and creaks.

"I'm not frightened of the submarine. I'm frightened I'll never get back to my father. Because I disobeyed him. I'm being punished."

With infinite sadness Lucia pronounced sentence on herself. She richly deserved her punishment. The submarine had just been invented to punish her for her transgression. There was no guilt in the world except her own. Such is the self-immolation of childhood.

"What did you do that was so awful?" Kore asked.

"I went where he told me not to go—Washington Square." Lucia's eyes were huge with sorrow. "I'll never see him again."

"You must," Kore said and felt in her little handbag for the gun.

- 16 -

— The Police copter was making such a racket that Cassidy and
Fletcher communicated by writing each other little notes. Fletcher
had the earphones on so he was the one who got the message. He
wrote it out and handed the yellow pad to Cassidy:

"Guppy has submerged."

Cassidy scowled at the three word message and expressed himself
with a single symbol:

"!"

Below them the lights were winking on, ribbons of light against
jagged pools of darkness. New York City at its most beautiful—from
fifteen hundred feet in twilight.

Fletcher had written on the pad: "Submerged submarines beyond
police capability. Must call in Navy."

Cassidy shook his head violently and wrested the yellow pad from Fletcher. "My daughter on that submarine. Calls for brains, not brawn."

He was thinking furiously. If the sub were underwater, it couldn't receive radio messages. Therefore they could communicate without fear that anyone would be listening. Well, hardly anyone. There was still that third force that Cassidy referred to as olive oil. He'd have to be careful.

Cassidy wrote on the pad: "Get me ship-to-shore—Channel 26," and handed it to the pilot. The police pilot threw the switches and handed the microphone to Cassidy who took the earphones from Fletcher's head and put them on his own.

"Calling Keefe! Calling Keefe! Come in, Keefe, you Hibernian tosspot. Where the hell are you, you malingering Celt, you over-educated lowlife!" Long ago in the Congo, Cassidy and Keefe had invented their own code, which consisted entirely of insults of a variety and color and ingenuity not seen since Falstaff took on Prince Hal.

"Come in, Keefe, you inebriated whelk, you contumacious Hippolyte, declare yourself."

What Cassidy had instructed Keefe to do was to come on the air and state his situation but be careful because the enemy was abroad.

Cassidy switched over to Receive, and his headset was inundated instantly with invective.

"Declare myself indeed, you dessicated medievalist, you spineless, bloodless turnip, you ineffable disestablishmentarian wimp! Where the hell have *you* been while here we are, hung up in the marshes by the palimpsest of inscrutable Providence, you scurrility of a theosophist, you closet Protestant."

Closet Protestant. Cassidy shook his head at that one. The top insult in all of Keefe's library of insult.

On the yellow pad Cassidy was writing: "They're hung up on the marshes by the tides. I want to check his position."

Switching to SEND, Cassidy said: "Closet Protestant, you unfrocked Papist! Did I hear you say Closet Protestant, you Cretaceous droppings off of a constipated Brontosaurus."

"I'll spell it out for you, you abominable atheist, you whore-mongering historian," Keefe said, and spelled it out or rather mis-spelled it out because the position on the charts was a big number and needed lots of letters. Cassidy counted the letters of abominable atheist, whore-mongering historian plus misspelled closet Protestant and put his pencil on the chart where the Navy tug rested and showed it to the police pilot, who nodded, heeled the copter over, and headed toward Horse Channel.

On the yellow pad, Cassidy wrote: "Have you got a tide chart on this whirly bird?"

Miraculously the pilot had one and handed it to Cassidy, who looked up the date and ran his fingers down the time line. It was now approaching 7:30 and high tide was 7:35. That meant the Navy tug could float free in about five minutes.

In his head Cassidy was trying to figure the odds. He knew where the submarine had submerged—just the other side of Governor's Island, knew it could go only five knots underwater, knew where the Navy tug was. What he was trying to do in his head was work out the time sub and tug would meet. It wasn't easy.

Nightfall had crept through the marshes, giving the wavy grasses an eery beauty. In the wheelhouse, Keefe put down the radio telephone. The wild Irish jollity he had displayed in his telephone exchange with Cassidy had vanished. He was very serious. Rattigan had listened to the exchange with his little clown smile. "Well," Rattigan said. For him a major policy pronouncement.

"Cassidy said to get moving," Keefe said. He signaled the engine room to Start Engines.

"There's more to it than that," Rattigan said who knew about the Cassidy-Keefe code though he didn't know the words.

Keefe was looking at the charts in their dim light. "We're in a three-cornered situation. On the one hand there is them wants to blow us sky high for their own selfish purposes. On the other hand there is them wants to steal the jewels for *their* own selfish purposes."

"And on the third hand?" Rattigan inquired.

"The third hand is the Archangel of Light, otherwise known as

Professor Cassidy, whose purity of motive shines like the radiance of heaven in this naughty world."

"What does the Archangel of Light wish exactly?"

"He'll tell us when he gets here."

Pindar came into the wheelhouse from the bridge. "We're afloat. Just."

The engines had come to life sending their shudder through the tug.

"We'll have to back out of here," Keefe said. "Pindar, go back to the stern and keep an eye on the rudder. I must know where it's lying— left, right, straight. Hand signal to Rattigan there, and Rattigan, you get out on the bridge and shout the word to me." Pindar started down the steel ladder, and Keefe called after him. "Get those Malays out on deck and tell them to be ready to cast off."

Keefe picked up the speaking tube. "Reverse engines when I give the signal but slow as they go. We're almost on the bottom."

"We could shear a pin," the engineer said. "It would take half the night to fix it."

"Try not to," Keefe said. "There's a good fellow."

Rattigan was shouting in the door. "Rudder's lying left." Keefe turned the wheel slowly until Pindar held his arms up straight. "Tell the Malays to cast off," Keefe shouted. He signaled the engineer Dead Slow, and the huge propellers started to turn.

"We're throwing up mountains of mud," Pindar screamed.

Rattigan relayed the bad news to Keefe, who scowled but kept on with the exercise because he had no choice. The tug backed slowly out of the narrow channel, between the waving grasses, toward the open water of Jamaica Bay. The narrow channel curved first right, then left. Pindar stood at the stern pointing with his arms, first right, then left. Rattigan would shout instructions at Keefe who would apply them to the wheel.

A clumsy system. Twice the stern of the tug missed the angle of curve and rammed into the mud. Each time the engineer stopped engines in the nick of time. Keefe pulled out of the mud by going forward, then resumed the rearward push.

It was ten minutes before the big blue Navy tug poked its stern into Horse Channel, which was dredged and marked by buoys that sent their warning flashes through the black night to the horizon.

"Rattigan," Keefe said, "come take the wheel." He picked up the flashlight.

Rattigan took over the wheel. "Where we headed?"

"Rockaway Inlet but Dead Slow. We're waiting for Godot if you catch my meaning."

Keefe went out of the wheelhouse to the catwalk, his eyes searching the night sky for helicopters.

Alison pulled off the headset and threw it on top of the radio telephone. The galley was very small, and the two men barely had room to move. "It's a code Keefe and Cassidy have been playing at for years," Alison said. "I don't know what games they're playing, and I'm not sure I'd tell you if I knew."

The man opposite him had a supple Levantine face of great intelligence. He still had his headset on and was fiddling with the dials of the radio-telephone. "They seem to have rung off," he said absently. He took off the headset and lit a cigarette. "What do you suggest now, Mr. Alison?"

Alison said coldly, "I don't wish to go any further with this. Mossad will have to do its own dirty work, Frame."

Frame smiled. A charming smile, containing the barest hint of menace. "You wish perhaps to return the money? Two hundred thousand dollars?"

"I haven't got it," Alison said angrily. "I've had expenses. Anyway I've done my bit. I gave those people very accurate information, and they bungled it."

The boat was burbling along at four knots, its two enormously powerful engines barely ticking over, the roar of Manhattan far distant in the background. Frame smoked in silence. He was a very clever operative and took his time. After a bit he said, "Those People, as you call them, have been promised two million dollars. They are not going to take kindly to any suggestion to stop now. I should like to point out that it was you who brought Those People into this operation. Not us."

"We've worked with them before," Alison said. "They're very good at—uh . . ."

"Stealing?" Frame asked.

"If Cassidy hadn't violated his orders, you'd have had the shells yesterday . . ."

Frame inhaled carcinogens into his lungs and exhaled them slowly into the narrow galley. "Cassidy was a mistake," he said. "Cassidy is his own man. If he were still in the Agency you could discipline him, but he isn't and you can't." Frame could have said a lot more. He might have pointed out that intelligence operations, once started, were almost impossible to stop, especially when armaments were involved and even more so, when the Mafia got mixed up into them. But Alison knew all that. Frame let him stew in his own juice and stood up, hunching his shoulders to avoid hitting his head in the little cabin. "You should do your own legwork, Alison." He let it go at that and climbed the three steps that led to the thick, wooden door leading into the main passenger lounge.

The passenger lounge was two-thirds of the vessel, and it was full of the leaden-faced characters, guns in their armpits, whom Alison referred to as Those People. The boat itself was a slender over-powered craft that had been a rumrunner in the 1920s, able to outspeed the swiftest Coast Guard ships, had later ferried weekend commuters to Fire Island, and for the last ten years had officially ceased to exist, had no papers, no license, no records, which was what made it attractive to intelligence organizations acting illicitly in someone else's country.

Frame threaded his way through Those People, looking neither to right nor left, and climbed the four iron steps into the pilot house, which sat above the passenger lounge. At the wheel was a young man who wore a white captain's hat rakishly over one eye as if it were a joke. His name was Abrams. Frame picked up a pair of binoculars lying on the chart table. "Alison's sulking," he said.

"Why?" Abrams asked.

"Wife trouble. *Rich* wife trouble, the worst kind."

The windows in the pilot house were the old-fashioned marine windows with leather straps that slid the glass down into the super-structure. Frame lowered a single pane of glass, letting cold night air into the pilot house. "I'd throw the son of a bitch into the Lower Bay, but he's fourth man in the Agency and they wouldn't like it." Frame poked his head out the window, listening.

Presently he brought his head back in and said, "Aha!"

"What's that mean?" Abrams asked.

"Listen!"

Both men listened.

Ratcheta. Ratcheta. Ratcheta, that unmistakable sound.

"Cassidy's up there in an eggbeater," Frame said. "It's way past bedtime for most helicopters, so it's my thought there is only one up there and he's in it." He was searching the sky, not using the binoculars because he didn't need them. The flashing white light could be seen for miles, far down the bay, headed right at them.

"Douse the lights," Frame said.

"The Harbor Patrol won't like it," Abrams said. He flicked the switch on the control board, and the craft went dark from bow to stern except for the little light on the compass.

They heard the helicopter beating its way down the Lower Bay five hundred feet over their head, its white light winking.

"Follow that helicopter," Frame said.

Abrams grinned. "The Harbor Patrol is going to like this even less." He thrust the two throttles all the way forward. Engines screaming, the ancient rumrunner leaped halfway out of the water onto its bottom plane and shot down the bay at sixty miles an hour. If we hit anything in this wooden boat at this speed, Abrams was thinking, the bay is going to be full of splinters, one of them me.

The helicopter pilot had passed over Rockaway Inlet when the pilot tapped Cassidy on the shoulder to attract his attention. He pointed to the fuel gauge whose needle stood halfway between quarter and empty. "I can only give you another ten minutes," he shouted. "We're running out of gas."

Cassidy nodded. The bird had already passed over Coney. The Navy tug should be . . . Cassidy pointed dead ahead where a pencil of light was making jiggly white lines in the sky. The pilot had already seen it and started his descent.

Presently the copter was hovering, twenty feet over the Navy tug; Cassidy was strapping the descent seat around his thighs. To Fletcher, he shouted, "Tell that Harbor Patrol boat to keep well out of it. If we blow up, it'll make a hole in the sky a mile and a half wide."

He lowered himself over the edge, suspended by the cable.

"I'm coming along," Fletcher said. "Hang on." Fletcher sat himself in Cassidy's lap, his arms tightly around Cassidy's shoulders.

"Why?" Cassidy yelled.

"You're under arrest. Didn't I tell you?"

Fletcher signaled the pilot to lower away, and down the two of them went, arms around each other like lovers.

"Under arrest! For what?"

"I'll think of something."

The steel cable deposited the two men into the huge embrace of Keefe on the catwalk of the Navy tug. They unhitched themselves from the cable and sent the helicopter on its way.

"Lieutenant Fletcher of the New York Police Department," Cassidy said. "This is Keefe, a very good man when sober, which isn't often. That bald fellow on the main deck who looks like a circus wrestler is Pindar, a Greek. At the wheel is Rattigan, who doesn't look like much but is a very good man with a gun or a knuckle in the eye."

Fletcher asked, "And all those crates on the deck?"

"Laser guided high technology projectiles. We're trying to restore them to their rightful owner, which is the arsenal at Raritan."

"Very noble of you, Cassidy."

"We'd welcome a little assistance, Lieutenant. We're badly outgunned."

Fletcher said, "I'll play it like it lays, Cassidy."

"What does that mean?"

"I'm reserving judgment."

"You're going to jump to this side or that, depending on which seems the most judicious, is that it? Well, let me tell you this, Lieutenant. If we blow up, there's only one way you're going and that's straight up." He pointed at the sky.

Fletcher smiled. "We all got to go sometime, Cassidy."

Cassidy took a deep breath. Clearly Fletcher was on the side of the archangel of light. "You had me going there for a minute, Lieutenant." To Rattigan Cassidy shouted, "Okay, get the scow moving. Full speed ahead right down the inlet."

"What do we do when we get out of the inlet into the bay?" Keefe asked.

"Wait," Cassidy said. "That submarine can only go five miles an hour. If he's going to waylay me, that's where it'll have to be. If he wants to use that deck gun, he'll have to surface."

The tug had picked up speed and was swooshing along now at fifteen knots in the deep channel.

"And when the sub surfaces?"

Cassidy knit his brow fiercely. "We grapple. My daughter's on that submarine, and so is Wenceslas . . ."

Also Kore.

In the control room Lebouef had raised the periscope and was walking on it, doing the full circle.

"Propellers bearing six-eight-oh from half mile at high speed," the sonar man reported.

"I can't see a thing," Lebouef said. "They must be traveling without lights. Wait! I see a blur. Come take a look."

Lebouef handed over the periscope to Wenceslas, who squinted through the eyepiece.

"Coming straight at us," reported the sonar man with the headphones on. "Quarter mile, still high speed. Too high pitched for a destroyer."

"Harbor Patrol?" Wenceslas asked. "No, the harbor patrol wouldn't travel without lights."

He'd seen the approaching blur, too, and now he handed the periscope back to Lebouef.

"No one would travel without lights unless they were illicit, illegal, immoral, and without shame," Wenceslas murmured. "Now who do I know who answers that description?"

Practically everyone.

The sonar man reported: "Propellers directly overhead now."

"What's our depth?" Lebouef asked.

"Thirty feet."

"Cut engines and hold it in the bottom. Where do we lie?"

The plotting officer showed him the position on the chart, Wenceslas looking over his shoulder.

The sonar man reported, "The other boat has stopped engines. Almost directly overhead."

"Well! Well!" Wenceslas said. "Fancy that!"

The sub had settled on the bottom now, engines stopped. The silence was stifling.

"Have you any idea who they might be, sir?" Lebouef asked.

"Oh, yes, indeed! Yes, indeed! I am afraid we'll have to deal with them before we get around to those others, or they will make difficulties."

The two men looked at each other.

"How do you propose to go about that, sir?"

Without a word, Wenceslas walked forward in the submarine, through the battery room, passing the officers' quarters to the torpedo room. There was only one torpedo, a three thousand pound fish that had a knifelike protuberance in its snout.

"Never saw one like that before," Lebouef said.

"The very latest technology," Wenceslas said. "Get those others back here. We'll need help wrestling that thing into the tube."

Aboard the Navy tug, Cassidy was staging a run through.

The searchlight was all important. It was huge and blinding, and it needed powerful muscles to swing it around. Cassidy put Keefe on it.

Rattigan was put on the wheel.

The five Malays were stationed on the main deck, with Pindar to give them their instructions.

Fletcher was appalled when he heard them.

"Trust me," Cassidy said with his Irish smile.

"Why?" Fletcher demanded.

"I'll think of something," Cassidy said.

The big blue Navy tug was chugging past Coney at that moment, everything dark on the ancient playground.

"Now, Lieutenant," Cassidy said, "if you'd just enjoy the crisp night air for a moment, a pause for philosophical reflection in the torment of our busy useless lives, shall we say, while Keefe and I go below . . ."

"What are you and Keefe doing below that you're trying so hard to prevent me from seeing?"

"We don't want any witnesses, and you wouldn't like it either because if you do you might have to go to court and tell tales about your old friend Cassidy and that would be a dreadful bore."

"I think I'll just come along and watch."

Cassidy's malleable face went mournful. "Lieutenant, my thirteen-year-old daughter is aboard that submarine. I have to . . . do a few things to get that submarine to surface. Try to be a little understanding."

Fletcher scowled. Not a very sincere scowl because he'd already made up his mind, just enough scowl to put himself on record. He said, "I'll enjoy the crisp night air, Cassidy, but I haven't the rank for philosophical reflection. Go on do what you have to do."

Cassidy and Keefe went below to the weapons room. It took a crowbar and all of Keefe's strength to break into the armory. The weapons were very lightweight Mallisons. Eight hundred rounds a minute, enough to cut a man in half. It would even the odds a little bit. Cassidy shoved a clip into each and handed two to Keefe.

"Tell Pindar to go easy on the trigger finger and be sure he's got something to fire at. You could blow the whole string in a minute," Cassidy said.

He went back to the wheelhouse by the back steps behind Fletcher's back and put Rattigan's weapon on the rack containing the maps, nudging Rattigan to be sure he saw it. Rattigan gave his little clown smile, and nodded.

On the old rumrunner Frame was passing out the grappling hooks to Those People, giving a brief lecture on how to use them.

They'll be coming from that direction," said the Mossad leader, pointing almost due north, "in about ten minutes if our calculations are correct. We'll be traveling without lights, and we'll go alongside as quietly as possible. Surprise is of the essence. We think there are only four men aboard, but they're all armed and very dangerous."

The soldiers of Those People listened icily. It was not the kind of odds they liked. They preferred the victims to be unarmed, unsuspecting, and totally helpless.

In the executive officer's quarters, Kore had screwed a silencer on the little .25, and now she put the gun behind her back, Lucia watching.

"No," Lucia said. She was talking in whispers because the sub's engines had stopped and it was very quiet. "It looks just like you have something behind your back. Haven't you a pocket?"

"Not in this skirt," Kore whispered.

"Put on another skirt," Lucia urged. "One with pockets."

Kore hastily fished out her luggage from under the bunk bed, found a blue wool skirt, and put it on. Now she put both hands in the pockets of her skirt—one with the gun in it.

"Much better," Lucia whispered.

"Do you love your father?" Kore whispered.

"Very much."

"Try not to look so scared," Kore said. "Here." She pushed Lucia in front of the mirror, and Lucia got a glimpse of her scared face. It made her giggle.

"That's better," Kore whispered. "Now get on with it."

Lucia walked boldly out of the door to the corridor.

Ali Heykal blocked her way. "Where are you going, miss?"

"To the toilet," Lucia said.

"There's one in the executive officer's room," Ali Heykal said.

"We can't get the door open," Lucia said. "Do you think you might get it open for us?" She essayed a smile, not a bad smile, considering the pressure.

"Of course," said Ali Heykal, the professional killer. He held the door open leading into the cabin and followed the little girl in, playing fly to the spider.

Everyone had his own plan of operation, four of them in all, each interacting on the other, and just at this point they all started to go very wrong.

- 17 -

— The submarine's electric engines had resumed their soft whir; the air conditioning was again whiffling, the old boat shook with life.

"Hold it at forty feet," Lebouef commanded, "dead slow, bearing three-eight-six."

The submarine nosed its way down the channel.

Lebouef was at the attack periscope. "It'll be a little like shooting a minnow with a twelve gauge shotgun," he said. "That fish was designed for bigger game."

Wenceslas's huge bulk was contained in one of the revolving chairs at the control panel for a crew member the sub didn't have. The arms salesman was in a state of high exaltation. Never in his life had he used one of the weapons he sold. Always he had insisted that the weapons were for peace, that the object of weaponry was stabilization, *not* use. Now here he was ordering the torpedo into the tube. It was all wrong! All wrong!

Yet indubitably thrilling.

"We don't want to be too near that explosion," Lebouef said at the periscope. "Quarter mile will be enough. Also, that fish will be more accurate with a bit of running room."

Wenceslas heaved himself out of his revolving chair, strode across the control room to the attack periscope, eyes alight.

"Stand by to fire," Wenceslas roared.

Lebouef sighed. This was not Wenceslas's thing to say. The words should have been spoken by Lebouef. Still, those in the control room seemed to have caught and executed the order.

The red light showed the number one tube stood ready.

Wenceslas clearly didn't know the rest of the drill. Lebouef said, "Bearing mark."

"Three five zero," the executive officer said.

"Set," Lebouef said.

The final data was set electrically into the torpedo.

Lebouef handed command back to Wenceslas.

"If you wish to issue the order, sir, go right ahead, but please wait until I give you that signal." A wave of the arm.

Lebouef put his eye back on the eyepiece of the periscope.

The rumrunner was now a good quarter mile away, sitting silently and without lights on the water but clearly outlined by the distant lights of the Jersey shore.

Until it was blotted out by the Navy tug, which at that moment sailed out of the inlet and lit itself up amidship to stern in the dazzling light of its own searchlight.

"Hold everything!" Lebouef barked. "Hold fire! Hold! Hold!"

"Stop engines," Cassidy commanded. He was back in the wheelhouse of the Navy tug, standing beside Rattigan, who sent the order down to the engine room. Out the window, Cassidy barked. "Okay,

Pindar, start the drill. Fletcher, get off the catwalk. You're a sitting duck out there."

Fletcher scurried into the wheelhouse to get out of the blinding light.

On the deck, in the full glare of the light, Pindar barked out an order. The five Malays, blinking in the terrible whiteness, heaved up one of the twenty-six crates containing roughly a million dollars worth of laser operated projectiles and dropped it overboard into New York harbor where it made a hugely visible splash.

Cassidy glowed with triumph. "High moral purpose combined with low cunning," Cassidy boasted to Fletcher.

"I don't understand any of it," Fletcher said.

"You will! You will!"

The second crate of projectiles was now on the shoulders of the Malays and they heaved it overboard. Again Cassidy felt a surge of righteousness. He explained: "Those shells will not now tear apart any small Iraqi children, and at the same time if anything will suck that submarine off the bottom, this will do it. Because out there somewhere very close Wenceslas is watching us through his periscope . . ."

As indeed he was.

Wenceslas had pushed Lebouef away from the attack periscope and was himself looking through the eyepiece. It was a beautifully lit scene, almost as if it had been designed for a film. Every lineament of the Malays could be seen as they heaved the heavy crates on their shoulders—and in color yet—and you could all but smell the sweat on them as they pushed the heavy crates into the water.

"It's a trick," Wenceslas roared. "Why would they turn the searchlight on? Why would they dump the stuff right there?"

"A very good trick," Lebouef commented. "If they dump all the shells you won't get your explosion."

"I'll dump the tin fish on *them,* blow them to smithereens." The arms salesman was alight with rage at the waste! "Stand by to fire."

"Wait!" Lebouef said. "You don't know what you are doing . . ."

"Fire!" Wenceslas roared.

The boat shuddered slightly as the big fish leaped out of the Number One torpedo tube.

"Number one running straight and hot . . ." the executive officer said coolly.

Ali Heykal tugged at the door of the head in the executive officer's room. "I believe it's locked," he said.

His last words.

Kore shot him twice in the back of the head with the little silenced .25, the weapon making a small plopping noise, lost in the hiss of the air conditioning.

Heykal fell forward onto the door he had been trying to open and rolled over on his back, his dead eyes pointed straight up to the ceiling.

Lucia burst into tears.

Kore wrapped her arms around the girl and held her head on her chest. "You can cry for hours later. Now we must get moving . . ."

Under her feet Kore felt the slight shudder that meant the torpedo was on its way, but she didn't know that. She was reaching down and searching the body. From under the armpit she fished out Ali Heykal's .357 magnum. Kore took the big gun and handed the little silenced .25 to Lucia.

"You sure you know how to handle it?"

"My father taught me." She held the gun straight out in both hands. "I've had lots of practice, and I'm not bad."

Kore opened the door of the cabin, and the two of them started toward the control room.

Aboard the old rumrunner, Frame shook his head slowly from side to side as if to clear his vision. He'd been on a dozen missions, and always something went wrong. He was prepared for a fuck-up—but this! *This!* "What the devil are they *doing!*" he said.

"Throwing the stuff overboard. There goes a million dollars worth!" Abrams said.

The crate made a hugh splash.

"We've got to stop that!" Frame yelled. "Get this crock going!"

Abrams pulled out the chokes on both his overheated engines—a serious mistake—and pushed the starter buttons, first the starboard engine, then the port engine. Neither engine started.

"Damn!" Abrams said. "I've flooded it. This may take a minute."

"We haven't got any spare minutes!" Frame raged.

It was Rattigan with his mysterious instinct for danger who had turned away from the brilliantly lit scene below and, for no reason at all, turned his gaze starboard and saw the white line of bubbles streaking at them at eighty miles an hour.

Rattigan grabbed Cassidy by the shoulders, spun him around and pointed.

"Mother of God!" whispered Cassidy, who didn't believe in God and certainly not in His Mother.

He was already signaling Full Speed Ahead to the engine room, a reflex action that he knew was useless. There was no way he could get the tug moving in time to get out of the way of that speeding fish.

The two of them, Rattigan and Cassidy, waited, mouths open, for the flash, the roar, the extinction . . .

On the conning tower of the submarine, Lebouef said, "Range three fifty. Counting one two three four five six seven . . ."

At twelve he stopped counting, his eye still at the periscope eye-piece. "It's a dud," he said calmly.

"You've missed!" Wenceslas shouted.

"At this range, impossible."

"It's the very latest technology," the arms merchant raged. "It cannot fail to go off!" Which is what he told all his customers.

"But it did fail," Lebouef said, an old submariner who knew the realities.

"Surface! Surface!" Wenceslas commanded in a fury of frustration. "It has torn them to shreds! You shall see!"

"Madness," Lebouef said. "The Harbor Patrol's up there looking for us. So are Cassidy and those others. Our advantage is to lie submerged."

"Surface! Surface!" Wenceslas was repeating the words like an incantation.

The executive officer was not quite sure who was in charge. He looked to Lebouef for instruction. Lebouef shrugged. "Surface," he said quietly.

Air hissed into the ballast tanks, blowing out the water; the bow planes went down hard, and the boat broke the dark surface of the water with such alacrity that Kore and Lucia, walking into the control room with the guns behind their backs, were thrown off stride and recoiled back into the passageway. No one noticed them.

The big, heavy Navy tug rocked slightly. That was all.

No blast. No flash.

"Jupiter!" Cassidy said changing deities in the middle of the crisis. "It's a dud."

The tug had come to life now, its engines beginning to churn at increasing speed, the big tug accelerating through the dark waters of the bay.

"Zigzag," commanded Cassidy to Rattigan who was back at the wheel. "They might throw another fish at us."

Cassidy was remembering Scapa Flow. The German commander Prien had sneaked his submarine into Scapa Flow and then in total frustration had watched four of his torpedoes, all duds, bounce off the steel sides of the British battleship *Royal Oak* before two good torpedoes slammed home, sinking her.

Rattigan spun the wheel to starboard. The Navy tug wheeled over sharply. From below came Pindar's agonized shout. "Take it easy up there! You don't want us to drop these firecrackers, do you?"

Cassidy stuck his head out the window and shouted, "Belay, Pindar! Cease and desist! We have a fresh problem to deal with. Keefe, turn off that light! Rattigan, you've zigged enough. Now zag!"

The light went out. The Navy tug heeled over on its side as Rattigan spun the wheel to port.

Wenceslas cradled the 155-millimeter shell in both arms. "This baby will not fail," he crooned.

"More high technology," Lebouef said and immediately wished he hadn't because Wenceslas glared at him with fury as if he'd committed a desecration.

"How do I get this weapon up that ladder?" Wenceslas asked furiously.

Lebouef signaled the executive officer to take the shell. The executive officer slung the shell in a canvas cradle around his neck and went up the steel ladder with it, closely followed by Wenceslas.

Lebouef was about to follow them when he felt the barrel of the gun against his neck.

"Sit down, Mr. Lebouef," Kore said politely, "right over there in that chair."

Lebouef didn't even look around. The barrel of the gun was very persuasive. He eased himself into the bow planesman's chair, facing the myriad dials and gauges and levers on the control panel.

"Just stay like that. If you turn your head, I'll shoot."

Lebouef didn't turn his head; he didn't need to. He could hear the sibilant sounds of feet going up the steel ladder.

The submarine lay quietly on the surface of the bay as the executive officer and Wenceslas emerged on the bridge. They climbed over the sides and down to the deck where the 155-millimeter cannon was oozing sea water. The executive officer removed the plug from the muzzle, the shell hanging from his neck.

"This shell is designed to fire a hundred miles, not a hundred yards," the officer said. Insanity, he was thinking, weapon intoxication. He'd seen it before, a kind of worship of devices that kill.

"Open the breech," Wenceslas commanded, reciting the litany.

The officer opened the breech and unslung the shell from his neck. just as Kore followed by Lucia emerged on the bridge.

The officer slammed the shell home and closed the breech.

Kore aimed the gun with both arms pointed straight before her. "Father!" she said, the forbidden word resounding on the steel deck like a witch's curse.

Wenceslas looked up into the .357 magnum aimed straight at him by his daughter.

Just then the moon broke through the clouds, an unscheduled happening that threw everyone's plans even more awry. The silvery radiance lit up the seascape for a dozen miles, changing the odds. Rattigan, caught between a zig and a zag, was first to notice the submarine, and he pointed it out to Cassidy.

"Aah," Cassidy said and took the wheel from Rattigan.

He aimed the tug straight at the submarine.

Fletcher stood at his side. "What now, admiral?" the police lieutenant asked.

"We're going to ram it," Cassidy said, "alert those people on deck to hang on tight."

On the ancient rumrunner, Abrams had succeeded in getting the engines going again. In the bright moonlight, Frame could see the Navy tug now heading directly away from them.

"Full speed," Frame directed, "to port. Everyone seems to be on the starboard side, so we'll board from the other side."

He went below to the passenger lounge where Those People, a full two dozen of them, were seated on the hard benches.

"Prepare to board," he said.

Frame didn't notice Alison at the very rear of the passenger's lounge, listening. When Frame went back to the pilot house, Alison turned quietly and went to the very rear of the craft where the inflatable life raft was, a round compact mass fastened to the deck by explosive bolts.

Alison knew the drill and pulled the lever.

The raft shot upward, inflating in midair, opening outward.

Alison took off his shoes and dove overboard.

Alison could smell a mission going sour way ahead of everyone else, and he was a world authority on survival.

Cassidy had once said that Alison always left the sinking ships five minutes ahead of the rats.

"Take the shell out of the cannon, Father."

A command. She who had never commanded, who had always obeyed. Sometimes reluctantly but always, always . . . Wenceslas turned his eyes to Heaven as if that was where the blame lay.

"Fire the cannon!" Wenceslas ordered, mad as King Lear and for the same reason.

Kore moved the muzzle of the gun so that it pointed now at the chest of the executive officer rather than at her father. I want no more of this father-daughter altercation, thought the officer, and dove over the side of the submarine into the moonlit water.

In the control room, Lebouef had taken the submarine commander's sidearm, a .45 automatic, from the locked drawer in which it was kept for just such an emergency and sprinted up the steel ladder. Gun in hand, he poked his head out of the hatch. Her back to him, the woman was pointing her gun over the edge of the bridge.

She was saying, "With deep love and hatred, Father! Hatred and love!"

Lebouef lifted his gun. Instantly he felt the round barrel at the nape of his neck, "Drop it," Lucia said, "or I'll kill you."

Lebouef dropped the .45 automatic, and it fell twenty feet to the floor of the control room with a huge clatter.

Now the Navy tug, bearing down on the submarine, was only fifty yards away, clamoring for attention.

Wenceslas turned woodenly away from his daughter, turned his back contemptuously on the .357 magnum and positioned himself behind the 155-millimeter cannon.

He knew it well, knew every grommet on it, its virtues, its vices, its strength, its weakness, and where the firing mechanism was—having sold a great many. He sighted down the barrel of the cannon as if it were a BB gun at the onrushing Navy tug and reached for the lanyard . . .

"Father!"

Kore shot her father twice in the back with the .357, the force of the explosion slamming him headlong into the cannon from which he ricocheted off into the bay.

The gun fell out of her hand to the deck. "I never knew what I was for," Kore murmured to herself. "*That's* what I was for."

Lucia rushed to her, putting her arms around her because Kore looked as if she might fall.

That gave Lebouef his opportunity. The submarine commander scuttled down the steel ladder, locking the steel hatch behind him. "Dive! Dive! Dive!" he yelled.

In the eery, sometime radiance of the room, Cassidy saw the scene on the deck of the submarine, saw Kore shoot her father, saw the arms merchant topple off into the water, saw his own daughter throw her arms around Kore—saw all of this too late, too late. He spun the wheel hard to starboard and managed to avoid hitting the bridge, but not to avoid the submarine altogether. The tug climbed right up on the back of the boat, the impact throwing everyone in the wheelhouse off balance.

When he regained his footing, Cassidy rushed to the catwalk and looked below. The submarine was slipping under the water. Kore and Lucia were pulled under by the force of the submarine submerging, but in a moment both heads popped to the surface, now three feet apart.

Cassidy climbed onto the rail running around the wheelhouse shouting, "Keefe, turn on the lights! Illuminate me, baby!"

The great searchlight went on just as Cassidy dove off the rail, lighting up the scene for hundreds of yards, and one of the things it illuminated was the approach of the old rumrunner, sneaking up on the Navy tug from what Frame had assumed was its blind side.

Keefe, who was working the light, saw it first.

He swung his Mallison to his shoulder, bellowing his old Congo battlecry: *"A moi, Auvergne! Voila les ennemis,"* which the Chevalier d'Assas a Wesel had shouted to his troops on the fifteenth of October, 1760, as every French school child knows.

Keefe's Mallison chattering away at the rate of eight-hundred-a-minute picked off eight of the Those People as they swarmed over the side. Then one of *les ennemis* put a bullet into the searchlight, and it went dark, leaving the light of the moon as the only radiance around. Another of the soldiers got Pindar in the chest, and the same man shot two of the Malays as they tried to dive below.

Rattigan was blazing away with his Mallison from the wheelhouse door. Next to him Lieutenant Fletcher methodically squeezed off one shot at a time with his .38 special.

The surprise was not total, but it was enough so that a good many of the Mafia soldiers got aboard the Navy tug, firing as they came, the sort of battle they would never have chosen if they had had the choice.

It was not a very long battle. What Cassidy had all along feared might happen happened. A stray bullet found its way into one of the crates of high technology projectiles.

The Navy tug blew up.

Cassidy had just swum to Lucia's side when the explosions started. Many explosions, mounting in crescendo and force and noise, an inferno of sound.

"Take a deep breath. Let it out and hold it," said Cassidy to Lucia. "Now."

The two of them ducked under the surface and swam, Lucia holding onto her father as he breaststroked down, down . . .

The air above them full of unexploded projectiles, bodies, flying steel, and fire . . .

When they could hold their breath no longer and came to the surface, they found both tug and rumrunner had disappeared.

"Kore!" Lucia cried. "Kore, where are you?"

Slowly the two of them, Cassidy and Lucia, swam through the litter of bodies and debris, searching for Kore.

The moon had gone back under a cloud, and again it was very dark.

A familiar voice. "Avast there! Help me count my fingers. I think I've lost a few." Keefe soberer than he'd been in years, his hand bloody but defiant.

They never found Kore.

When Lucia could not tread water any longer, Cassidy put her hands on his shoulders and himself lay back in the water and kicked slowly, pulling her along after him.

Himself thinking; we'll never make it, we're too far out.

Ten minutes later Alison paddled up in his rubber raft.

"I'm not usually glad to see you, Alison," Cassidy said, "but this time I'll make an exception."

"Always the needle," Alison complained, "even when I'm saving your life. Why do you do it?"

"Because I can't help remembering, . . ." Cassidy was clambering into the rubber boat, pulling Lucia in after him, "that it was you got me into this in the first place."

The Harbor Patrol came on Rattigan, holding Lieutenant Fletcher's unconscious head out of the water, and pulled the two of them out. When the harbor police tried to question Rattigan, all they got was a little clown smile.

Only three of the Mafia soldiers were fished alive out of the bay that night, and they were even less helpful to the police in explaining the battle of the Lower Bay as it came to be called.

A very mysterious sea battle in every respect, and about the only clear conclusion anyone reached was that the Mafia shouldn't go to sea. Water wasn't their natural element.

Epilogue

— They were in the back room of the Spumi before the lunch crowd arrived, Cassidy running his eyes over Alison's new suit, which fitted loosely like the skin of a chameleon, which was what Alison was, changing his color, his opinions, his very texture to fit this new Administration. A survivor. One mustn't underestimate survivors, Cassidy thought. In the long run the human race needed survivors more than it needed heroes, and, Keynes to the contrary, in the long run we're not all dead. Only the nonsurvivors are dead.

Alison was grumbling, "If you'd followed orders, it would never have happened."

Cassidy grinned evilly and drank his Wild Turkey. "Think of all those Iraqi children who will not now be torn to bits."

"You weren't hired to make moral decisions," Alison said in his silken voice that meant bad news.

"I missed four days of teaching," Cassidy said. "I want my money."

Alison laid the envelope before him, and Cassidy immediately tore it open. Very bad undercover manners. The agent was supposed to count it later, but Cassidy knew he'd been bilked and he wanted to know how badly bilked.

"Four thousand," he snarled. "I was promised twelve."

"You didn't deliver, Cassidy. You disobeyed. You're lucky to get four."

Cassidy ordered another Wild Turkey—on Alison—and throttled his rage because, as a matter of fact, he hadn't expected to get four thousand. More like two. Alison was going soft.

"I paid your disgraceful bar bill, too, Horatio. You're drinking too much."

"That's because I have emotional problems," Cassidy said. "How are your emotional problems?"

"She's gone to Honolulu, but she'll be back."

I saved the bastard's life, his job, and his marriage. Why?

For four thousand dollars, that's why.

"What's the news on the submarine?"

"The Navy lost it. They thought they had it pinpointed, but they were wrong."

All that marvelous detection equipment that was supposed to track a dime across the Atlantic, like those wonderful bomb sights in World War II that could drop a bomb down a pickle barrel—at least in the newspapers. None of it worked. The history of armaments was one long catastrophe. Cassidy thought of the French who clung to their bright armor for a hundred years after Crécy because the French aristocracy couldn't bear to part with the beautiful expensive stuff.

Cassidy walked out of the Spumi into the bright spring weather and climbed the steps to his apartment.

Lucia was belly down on the sofa reading her dragon book. "The elven pantheon is largely headquartered on one of the planes of

Olympus, in an area known as Arvandor, 'The High Forest.' Here dwell a large number of elven deities who collectively refer to themselves as the Seldarine, which roughly translates as the fellowship of brothers and sisters of the wood . . ." and so on.

Lucia had gone through Dungeons and Dragons and was now deep into elves, an even more mystical games-playing flight of imagination than the original Dungeons and Dragons, and one Cassidy couldn't follow her into though he tried. God knows he tried.

He looked over her shoulder now and read: "Evil elvenkind have nothing to do with the gods of the Seldarine. They frequently find the demon princes, arch-devils, and other gods of the lower planes more to their liking . . ."

"That's because they haven't had any wars," Cassidy said. "This yearning for devils and archdevils is because we've had forty years of peace, that boring thing."

"Oh, Daddy," groaned Lucia, who'd heard it all before.

Cassidy was suffering the anguish of a father whose daughter was getting into areas he couldn't penetrate. Actually these were very sophisticated games, and it wasn't simply that he didn't want to play the dragon games. He couldn't. She was outstripping him, his own daughter!

Lucia rolled over on her back and looked at Cassidy.

"I dreamt of Kore last night," she said.

Damn, Cassidy thought. Lucia had taken Kore's death even harder than he had. She felt guilty about it, as if they hadn't tried hard enough to find her.

"What did you dream?" he asked gently.

"She was dead, but she said she didn't mind being dead. She said it wasn't all that different from being alive. That's what she said."

Lucia's black eyes full of colored lights and behind the eyes the thirteen-year-old mind in its shadowy world of elves and evil. Trying to find an accommodation. Cassidy was not going to interfere though he violently disagreed.

He kissed her on the forehead. "Well, that's all right then."

"It's not *that* all right," Lucia said. "She would rather be alive than dead. But she had to go through this death period as atonement because she had killed her father. After the atonement, she'd be born again . . ."

"My goodness," Cassidy murmured.

"Not *here,* Daddy." Lucia trying hard not to be too contemptuous of her stupid father. "She'll be born again in another place and in a much higher civilization than this dumb place."

"I see," Cassidy said. But he didn't see, and she knew it. In the matter of otherworldliness, Lucia's generation was beyond the communication barrier.

Cassidy talked it over with Keefe, the two men playing the match game in the back room of the Spumi.

"It'll get worse before it gets better," Keefe said. "I know a chap was *summa cum laude* at Harvard, and he says to me he cannot understand a single word of what they're teaching his young nephew at Harvard these days. Not a word—and him the brightest student of his generation. We're out of date, Cassidy. On the shelf. Two," he said and opened his hand and won the game.

Cassidy said: "Kore's last words were: 'I never knew what I was for. That's what I was for.' Killing her father was what she was for. A terrible thought, a terrible deed. She couldn't have lived with it so she didn't. You open."

"Three," Keefe said, the conventional opening.

Cassidy said, "I don't think Kore ever forgave me for saying to Wenceslas I would shoot his daughter if he harmed mine."

"And would you have?" Keefe asked.

Cassidy scowled. "Two," he said. And lost again.

To his summer school classes Cassidy was in great form—using all his old Alfred Lunt acting tricks—opening his eyes wide, dropping his voice to a whisper, striding about the platform like a Renaissance prince, or collapsing into a snarling, whining Fagin—all to make them pay attention to the Middle Ages in order, he told them, to avoid them having to relive them.

He worked the arms trade right into his lectures: "The only thing you can rely on absolutely in armaments is that the experts will *always* back the wrong horse. The German High Seas Fleet, which was built at great cost to prepare for World War I, was of no use whatsoever, whereas the submarine the experts looked down their long noses at almost won the war for them against their better judgment. In World War II the Maginot Line, constructed at hideous expense, might just as well not have been there, and in World War III the one thing we can count on with absolute certainty is that the MX missile now being built at such obscene cost will not work or will work in totally unexpected ways, probably disastrously.

"There's the bell. I hope I have started a tiny fire in your tiny minds. Next week I shall talk to you about the nature and symptoms of social disintegration, a lecture of such cheerfulness you will leave the classroom singing like larks. Good day."

Deborah waylaid him as usual, and he walked her to Twelfth Street.

"This is my last class," she told him. "Starting next week, I'll be teaching social science in summer school at P.S. 26."

What she was really saying, they both knew, was that now she was no longer his student there would be no moral obloquy in his screwing her. Cassidy stole a look at Deborah's ample thighs and womanly breasts. Not his type at all, certainly she wasn't in Kore's league.

Still, at his age, he supposed he had to be content with whatever was offered.